THE MARTY GRAW BOOK

THE MARTY GRAW BOOK

A NOVEL BY

TOM BALL

From the time I was Liam's age,
my mother Lolita encouraged me to write –
even going so far as to lend supportive approval
to the ridiculous notion of possibly pursuing it as a career.
By contrast I, ever practical in nature, came to regard writing as a
somewhat unsteady occupational choice,
flaky, fraught with both artistic and financial peril.
So instead I became a blues harmonica player.

She's been gone a few years now, but I often felt her
reading this over my shoulder as I typed late into the night.
Every now and then she took issue with the content,
but never with the process.

This is for her.

Works by Tom Ball:

<u>Non-fiction</u>

Blues Harmonica: A Comprehensive Crash Course and Overview
The Nasty Blues
Sourcebook of Sonny Terry Licks for Blues Harmonica
Sourcebook of Little Walter/Big Walter Licks for Blues Harmonica
Dropped-D Tuning for Fingerstyle Guitar

<u>Commercial Recordings (solo)</u>

18 Pieces for Solo Steel-String Guitar
Guitar Music

<u>Commercial Recordings by Tom Ball & Kenny Sultan</u>

20th Anniversary - Live!
Double Vision
Filthy Rich
Too Much Fun
Bloodshot Eyes
Who Drank My Beer?
Confusion

<u>Fiction</u>

The Marty Graw Book

September 18, 1960

You're not allowed to read this. Ha ha! Good morning, my name is Liam Freddy McAfee and next week I'll be ten years old. I'm hoping to get a dog for my birthday but I'd settle for a spaceship or a BB gun. A great big German Shepherd dog like Rin Tin Tin would be the best, but I don't have much hope for that because Mom says she's allergic to dogs even though Uncle Mick told me she's really just allergic to dogdoo. And I don't think I'll get a BB gun because my dad says I'd probably shoot my little brother Colin with it, or else put somebody's eye out, which I think is almost impossible.

I wonder why grownups always worry so much about putting somebody's eye out? I never heard of anybody getting their eye put out, have you? I guess parents have to worry about something, since they can't worry anymore about Hitler or the Great Depression or all the snow they used to have to walk through to get to school and back.

We don't have snow here because we live near the beach in California and it doesn't snow. Dad says, "It hasn't snowed here in a goddamn coon's age." Mom says that's not a nice way to talk around the boys. She's always telling Dad what not to say around us after he's already said it. He cusses sometimes and I guess Mom thinks that's a bad example or something, like we never hear it at school. It's a good thing Mom doesn't come to our Little League games.

I play Little League baseball for the Tocaloma Huskies. That's the minor league team for the Tocaloma Yankees. We suck. We play every Saturday and we've only won two games this season and one of them was a "forfeit." (That's where the other team doesn't show up or gets in trouble.)

The forfeit happened yesterday. We were behind 14 to 4 to the Morris Hardware Panthers when one of their guys, Tony Little, got called out at third by the ump. Tony's dad went kind of nuts and ran out onto the field and called the ump a cocksucker, so the ump kicked Mr. Little out of the game. Only trouble is Mr. Little is the

Panthers' manager, so they had to forfeit which meant we won. We all threw our mitts in the air and yelled, "Two, four, six, eight, who do we appreciate, cocksucker, cocksucker, yay!"

They say next year I'll be old enough to play for the Tocaloma Yankees if I can find my game. That's a weird expression if you ask me, "find my game," like it's missing somewhere or something. That's Coach Cunningham's way of saying I stink, which is pretty much true. It's on account of my eyes, which don't see that good. I got my first glasses when I was only two, so my baby pictures look sort of dorky but I don't mind my glasses now, because Marie Blessing says they make me look "studious" and "debonair."

Marie Blessing is the most beautiful girl in the whole 5th grade -- she looks like Natalie Wood. I bet she'll grow up to be a fashion model or something. If I look at her really hard and concentrate, I get kind of nervous and one time when I was looking at her, Miss Kleinholz asked me if I wanted to go see Nurse Norwich because my cheeks were flushing. I didn't want to go because I wasn't actually sick, and besides Nurse Norwich is a big, fat, angry old hag. She yells at us kids just for being sick -- like we can help it? We call her Nurse Norbitch.

The only time I ever went to Nurse Norbitch was when I barfed a lot of yellow junk all over Betty Bachelis in second grade. I didn't mean to barf on Betty -- she was just in the way when I barfed, but she's still sore at me about it, three years later. Some people can sure hold a grudge.

September 19, 1960

It's Monday and guess what? Today was the first day of school. It was kind of depressing to have to get up early and go on back to Room 27 after a whole summer of playing ball and going to the beach and stuff. Everything at school is pretty much just like it was last year, except we're in the A5 now instead of the B5. But it's the same kids, same teacher, same principal. Disgustomatic, if you ask me.

Dad just got home from work. He makes car windshields all day at someplace called Tri-Flex. It's out in the Valley and it's really hot there. Mom always brings him a cold martini when he gets home. Once I took a sip of it and it smelled like that Testor's Glue you put model airplanes together with, and it tasted sickening. I liked the olive with the pitento, though.

Uncle Mick says they make pitentos out of cow's eyeballs. When I was little I didn't know he was just kidding, so I wouldn't eat olives. He also told me that butter was made out of ear wax, but I didn't fall for that one.

Uncle Mick won't drink martinis with Dad. He says martinis are for wimpshits and are a disgrace to the Irish Race. He drinks black beer and whiskey and says he has to, because it's his social responsibility as an Irish-American. So I guess we're Irish-American. Mom says we've been in America for so long we're mutts by now, but Dad and Uncle Mick say we're still Irish and that St. Patrick was the greatest saint because he drove all the snakes out of Ireland.

Just between you and me, I think St. Patrick sounds like a royal shitburger. I like snakes. When I was eight I had a snake for a pet, a little black snake with a red ring around its neck. They're called Ringworm Snakes. I found him in the canyon and brought him home and snuck him into my room and fed him flies. His name was Finfer.

I knew Mom and Dad wouldn't let me keep him, so I hid him in my box of baseball cards. For a week I ran around with a fly swatter to get flies for him. I couldn't tell Mom or Dad why I was swatting all the flies and I think Mom was worried about my mental health or something, swatting flies all the time like that.

Then one day while I was away at Little League, my brother Colin accidentally stepped on Finfer with some high-top Keds and squarshed him flat. Colin was afraid I'd pound him when I found out, so he hid Finfer in the clothes dryer and then Mom tried to dry some sheets, and Dad sniffed and asked, "What's that you're cooking for dinner, Dearie?"

Being grounded from TV is the worst, isn't it? Our TV is in the living room, right under the picture of Michael Collins. It's not a colored-TV like the Vanderhoeven's have, but at least it works. It gets all seven channels: two, four, five, seven, nine, eleven and thirteen, but there's never anything good on channel thirteen.

I once asked Uncle Mick why TV doesn't have a channel one and he said there really *is* a channel one, but kids can't see it because it only comes on at midnight and it shows bare-naked ladies. I asked him which naked ladies it showed and he said, "Who would you like to see naked?" and I said Miss Kleinholz. She's my teacher and she has really big titties that come to a point like ice cream cones. I don't get why her's are so pointy and most ladies' titties are kind of round, so I'd like to see her naked. Uncle Mick said they have a whole movie of Miss Kleinholz bare-naked on channel one, and that it starts at midnight.

So that night I decided I'd stay up real late and see if it was true. I asked Mom for a cup of coffee since that's supposed to keep you up, but she looked at me like I was crazy, so after everybody left the kitchen I got a big tablespoon full of Folger's Instant Coffee and ate it.

It tasted gross but it worked (or maybe, as Mom says, it was just cyclelogical) but anyhow I stayed awake and snuck downstairs at midnight and turned on the TV.

Uncle Mick is full of it. The only thing on channel one is a picture of an Indian inside some circles, and plus the instant coffee gave me a stomachache and the poops. That's the last time I'll trust Uncle Mick.

September 20, 1960

Miss Kleinholz took us on a field trip today. Everybody in class piled into a big bus and this nice colored man drove us downtown to see this opera called 'Hansel and Gretel.' Every time the lady started to sing, Bobby Del Valle would make a armpit fart and finally Miss Kleinholz had to take him out into the lobby and give him a good talking to. I don't know what she said to him, but he stopped doing armpit farts. Maybe Miss Kleinholz threatened to put his eyes out with her big pointy bazoombas? Ha ha! Guess what? Pinky and Stinky got a duck! Those are my next door neighbors. Pinky and Stinky aren't their real names of course -- Pinky's name is actually Darlene Vanderhoeven and Stinky is her older brother Donny, but everybody calls them Pinky and Stinky, even their parents. Pinky is a year younger than me, and Stinky is 2 1/2 years older. I guess they nicknamed Darlene 'Pinky' because pink was always her favorite color. Personally, I wouldn't mind being called Pinky (if I was a girl, of course,) but I sure wouldn't like to be called 'Stinky.' But Stinky doesn't seem to mind it, so that's that.

Anyways they live next door with their parents Alva and Ted Vanderhoeven. They're from the south somewhere, and they all talk funny. Dad doesn't trust them because they're some weird kind of Baptists or Holy Rollers and I guess we're supposedly Catholic although the last time we went to Mass I was just a kid. Mom says we're "Collapsed Catholics."

Anyhow Pinky and Stinky got a duck! They built a little pen next to our fence beyond the woodpile, and the duck lives there now. It's name is 'Ducky' which seems pretty unimaginative to me, but what can you expect from two kids named Pinky and Stinky?

I told Stinky that I was getting a big Rin Tin Tin dog for my birthday, and that my dog was going to have duck soup for lunch, but Stinky didn't think that was funny so he slugged me in the stomach. Dad says Southern Baptists have no sense of humor. I told Colin what happened and he said, "Stinky blows dead worms," which I thought was an awful smart thing for a seven-year-old kid to say.

Pinky and Stinky's mom Alva won the Miss Peaches of Jonesboro County contest way back before I was born, so I guess that makes her some sort of a beauty queen. Big deal. Dad says Mrs. Vanderhoeven doesn't have the brains she was born with (but then he said, "You didn't hear that from me, Liam.") I don't know. I guess she's nice to me, but I don't really like to be in their house. They're always saying prayers and there's lots of candles and pictures of bloody Jesuses all over the walls, so it's kind of spooky. Plus they eat totally disgusting food like fried Spam sandwiches and creamed tuna on toast, and they'd rather watch Korla Pandit than Sky King, can you imagine? Pinky's OK, though, for a girl. But she's just a little kid -- she's only 8 1/2 and I'll be ten.

Now that I'll be ten, I can be a Webelo if I want. Webelos are boys who are too old for Cub Scouts and too young for Boy Scouts. I think I'm supposed to be excited about this, but unless they make me, I'm not going into Webelos.

Last summer Mom and Dad let me spend a weekend at the Webelo camp to see if I liked it, but it just seemed dumb. The only cool part was you can cook marshmallows on a campfire and they tell good ghost stories, but in the morning some fat guy with a horn wakes you up at six by blowing music through a microphone. They also blow whistles and make you march around like you're in the Army or something, and for breakfast you have to eat powdered eggs, which taste farty.

It was cool sleeping outside in the Webelo tents, but I didn't actually get much sleep because Mr. Cuchinello, the Scoutmaster, snored so loud that nobody could sleep -- not even Frankie Dupoy who sleeps in the sandbox every day during recess. Finally Mr. Bernstein, who had been drinking from a flat silver canteen and swearing for a couple hours, went into Mr. Cuchinello's tent and put two acorns in Mr. Cuchinello's nose, and Mr. Cuchinello woked up and yelled a whole bunch of words my mom thinks I've never heard before.

September 21, 1960

Mom just told me I don't have to go to school tomorrow because it'll be my birthday! That's the best present of all, because Miss Kleinholz is giving an arithmetic test tomorrow. I hate arithmetic.

I do pretty good in the other subjects -- A's and B's -- but I can barely survive arithmetic.

Uncle Mick says not to worry about it, it's genetic. He says none of the McAfees have ever been any good at numbers which is why we couldn't pay the goddamn British landlords the goddamn rent money and we got run out of goddamn County Kilkenny and had to emigrate to the goddamn United States. All this stuff happened about 3000 years ago, but Uncle Mick is still mad about it. He's worse about holding a grudge than Betty Bachelis.

After school Mom took me to Vince's Barbershop to get my hairs cut. There's always a bunch of men hanging at out Vince's which seems to make Mom nervous, so she usually just drops me off and goes shopping, then comes back and picks me up.

Sometimes Vince himself cuts your hair, but he always cuts it too short, and then he brushes all the clipped off hairs down the back of your shirt until your back itches so bad it's worse than poison oak. Then he puts this pink goop called Butchwax all over your head. It's like stinky pink tar. He rubs and rubs your head like it's a crystal ball or something, then he combs all your hair straight up. You come out like Chucko The Clown when Vince cuts your hair, so I always try to get my favorite barber instead, whose name is Cecil.

Cecil is a card -- sometimes he takes out his false teeth and clacks them at you. He tells jokes the whole time he cuts your hairs, and he doesn't use Butchwax. One time I asked him where he came from and he said, "I was born in my ammy," so I said, "Where's your ammy?" and all the barbers laughed. I didn't get it then, but I get it now. Ha ha! And guess what? Cecil the barber is bald! That cracks me up.

A couple years ago when I was a little kid, Cecil said he'd go to Pluto with me. No, not Pluto the Dog on Walt Disney's Wonderful World of Color -- I mean Pluto the planet. Mrs. Brubaker had just taught us about the Solar System and I thought Pluto seemed really neato and Cecil agreed, so we decided we'd go. All I had to do was build the spaceship.

Across the street Volker Dortmunder's dad was having a new bathroom stuck on their house, so one night after dinner I swiped a couple pieces of plywood and started sawing the rocketship. I thought it would really work, too! Boy, was I a dumb little kid!

Volker finked on me and Dr. Dortmunder came over and asked for $3 for the plywood. Dad gave him the money and I was sure I'd get grounded, but I didn't. Instead Dad just told me, "Liam? Stay away from that Gestapo fuckwit," which sounded so funny I laughed until my stomach hurt. Dad fought in the war so he's not very friendly with Germans.

He talks bad about Germany, but the only time I ever see Dad get angry with Ireland is when he talks about the war and about how Ireland stayed neutral. He thinks they should have helped more. "There's a whole lot of things wrong with England and America," Dad says, "but nothing Hitler would've fixed."

September 22, 1960

Right in the middle of opening my presents, somebody rang the doorbell. It was some of those Jehovah's Witness people who try to sell you newspapers about Jesus. Even though we're Collapsed Catholic, Mom always tells them, "Guess what? We're Jewish and so was Jesus," and they leave right away.

I didn't get a dog or a spaceship or a BB gun, but I knew I wouldn't, so that's OK. I did get an Erector Set and a airplane model (a Spad!) and some great cowboy boots. Also some dumb stuff like clothes. It's been great! And Uncle Mick gave me ten packs of baseball cards, and one of them had Sandy Koufax right on top! I'm pretty busy today so I can't talk anymore.

September 23, 1960

Today after school I went down to the park to play tether ball. I'm good at tether ball, maybe not the best in the world, but pretty good. It's a big yellow ball on a rope, so you can see it better than a baseball. The way it works is when you win, you get to keep playing new guys until you lose. So I won six games in a row until this new kid named Fred Brown beat me 15 to 9. He's a colored kid and a really good tether ball player.

We don't have too many colored kids in our town, I can only think of about ten in the whole school. Some grownups don't like the colored families, but I do. They're always nice to me and their kids always make jokes and are good at sports. My dad says that if the colored man was good enough to fight for America in the war, he ought to be allowed to live any goddamn place he wants. He says prejudice is a bad thing, so I guess it is, unless you're German.

Cookie Swansea is the only kid at school who's half-and-half, and she's just about the best singer in the whole state of California, I bet. She likes to sing Spiritual songs that she learned in church. Spiritual songs are fun because everybody gets to clap and sing whether you're any good or not, and it's all in English, not in Catholic. Spiritual songs come from Africa and Detroit.

Cookie says she goes to the Baptist Church but it must be a different one than where Pinky and Stinky go, because they don't know any Spiritual songs. One time Cookie Swansea sang two solos for the whole school and all the teachers and parents were there too, and she wasn't even nervous at all. I think I would have barfed.

Anyways, Fred Brown seems like a OK kid and it was fun playing somebody so good, even if I did lose. I asked Fred Brown if he had a nickname and he looked at me cockeyed and said, "No, just Fred Brown." I bet nobody would dare call Fred Brown 'Stinky.' Fred Brown would probably pound them.

While we were playing, Coach Cunningham who manages me in Little League came over and said, "Hey, McAfee! What are you doing over there with that darkie?" and I said, "Playing tether ball." Coach Cunningham doesn't like Negroes. I know this because earlier this season Drew Tenzer and me were riding the bench and trading baseball cards, and I traded Mickey Mantle for

Willie Mays and Hank Aaron, and Coach Cunningham made a face and said, "Nigger lover."

If I can find my game, I'll be happy to join the Yankees next season because then I won't have to be managed by Coach Cunningham anymore. Personally I think he's a royal shitburger.

Speaking of Negroes, I should tell you about this great old man named Nathan who works in the parking lot of the Mayfair Market. There's this little building there called 'Archie's Shine Parlor,' and that's where Nathan works, he's a shoeshiner. (I don't know why it's called Archie's when the only guy who works there is called Nathan -- I guess you'd have to ask Nathan that.)

Anyways Nathan's real old, at least 40, and he has a little beard. You just leave your shoes and Nathan shines them and fixes them if they're broken, then you pick them up the next day. Sometimes I go there just to talk to Nathan because he has a lot of funny stories about the people in our town. Like did you know that Mr. Harrington from the bank has two completely different wives and families in two different towns and they don't even know about each other, which seems like they must be really stupid?

Nathan also told me there was a house in town where bad girls worked. I asked him why anyone would want to give jobs to bad girls, and he winked. Also Nathan knows how to trick the Coke machine into giving you a free bottle of Coke. Nathan is cool. He gives all the shoes their own names, and he says they are his pets. He has a gold tooth and a tattoo (which I didn't even know colored people could have,) and he listens to Nat King Cole all day long. I like Nat King Cole.

My dad also listens to Nat King Cole, but Uncle Mick doesn't like Nat King Cole or Elvis or Connie Francis or anybody who's American. All he listens to is Irish music by Irishmen like John McCormack or the Clancy Brothers or Mickey Rooney. When he drinks whiskey, Uncle Mick always cries and sings Irish songs. He must know a million of them and they're always real sad, about how beautiful and wonderful Ireland is, which makes me think if it's so wonderful and beautiful in Ireland then how come Uncle Mick lives in California?

September 24, 1960

It's Saturday and we played our last game of the season, against the Chicken Delight Leopards, and guess what? We tied 12 to 12, which is a lot better than losing. I only played the last two innings, but I came up twice and only struck out once. The other time I hit a single and stole two bases, so it was a pretty cool game. The best part about it was that Coach Cunningham took the whole team to 31 Flavors after the game and bought us all ice cream. I had a double cone with pistachio nut and rocky road. Maybe Coach Cunningham isn't such a buttworm after all?

It was a good thing I ate so much ice cream because Mom made Meat Loaf Surprise tonight, which tastes like goatboogers. The big 'surprise" in Meat Loaf Surprise is that it has some hard-boiled eggs hiding inside it. What kind of moron would think that up? Luckily Colin loves the stuff, so when nobody was looking I gave him most of mine.

After we went to our room, Mom got a bad telephone call. They thought I couldn't hear but I could hear some of it. Gramma is really sick. She has a cancer, but it's not the kind that kills you -- I don't know what kind it is. Mom must be real worried because I heard her ask Dad if we could all go to Mass tomorrow, which would be the first time in about two years. Dad said it was real important for him to mow the lawn tomorrow so he couldn't go, but that Mom and Colin and me could go, so it looks like I'll have to dress up and go. Ugh.

Here's some other bad stuff: this kid named Danny Beedy died from Leukemia today. Danny lived around the corner from us and was one year older than me. I didn't know him very well, but everybody's really sad. His little brother Duane is one year younger than me and is a pretty neat kid -- Mom says we should be especially nice to Duane now since his big brother died.

September 25, 1960

Well, we got all dressed up and Mom took Colin and me to Our
Lady of Sorrows for the Mass. We asked Uncle Mick if he wanted
to come with us and he said, "Going to Mass doesn't make you a
Catholic any more than standing in a garage makes you a car."
Anyhow, Mass was just like I remembered it the last time, with
singing and kneeling and praying and the foreign language.
Father O'Dowd said a special prayer for Gramma and that made
Mom feel better.

Colin was only about five the last time we went to Mass, and I
don't think he even remembered it, so he got kind of restless and
kept fidgeting in the pew and fooling with his wiener, and Mom
had to slap his hand a couple times. But we went to Hamburger
Hamlet afterward, and once we got our ties off, Colin was fine
again. I don't think he'll become a priest though.

September 26, 1960

Tonight we watched the debate on TV between Senator Kennedy
and Vice President Nixon. We're for Kennedy, duh! He's Irish-
American and a Catholic and a Democrat, so Mom and Dad think
he'll be good for the country, even though they're not sure he'll
win. Dad says that Nixon is a goddamn liar and a dickhead and he
wouldn't trust him as far as he could throw him, and that he'll
probably drop the H-bomb on the Russians.

Everybody seems scared about the H-bomb. In school sometimes they have drop-drills, which is where Miss Kleinholz
suddenly yells "DROP!" and all us kids have to jump onto the floor
and hide under our desks and put our heads between our knees
and kiss our ass goodbye. I guess that's a good idea if the
Commies drop the H-bomb. Also they have an air raid siren that
they test once a week, which makes all the dogs in town go nuts,
but I bet Rin Tin Tin wouldn't go nuts. He'd probably bite the
Commies and win the whole war all by himself, I bet.

September 27, 1960

Today at school we were talking about the debate so we held an election, and me and Toren Shumaker got nominated for Class President. Miss Kleinholz made us all put our heads down on our desks while we voted, so that nobody could see who voted for who. But I peeked and guess what? Every boy in the class voted for me, and every girl in the class voted for Toren. But there's 16 girls and 13 boys in the class, so Toren won and now she's Class President. That's the way the cookie crumbles.

Aunt Gwen came to dinner tonight. I think her and Mom wanted to talk about Gramma. Aunt Gwen is Mom's sister. They went out in the back yard for an hour after dinner and talked real quiet, and I tried to spy but I couldn't hear anything. After awhile they came back in and we all watched I Love Lucy on TV.

Aunt Gwen is a card. She was yelling at Lucy the whole show, saying stuff like, "Hey, um, Lucy! It's called lipstick, Lucy, not *facestick*! Uh, you don't have to smear it all over your face, Lucy!" Stuff like that. And you know that lady who plays Ethel on the show? Vivica Vance? Aunt Gwen says she shops at the Hughes Market right here in town, every Saturday afternoon. I'd really like to see her and get her autograph, but we go to the Mayfair, not the Hughes.

After Aunt Gwen left, Uncle Mick came by with two bottles of black beer. I was glad Aunt Gwen was gone because she and Uncle Mick don't get along, even though I think they'd be a great couple. Neither one of them is married and they're both about the same age, and they're both really funny. I told Dad they should get married, but he rolled his eyes and said, "One McAfee-Owen couple is enough for this world." (That's Mom's maiden name, 'Owen.')

I still think it's a good idea, though. They wouldn't even have to change their titles, because they'd still be Aunt Gwen and Uncle Mick. Mom said they're already kind of related, so if they got married it would never work, because it would be almost like incense.

Uncle Mick went out in the garage to smoke a Tiparillo (they stink!) and he said, "Hey Liam! Come with me," so I did. When I got there he showed me an old magazine called "Eyeful" that was full of pictures of ladies in their underwears. There were articles like, 'High Heeled Honeys,' and 'Rootin' Tootin' Tootsies,' and 'Curvy Corset Cuties.' It was great!

Uncle Mick says they don't make magazines like that anymore. All the ladies wore really funny underwears with straps and belts and buckles -- I never saw Mom wear any underwears like that. I wonder if the girls at school wear undies like that? I bet Miss Kleinholz doesn't, because her pointy titties would never fit into those things.

September 28, 1960

I got in trouble at school today. See, I'm in room 27, which is actually called a "bungalow." Bungalows are these rooms on stilts in the playground and you have to go up three stairs to get in. So I figured out if you go underneath the bungalow you can hide under the stairs and look between the cracks in the wood, and when the girls go on the stairs you can look up and see their underwears. I wanted to see if Marie Blessing wore the kind of underwears like in 'Eyeful.' Well, I got caught and Miss Kleinholz sent me to the Principal's office.

Our Principal is named Mrs. Palolozzi and she's about 150 years old and has a face like a prune and a boy's haircut. I wonder if Vince cuts her hair? Ha ha! I told her I was just playing Hide and Go Seek under the bungalow, but she didn't fall for it.

She asked me a lot of questions about my family and whether any grownups ever did anything weird to me. I was scared that she'd call my mom and tell on me, but she didn't -- she just benched me for a week, which means I can't play games at recess, I just have to sit on the bench like The Blob or something. Miss Kleinholz said, "This will give you a good opportunity to attend to your homework, Liam." Don't make me laugh.

The only way I'm allowed to get off the bench is if there's a fire drill. They have a fire drill about once a month, and all the kids have to go marching out of class and line up on the playground. You know what's weird? In case of fire you have to line up in a single file line from smallest to tallest. I may be only a kid, but what is the reason for that? Do tall people burn slower?

Oh, that reminds me, last year we had a heat wave and it was real hot, and Bobby Del Valle came to school one day barefoot so they sent him home to get some shoes. Bobby hates shoes. So Bobby came back with these old tennies that he cut the bottoms out of -- so it looked like shoes from the top, but he was really barefoot underneath, do you know what I mean? Bobby Del Valle can be pretty smart.

So anyways, Bobby got away with wearing his barefoot shoes for a whole week. Nobody finked on him because nobody wanted to get pounded. Then one day there was a fire drill and we all had to march across the playground, and there was water on the playground, so Bobby's wet footprints came out barefooted and he got benched.

September 29, 1960

They had to take Pinky Vanderhoeven to the Emergency Room today. After school Pinky and Stinky and me were making Ducky quack, and Pinky said, "Let's play duck," so we all got in the pen with Ducky and started quacking and pretending like we were ducks.

You don't want to know what Ducky eats -- it's pretty disgusting but I guess I have to tell you, because if I don't tell you this won't make any sense. Ducky eats snails. I'm serious! That's what ducks eat! So Pinky said if we want to play duck right we should eat snails too, so she did. They crunched just like Fritos when she ate them. Me and Stinky wouldn't do it, but Pinky ate a lot of them and got a stomachache so she had to go to the Emergency Room.

I told Mom about it and she said Pinky should be just fine because French people eat snails all the time, which personally makes me glad we're Irish-American. I wonder if French people eat Meat Loaf Surprise too?

Anyways I hope Pinky's OK. Come to think of it, it hasn't been a very good few days for Colin either. The last couple nights he woked up yelling and crying with nightmares and Mom and Dad didn't know what to do. They called Dr. Dicksau and he said it's probably pinworms. Pinworms are these little worms that live in your blood. They sleep in late during the daytime, but at night they go crazy and swim all around you in your blood, and they fire things up and it gives you nightmares. You get them from the sandbox at school, or else you can also get them if you forget to wash your hands after you take a dump.

September 30, 1960

This new TV show came on tonight for the first time, and it's a cartoon show but it's not just for kids, and it's called 'The Flintstones.' Did you watch it? We did and everybody liked it, even Dad who usually says all cartoons are stupid except for Betty Boop. It takes place back in the dinosaur times and it's pretty silly but in a good way. So now there's at least one show we can all agree on. Usually we all fight over the TV. I like Sky King and Roy Rogers and the Dodger games. Colin likes Romper Room and Sheriff John and Engineer Bill. Dad likes the Friday Night Fights and Ed Sullivan and Dragnet. Mom likes Perry Como and Bonanza and I Love Lucy. It's a mess.

If my allowance was bigger I'd save up and get a portable TV of my own, but since I only get 35 cents a week I'll be a old man in a wheelchair before I get one, I bet. Mom says I could get work mowing lawns or else I could get a paper route and save up money that way, but I hate mowing lawns because the grass makes me itch, and my bike's not good enough to do a paper route. Dad says I'm not very ambitious, which is pretty much true.

Oh I almost forgot, today while I was sitting on the bench during recess, this girl came over and sat next to me and asked me if I liked to play cards. She was real friendly and we played Go Fish and Crazy Eights and then War. Her name is Mary-Ann Lindstrom and she has red hair and freckles and band-aids on her knees. I never really noticed her before, and to tell you the truth I would've rather played cards with Bobby Del Valle because Mary-Ann doesn't know how to play poker, but still it was nice to have somebody to play with during recess for a change. And Mary-Ann is really smart. I only have three more days until my benching is over and then I can go back to sockball and dodgeball.

Tomorrow is Saturday and it's the first one in a long time where I won't be playing Little League. It's hot out so I'm thinking of going to the beach if I can talk somebody into it. If Mom and Dad are too busy, maybe Uncle Mick will take me to State Beach? He likes State Beach because there's always lots of really stacked girls in bikini bathing suits playing volleyball there. Also one time we saw Wilt Chamberlain playing volleyball there, and lots of girls were talking to him and getting his autograph. Uncle Mick says it's easy to get girls in bikinis to talk to you when you're famous and rich and seven feet tall.

October 1, 1960

There was nothing to do this morning so I went across the street and sat on Old Lady Kroot's lawn and looked for four-leaf-clovers, but she saw me on her lawn and turned on the sprinklers! She doesn't like kids.

Nobody could take me to the beach and I'm not supposed to go by myself. Sometimes I do anyway, but today Alex Eisenbaum and me walked downtown to the Royale Theater and saw the best movie I've ever seen in my whole life called 'The Magnificent Seven.' Have you seen it yet? You have to go see it! This bald headed guy is the leader of a gang of really cool gunmen, and they save a townful of poor Mexican farmers from a bad guy's gang.

You should see all the stuff that happens to them, it's the best! I ate Jordan Almonds and Jujubes and Good and Plentys and Red Hots, and they also had a Bugs Bunny cartoon.

One funny thing about the movie is that there's this one good guy in it who's supposed to be a Mexican but he sounds kind of like a German, and the bald guy is supposed to be an American but he sounds like a Polish guy or something. Alex pointed it out to me, and he ought to know because he's got the gift for languages.

I should probably tell you about Alex Eisenbaum. He lives around the corner on Palomar Street, and his real name is Aleksander. His Dad's first name is Wlodzimierz and his mom's first name is Feigl, but don't ask me how to pronounce that -- I had to ask Alex for the right spelling. He also has a baby sister named Sarah. They're from Poland and really nice. At least I *think* they're really nice -- actually his parents can't talk in English, so Alex turns everything into Polish and then back again. Sarah's too little to talk in anything except goo-goo-talk.

The parents came here to get away from Hitler. They're Jewish so they go to church on Saturday instead of Sunday, and they don't have Easter or Christmas but they have Passover and Honica instead, which seems just as good to me. You still get presents and stuff, they just come from your family instead of from Santa. What's the difference?

I bet it would be hard if you didn't talk English. You couldn't read the menu at Hamburger Hamlet or even the stop signs or anything else. His parents have been here a long time but they still can't do it, but Alex can talk Polish even though he's never even been to Poland, which is weird. Aunt Gwen said, "Some people just have a gift for languages, and, um, other people don't. It's just like you, Liam, you do well in science and reading, but you don't do very well in arithmetic, right? Some people just have the gift for certain things."

So I guess Alex has the gift. The best part is when I go over there and watch TV with Alex, we can watch anything we want to because Mr. and Mrs. Eisenbaum and Sarah don't care what they watch since they can't understand what's on anyway.

October 2, 1960

There's nothing to do when it rains, you can't ride your bike or go to the canyon or play hit-the-bat or anything. I can't even play with Colin because he's next door at Pinky's. Dad's watching golf on TV which is boring and Mom's busy washing clothes, so all there is to do is talk to you in this silly old Marty Graw Book.

Oh, I probably never even told about this book, did I? Well it started two weeks ago when they had Marty Graw at school. It's this big thing they do every year right before the fall term starts, and all the kids and parents go. It lasts all day long and they have a magician and a strong man and a bunch of bands and a cakewalk and skits and stuff like that. Also they have cotton candy and popcorn and hot dogs, and they have games where you can win stuff if you do good, like you can win a teddy bear if your darts breaks enough balloons, or you can win a goldfish if you can throw a ping pong ball into a little fishbowl.

Three years ago when I was almost seven, I threw the ping pong ball into the fishbowl and I won a goldfish. They give it to you in a little plastic bag. Mom and Dad always told us never to play with plastic bags because you can suffocate, and I thought maybe the goldfish might suffocate too, so I took it out of the bag and put it in my 7-Up.

I probably shouldn't have did that because it rolled over and floated, so I went back to the Goldfish Guy and tried to get another one but he wouldn't do it, so I ran and got Mom and Dad. Dad just said, "They don't make goldfish like they used to, Liam," and Mom said, "If that stuff will kill a goldfish that fast, imagine what it's doing to the kids' teeth?" I cried. I wouldn't cry now, but I was just a little kid then.

Anyways, one of the cool things about Marty Graw is they have this big General Store where they sell all kinds of good stuff really cheap. They have millions of records and books. I like records and books. They had this big book that was completely blank inside, which is a great idea because then you can make up your own book if you want to. I bet it would've cost about $1.44 in a real store, but it was only a dime at Marty Graw because it had a mustard stain on one page. Big deal! So Aunt Gwen bought it for me and that's why I'm talking to you, whoever you are.

Aunt Gwen told Mom I could make it a "Diary." Actually, it was sort of funnier than that because Aunt Gwen has this habit of saying "er" and "uh" when she talks, so what she really said was, "Um, Liam could make that into a diary, uh, couldn't he?" And I started laughing because I thought she said, "Liam could make that into a diarrhea, couldn't he?" and I couldn't figure out why a book had anything to do with the shits, unless you were supposed to wipe with the pages, which seems stupid since toilet paper is softer.

Uncle Mick says toilet paper is only really softer in America. He fought in the Korean War so he's been all over the place, and he says in some places the toilet paper is really hard and brown and has little bits of sand in it. He also said that in Siam and Persia and places like that, they don't even have toilets -- they just have two little footprints painted on the ground like at the Arthur Murray Dance Studio, and you're just supposed to stand on those footprints and poop right down into a little hole, and when you're done they don't even have toilet paper, you just wipe your butt with your hand! I don't believe Uncle Mick – sometimes he's just plain full of it.

So anyhow Aunt Gwen says it's called a diary and that you're supposed to write in it every day, and that at the start of each day you're supposed to write, "Dear Diary." But that seems really stupid to me, like the pages are an imaginary person or something. I asked her if she says, "Dear Telephone," every time the phone rings, but Mom gave me one of Those Looks so I shut up. But I still think saying "Dear Diary" is dumb, so I'm not going to say it and that's that.

And that's how come this book's being writ. I don't know if I'll write in it every day because some days are pretty boring around here, but if there's anything going on worth talking about, I'll tell you. Mom says I can write anything I want and that nobody is allowed to sneak in and look at it, and when I'm an old man I can read this and remember being a kid, but I sure hope I have a lot better stuff to do by then.

October 3, 1960

I accidentally got Scotty McDonald in trouble today, because he called me a "slut" and I didn't know what that meant so I asked Miss Kleinholz and she said, "Where did you hear that word, Liam?" so I said Scotty called me it. So she asked Scotty where he heard it. He didn't know what it meant either, but he showed her this book called 'A Bell For Adano,' which is about the war, and there's this part where one guy says to another guy, "I'm going to screw me one of these sluts yet." Scotty thought that was funny, so he called me one.

Miss Kleinholz didn't really get mad at Scotty, she just told him not to bring the book to school again. When I got home, Mom and Gramma and Aunt Gwen were all sitting around playing cards so I asked them what it meant, and Mom said, "Ask me again in about 100 years," and Gramma said, "He'll find out soon enough won't he?" and Aunt Gwen said, "Uh, go look it up in the dictionary." Gee, thanks.

Scotty McDonald lives over on Quinto Street, which seems far away if you walk it, but it's only ten minutes by bike. Sometimes I go over there and visit. His dad's dead so he lives in this little apartment with his mom and two older brothers who are always in trouble for something or other.

I like hanging around Scotty's place -- it's different. But Scotty just likes to get out of there. He rides his bike everywhere, and keeps it inside at night so the dope attics don't swipe it.

Dad thinks Scotty will grow up to be a juvenile delinquent like his brothers did, but I don't think he will, because he's pretty smart and his brothers are dumber than doornails. I'm not exactly sure all the bad stuff his brothers have done, but their pictures have been in the paper a couple times so I know they've done some bad stuff.

I do know that his oldest brother Milo once hit this guy named Muggsy Green over the head with a pool cue one night at The Golden Frog. That's not smart -- Muggsy Green is an awful tough guy. I bet Milo's too stupid to read 'A Bell For Adano.'

October 15, 1960

Well it's been almost two weeks since I talked to you, which is the first time that's ever happened. That's because I've been real busy. Some good junk happened and some bad junk and some stupid junk. Which do you want to hear about first? OK, I'll tell you the good junk first.

First of all, I got unbenched. Also the World Series came and went and the Yankees lost, which is great! I hate the Yankees. They got beat in the last inning of the last game on a home run by Bill Mazeroski so the next day at school everybody wanted Bill Mazeroski's baseball card, and since I had about 16 of them, I made some great trades for guys I like: old cards of Roy Campanella and Eddie Mathews. Miss Kleinholz even let Bobby Del Valle bring a transistor radio to school and let us listen to the games. Everybody at school was really happy the Yankees lost.

Everybody hates the Yankees. In fact, my favorite baseball movie is called 'Damn Yankees' -- it's the best. It would've been a lot more believable though if it didn't have all that singing and stuff. I mean how many ballgames have you ever seen on TV where the whole team suddenly just starts singing and dancing like that? Miss Kleinholz says that kind of movie is called a musical. It was still great and everything, but it could've been really great if nobody sung, I bet.

OK, so here's the bad stuff: Gramma had a stroke and now half her face is frozen. It's weird to talk to her now because she smiles and talks out of one side of her face, but the other side just sits there like it's stuck or something. The doctors said a lot of that will go away after awhile so that's good, but right now it's pretty strange.

You know how when you go to the Eye Doctor he holds up a card in front of one eye, and then in front of the other one? Well, that's kind of how I felt with Gramma -- I wanted to hold up a card to cover the frozen half of her face so I could figure out how she was supposed to look. I told Mom that, but she called me a "smart aleck" even though I was being serious.

Anyways, Gramma was in the hospital for awhile, but they sent her home because she kept smoking near the oxygen tanks and the nurses were afraid she'd blow the whole place up, so she got to go home.

OK, so here's the stupid stuff: Scotty McDonald's brother Milo robbed a bank and got caught and now he's in jail! No kidding! And the really stupid part isn't so much that he just robbed a bank -- he robbed the bank right here in town, the one about two blocks from where he lives! And the teller was this girl he went to high school with! Is Milo a idiot or what?

Sure he wore a disguise, but alls it was was dark glasses and a fake mustache and a Dodger cap. And he walked right up to this girl he went to high school with, and gave her this note that said, "Give me all the money. I have a gun." Then he took the money and walked on home two blocks away, just like nothing happened! Scotty was so embarrassed he didn't come to school for two days. I mean, it wouldn't be too bad to have your brother be a bank robber, but nobody wants his brother to be a *moron* bank robber.

Mrs. McDonald hasn't come out of their apartment for four days and Mom's really worried about her, but when I asked Scotty about his mom, he said she's OK -- not great but OK. He said she's been drinking a lot of wine and lighting candles, but she's not nearly as messed up as when his dad died, so he figures she'll be fine after awhile.

I think they took up a collection at Our Lady of Sorrows, because Scotty said that Father O'Dowd brought over a lot of food and some money, which is actually pretty neato if you think about it. I mean, they don't even have a racket selling Jesus newspapers like the Jehovah's do, so when they give somebody some money it must mean they really care, I guess.

October 16, 1960

Here's the latest news. Some guy from the FBI called Mom today, and Mom's brother, Uncle Jake, got in trouble for smuggling some loco weed from Mexico into Texas. I guess there was a lot of it because now he has to go to prison for three whole years. Mom's not very happy, and Aunt Gwen is really mad -- she says Uncle Jake was always a bad seed and she knew he'd go to the hoosegow someday.

To tell you the truth I hardly remember Uncle Jake, but he seemed all right to me. When I was really little he used to come visit sometimes, and he always brought me some foreign coins to play with. Dad didn't like him much, but Uncle Jake was OK to Colin and me. When I was about six or seven and I used to say my prayers at night, I always used to say:

Now I lay me down to sleep,
With my peanuts at my feet,
If I should die before I wake,
Give my peanuts to Uncle Jake.

Anyways I guess he has to go to prison now. I hope he'll be OK there. I once saw this movie about prison with Jimmy Cagney, and it looked pretty rough in there. I forget the name of the picture, but there was this part where Jimmy Cagney smashed a grapefruit in somebody's face, which made me laugh. Maybe Uncle Jake can go to Alcatraz, and his cellmate will be Milo McDonald, and Uncle Jake can smash a grapefruit in Jimmy Cagney's face?

October 17, 1960

Today at recess I was playing four-square with Duane Beedy, the kid whose brother died of Leukemia, and we were talking about Danny. Duane said he still talks to Danny late at night, but that it's not really Danny, it's just Danny's "Monitor," and that Danny is getting younger every day and is scared of coyotes. I wonder if Duane might be losing his marbles?

Do you remember Mary-Ann Lindstrom, the little red-haired girl with the freckles who played cards with me when I got benched? Well, she finally got around to asking me why I'd gotten benched, and for some reason I didn't lie. I just told her the truth, that I wanted to look at girls' underwears to see if they had those funny straps and things like in 'Eyeful.' And Mary-Ann said she'd show me her undies if I really wanted to see it, so I said, "Yes please," and she did. And guess what? They look exactly like boy's underwears, just plain old white underpants, that's all. Man was I disappointed!

October 18, 1960

After school I was at the park and I was talking to this older kid named Brian Evans about how Uncle Jake got caught smuggling loco weed at the Mexican border. So then Brian told me about how their whole family went down to Mexico last summer to go camping. Brian and his mom and dad and sister and gramma all went.

So they were camping in tents on the beach, and one night their gramma died of old age. She was about 100 years old so nobody was too surprised. But Brian's parents were scared that the Mexican Police would take Gramma's body away and bury it in Mexico, and Gramma wanted to be buried at Forest Lawn next to Grampa. So Mr. Evans got this great idea: they didn't tell anyone what happened, they just wrapped Gramma in a blanket and put her in the trunk and brought her back to America.

Brian said that everybody in the car was real nervous at the border, because there would have been a lot of explaining to do if the Border Cops found a dead gramma in the trunk. But the cops didn't even look in the trunk, so the family drove right back into America, no problem.

When they got to San Diego, Brian's mom and dad were so nervous they decided they needed a Margarita, so they stopped somewhere and the kids got a coke, and the parents had a couple Margaritas. Then when they went back out to the parking lot, their car had been stolen.

October 19, 1960

Aunt Gwen works down at the Rexall Drug Store so sometimes I go there after school just to say hello. Today she looked kind of sick and she said, "Liam, um, I have to go to the ladies room for five minutes. Can you please watch the store for me?"

I said, "But I don't know how to work the cash register!"

Aunt Gwen said, "Don't worry about that, if anybody comes in, just call them 'sir' or 'ma'am,' and tell them I'll be right back."

So I said, "OK."

A couple of minutes later this fancy lady carrying a little tiny dog came in, and she said, "Excuse me, who's in charge here?"

I was afraid the little dog would poop on the floor and I'd have to clean up the dogdoo, so I hurried over and said, "My Aunt Gwen is in charge here, but she had to go to the toilet really, really, really bad, so she won't be back for awhile, ma'am. I can't work the cash register, but if I can help you some other way, I will."

So the lady smiled and said, "Can you please direct me to the women's products?"

"Sure!" I said. "What kind of women's products? Perfume? Soap?"

And she said, "I would like to buy sanitary napkins."

Well, that was easy enough -- I took her where the napkins were, but she said, "No, son, I'm looking for sanitary napkins,"

So I told her, "All Rexall's napkins are quite sanitary, ma'am," and she said maybe she'd better wait for Aunt Gwen. Some people just don't trust kids, I guess.

October 20, 1960

Today in school there were two new kids in our class, these twins named Vicki and Rikki Drinkwater. They're supposed to be identical twins, but I've already figured them out because Vicki is really talkative and funny, and Rikki is a little shy and quiet and can't stop picking her nose. It's disgusto!

I mean it's one thing to pick your nose once in a while when there's something in there that you just *have* to get, but Rikki Drinkwater can't stop -- all day long she had a finger up there, and sometimes even a thumb too. Do you think she's got some kind of Nosepicker's Disease or something? At least she doesn't eat her boogers like James Watson does. He rolls them up into little balls and eats them like Kandy Korn.

Speaking of diseases, after lunch today the whole class had to march down to Nurse Norbitch's office and we all had to eat these sugar cubes that are supposed to keep us from getting Polio. I can't figure out why we have to do this, because all us kids already got Polio shots years ago. I mean, how many times can you not get Polio? Polio must be awful, though. Danny Sweppston got it, and he has to walk with a brace now.

There's lots of diseases that are mysterious. Some diseases you can get from rotten milk and some from dirty water, and some from if a moron in the cafeteria sneezes on your hot dog. And there's other ones you don't know *how* you get them. Like I heard Uncle Mick tell Dad that when he was in the Korean War, he caught a bad Vetrinerial Disease from a young girl there, and I thought only dogs and cats had Vetrinerial Diseases, not young Korean girls.

October 21, 1960

Miss Kleinholz had a Poetry Contest today, and I came in third. Toren Shumaker was first, which doesn't surprise me because she's Class President and kind of a kiss-ass. Mary-Ann Lindstrom

was second. I'll read you all three poems and you can be the judge.
Toren's first-place poem was called 'Faith:'

The Lord created snow capped peaks,
So we may know His breadth and reach,
The moon and sun beguile us and,
Remind us of His guiding hand.

Now just between you and me, I bet she swiped that whole
thing from some Sunday School book or something. It doesn't
sound to me like something a 10-year-old kid would think up, do
you know what I mean? Mom would say, "Something's rotten in
Denmark." Mary-Ann Lindstrom wrote the second-place poem.
It's called 'Friday Night:'

If my mother,
And my brother,
Had their druthers,
They would blister,
My big sister,
And the guy who kissed her.

Now I thought that was a pretty good poem and should've won!
Anyways, my own poem was called 'Pickles:'

Pickles, pickles, all over the house,
Pickles, pickles, attracting that mouse,
Pickles, pickles, all over the floor,
I ain't going to eat no more pickles no more.

I got downgraded because I used the word 'ain't.' But Mickey
Mantle uses the word 'ain't' all the time and he's the most famous
man in the world, even more famous than President Eisenhowler,
I bet.

Bobby Del Valle got in trouble for his poem. He wrote:

I like coffee, I like tea
It's a shame they make me pee.
Animal crackers in my soup
Makes me want to take a poop.

October 22, 1960

Do you have a Helms Man? I bet you don't -- Dad says the Helms Man only comes to a small part of the state, so I guess I'll have to tell you about him.

You know how there's the Milkman who drives a truck and brings milk and butter and eggs? Or how there's the Ice Cream Man? Well the Helms Man is kind of like that, except Helms is this big bakery, so instead of milk or ice cream, the Helms Man brings doughnuts and cookies and cakes and pies and bread and stuff like that.

The Helms Men all drive these little wooden trucks with drawers inside, so you can walk right up into the Helms Truck and slide open the drawers and smell all the doughnuts. It's the best! Glazed doughnuts cost a nickel and jelly doughnuts are six cents. Creampuffs cost a fortune -- they're fifteen cents!

On the back of the Helms Truck, there's this big bumper that sticks way out. It has to be big, because sometimes the Helms Man has to stand on it to load and unload the truck. So when nobody's looking, sometimes us kids run after the Helms Truck and sit on the bumper and ride all over town on the back of the Helms Truck. If the driver catches you he gets really mad, but usually he doesn't see us, so it's fun.

Except today me and Stinky jumped on there, and I guess it was quitting time for the Helms Man, because he got onto the Coast Highway and drove all the way back to the bakery which is about 15 miles away in Culver City. There's no stop signs or traffic lights on the Coast Highway, so he never stopped once, which meant me and Stinky couldn't jump off without getting squarshed, so we just hung on and yelled a lot, but the Helms Man must be hard of hearing.

When we finally jumped off in Culver City we had to borrow a dime from a wino and call Mrs. Vanderhoeven to come pick us up. Naturally she told Mom and Dad, and boy oh boy, I am in some deep dogdoo this time! I got spanked and I can't play with Stinky for a week, no TV for a week and no Helms doughnuts for a month!

October 23, 1960

Today is Sunday so Bobby Del Valle and me rode our bikes down to the beach. We're not supposed to go down there alone, but sometimes we do it anyway. This time we rode out to the Santa Monica Pier, which is really a fun place because they have a Penny Arcade and bumper cars and pinball games and stuff like that. I told Mom I was just riding to the baseball diamond, so I sure hope nobody saw me at the pier. After what happened yesterday, I'd be grounded til Christmas if I got caught at the pier!

I had about $3 that I made at the Nursery Game, so I was able to play pinball and stuff for a little while, and ride the bumper cars once. I could've paid thirty cents to see Jerry The Alligator Man ("IT CAME FROM THE SWAMP! HALF MAN! HALF REPTILE! THE MISSING LINK! JERRY THE ALLIGATOR MAN!") but Bobby told me he saw it once and it was a gyp.

I guess I never told you about the Nursery Game, did I? Well, that's the way I made my $3 and it's kind of illegal, so you have to promise not to tell, OK? Cross your heart and hope to die? OK. Here's the Nursery Game:

There's two nurseries here in town. Not the kind of nursery where you store your little kids, I mean the kind where you buy plants and trees and fertilizer and stuff like that. There's Mr. Sampson's Nursery, and then just down the block and across the street, there's Yoshida's Nursery. They compete with each other and have sales, and try to drive each other out of business, but so far both of them do OK and neither one is winning what Dad calls "The Nursery Wars."

So anyway, both of these nurseries will sell you small plants, and they come in square wooden boxes called 'flats.' Flats are about two feet by two feet, and a couple of inches deep. When you buy strawberry plants or something like that, you buy a flat full of them, filled up with dirt. The nursery makes you pay a 25-cent deposit for the wooden flat, then you take home your plant and stick it in the ground, and then when you return the flat they give you your 25 cents back.

Now here's what's weird: both of the nurseries use the same kind of flats, and they both store big piles of flats outside, behind a fence. So if you wait til it's dark you can climb over the fence at Sampson's and toss a few flats over the fence and hide them somewhere. Then you can wait a day or two and take those flats over to Yoshida's and get 25 cents each for them. Then you wait a few more days and climb Yoshida's fence and swipe them back again, and take them back to Sampson's and get another 25 cents each for them. The same flats!

The only thing is you can't be greedy and do this too often, because after all, kids like us don't really buy a lot of plants, you know? So you don't want to make anybody suspicious. I only do it maybe every two or three months, and also I make sure I never go into either nursery with Mom or Dad so I won't be recognized.

Other than the Nursery Game, the only other bad thing I do to get money is to sometimes take the Coke bottles from the racks on the Coke machines at the gas stations, and then I take them to the Hughes Market and get two cents deposit for each one. I never take the bottles to the Mayfair, because everybody knows me at the Mayfair and they know my family would never buy whole cases of Coca Cola at a time. But they don't know me at the Hughes. I keep looking for Vivica Vance there, but so far I haven't seen her.

October 24, 1960

What do you do when you're stuck inside an elephant?   Run around until you're all pooped out. Ha ha!

October 25, 1960

Standing outside school today there was this weird guy in a Frankenstein mask, and he was handing out these flyer thingies that advertised a big Halloween Show at the Royale Theater. Here's what the ad says:

SUNDAY NIGHT, OCT 31.
BIG HALLOWEEN SHOW AT THE ROYALE THEATER!
3 super shock shows! On stage, in person:
Mad monster impersonator
Dr. Evil and his Terrors of the Unknown!
First time here!
Unlike anything you have ever seen before! All new!
Living dead sit next to you!
Monsters grab girls from audience!
See girls head chopped off right before your eyes!
You'll have nightmares for a week!
Anything can happen and usually does!
Live snakes roam theater! Also, in person:
THE MUMMY! KING KONG!
See! We can't advertise what happens when Mummy grabs slave girls and lights go out, but WOW!
Something you never dreamed you'd see!
TWIST CONTEST!
IF YOU ARE BRAVE ENUF - YOU WIN A REAL DEAD BODY
FREE!
admission 75 cents

I showed the flyer to Dad, but he says the guy who's putting on this show must be an idiot to have it on Halloween night, because all the kids will be out trick-or-treating. He says Dr. Evil will lose his shorts. I mean it does sound scary and cool and all that, but Dad's got a point -- would you rather pay to go to the movies, or would you rather go around and get a huge bagful of free candy? Well? Would you?

October 26, 1960

On the way home from school I was talking to Duane Beedy a little more about his dead brother Danny. He told me Danny's "Monitor" lives sort of under the ground. So I asked him if "Monitors" were like ghosts, and he said, not really; they were more like reflections. He said it was kind of like when you go to the movies and you look real hard at the light rays coming out of the projection booth, you can see movement and color in the light rays, but if you reach out to touch it, there's nothing really there? That's what "Monitors" are like, he says.

Duane says they give advice, but they warn you to listen to their advice right away rather than a week from now, because Monitors get younger and younger every day, so their advice gets worse.

He also says although you can't touch Monitors, they can touch you -- but it just feels like a whisper of wind, and it makes your TV go all static and makes electrical stuff happen, like your toast burns and the radio goes on by itself. Stuff like that. It all sounds kind of crazy-like to me, and I sure hope nobody I know dies of Leukemia anytime soon.

Do you remember I told you about Marie Blessing, the most beautiful girl in the whole 5th grade? Well, she moved away! Her family had to move because her dad lost his job at some airplane company, so they went away and that's that. I didn't even get a chance to say goodbye or to even tell her I thought she was perfect. Mom said, "Liam, there's a lesson there. When you like somebody, tell them, because you never know if you might never see them again."

I think maybe she was thinking about older people and when they die, but still that lesson makes sense even for kids, I guess. I would've liked to known Marie better, but she was so pretty she made me nervous.

October 27, 1960

After school today I got to watch whatever I wanted to on TV, because Colin got grounded from TV for a night, for smart mouthing Dad. It happened when Dad sat down after work last night and said, "So, what's on the TV?" And Colin said, "The antenna, duh!" Dad didn't think that was funny, but I do.

Tonight the moon was full and I went outside to play with Pinky (I'm still grounded from Stinky over the Helms Truck thing,) and I didn't get home til about nine. We were playing Cowboys And Indians on Old Lady Kroot's lawn and she turned the sprinklers on us again. What a royal shitburger! So we rang her doorbell and ran away a few times, and then we put a dogdoo in her mailbox.

We looked all over the neighborhood for a big fresh dogdoo like Rin Tin Tin would've made, but we couldn't find one, so we settled for a little white one that's not much bigger than a duckdoo. But still, that'll fix her!

October 28, 1960

These two special teachers came to school today, one man and one woman. They were kind of like plastic looking -- Mary-Ann Lindstrom said they looked just like Ken and Barbie, which cracked me up because they did. Anyways they were health teachers, and Ken took all the boys into one room and Barbie took all the girls into another. Then they showed some movies.

The movie they showed the boys was called 'From Boy To Man,' and it was about penises and reproduction and sperms and that kind of stuff. Most of it I already knew about anyways. At lunchtime Mary-Ann said she'd tell me about the girl's movie if I told her about the boy's, so we talked and she said the girl's movie was called 'From Girl To Woman,' and it was also about reproduction and babies and stuff, but it had some things I didn't know about before, like periods and vaginas and stuff.

Oh, I almost forgot, Aunt Gwen is a widow! Well, sort of, anyway. Tonight she came over for dinner, and she was really sad because she just found out one of her ex-husbands died. Aunt Gwen has three ex-husbands (well, two now if you want to get technical,) which seems pretty many considering she's only about thirty.

Anyways, the one who died was named Freddy Gatlin and he was her second husband. I don't remember him too good at all. He drownded in the Marina. Him and two other guys were drinking Pabst Blue Ribbon all day and they decided they'd steal a yott and drive it to Catalina, so they did, but they were so drunk they drove it about fifty feet into the jetty and it sunk. The other guys got saved, but Freddy Gatlin got drownded.

Aunt Gwen seemed pretty sad about it. She said Freddy wasn't the worst husband she ever had. Aunt Gwen also said the reason lots of marriages don't work is that most women act wild when they're trying to attract a man, but once they get him, they change and become normal housewives. Meanwhile (she says) most women are attracted to the slightly dangerous type of man -- they figure they can marry the guy and change him later. But the men don't change later, plus they don't like it that their wives changed.

I don't know about any of that stuff, but Mom decided Aunt Gwen was getting "too philosophical" and needed some cheering up, so they broke out some champagne to drink to Freddy Gatlin's memory. Aunt Gwen said, "Bigamy is having one husband too many. Monogamy is the same," which made Mom laugh. The champagne must've worked because after awhile Aunt Gwen was giggling and having fun and she even let Colin teach her how to do

The Twist. That was a pretty funny sight -- a 30-year-old lady doing The Twist with a 7-year-old kid. Aunt Gwen says if Colin was older, she'd marry him.

October 29, 1960

Toren Shumaker got a tooth knocked out today at school! She was running in the sandbox and she tripped over Frankie Dupoy who always sleeps there during recess, and she hit her mouth on the edge of the sandbox and knocked her front tooth clean out!

She started screaming and Miss Kleinholz took her to Nurse Norbitch's room. Frankie found her tooth on the playground and brought it to her. Miss Kleinholz said it was a good thing Frankie found her tooth, because it was a permanent tooth and the dentist could probably shove it back in.

After school today I went to say hi to Aunt Gwen at the Rexall, but she wasn't in a very good mood -- she said she had a champagne hangover. This other lady overheard her and laughed and said, "Gwen? Here's my advice for the day. If you're hung over, do exactly the two things it says on the Aspirin bottle: 'Take two Aspirin' and 'keep away from children.'"

Halloween's coming up on Sunday, and I still haven't figured out what I want to be this year. Colin is going as a pirate -- Mom made him a cool costume with an eye patch and a phony parrot, and a red scarf to wear around his head and a big cardboard sword and a fake scar. I'd like to be the Wolfman, but the really good Wolfman masks cost a lot at the Hobby Shop. Maybe if I take out the trash and do the dishes and mow the lawn I can get Mom to buy me the Wolfman mask?

October 30, 1960

I got Mom to OK me getting the Wolfman mask, sort of. Actually what she said was, "Go ask your father," so I told Dad, "Mom says it's OK with her if it's OK with you," and Dad said, "Well, as long as it's all right with your mother..." The thing costs $3.99 plus tax which is a lot, and I have to promise I'll use it again next year too, but it looks like we get to go to the Hobby Shop this afternoon and pick it up. Yay!

I don't know any kids who are going to the Royale Theater for the Dr. Evil Show tomorrow night -- everybody I know will be out trick-or-treating. But Scotty says his brother Jimmy will be going, along with some other teenagers who are too old to trick-or-treat. I guess Milo had a ticket too, but he's still in jail for robbing the bank. I want to talk to Jimmy afterward and find out how they gave away "a real dead body free!" It couldn't be real. Could it?

October 31, 1960

Happy Halloween! I don't have time to talk because I'm getting ready to go trick-or-treating with Colin and Pinky and Stinky and Alex Eisenbaum. Mom says she has to go with us "to protect us," but she promised she'd stay in the background and not actually come up to peoples' doors with us. We're getting too old for that!

November 1, 1960

Well, Halloween came and went and boy was it ever interesting. Alex didn't have any costume because his mom and dad don't really understand about Halloween, so Colin suggested he could just go as a ghost -- we could hang a sheet over him and cut some eyeholes. But then Uncle Mick said, "Naw, that's dumb. And how do we know that a kid who wears a sheet is really dressed up as ghost, anyway? Couldn't he just be dressing up as a mattress?"

In the end we fixed up Alex with a quick Cowboy costume by letting him wear my boots and Dad's Stetson hat and Stinky's toy guns. Stinky was Frankenstein and he looked pretty cool. Colin was Bluebeard the Pirate and he looked great. Pinky was a Magic

Ballerina, which was easy to do because she takes ballet anyway so she already had the pointy shoes and the too-too thingy, and all she needed was a magic wand which her mom made out of a barbecue skewer.

The night started out fine. Everybody on our side of the street was really cool and gave us good candy. Mr. and Mrs. Bradley even turned their house into 'The Haunted Castle' and made us all walk through it -- it was full of scary stuff! The Morrisons gave out whole nickel candy bars so we wanted to go there twice, but Mom said that would be greedy, so we couldn't.

Then we went across the street and everybody there was nice, even the Dortmunders, until we got to Old Lady Kroot's. Pinky and I looked at each other and remembered we'd just stuck a dogdoo in her mailbox a few days ago, so we said, "Let's just skip this house." But Alex and Stinky said, "Why?" and Mom said, "Go ahead, Liam, she won't bite you," so we had to go.

So we counted one-potato two-potato to see who'd ring the doorbell and we yelled "Trick or treat!" and Old Lady Kroot came to the door and smiled and gave each of us some cookies. So far, so good. We stuck the cookies in our bags and got the heck out of there.

About twenty minutes later we were around the corner on Palomar Street and just as we were about to bang on Duane Beedy's door, Pinky started screaming for water and yelling, "I've been poisoned!" She was eating Old Lady Kroot's cookie, so Mom took a look at the cookie and sniffed it, and it was full of red pepper! Old Lady Kroot tried to murder us! So Mom took all the Old Lady Kroot cookies from our bags, and each one was like that, filled up either with red pepper or hot chilies.

I have never ever seen my mother as mad as she was then! She marched us all home and said, "You all wait here for ten minutes, then we'll go out again, but right now I'm going to have a word with that witch across the street!"

We tried to watch through the window but we were blocked by the oak tree so we couldn't see exactly what happened, but Mom came back about five minutes later.   "What happened, what happened?" we all yelled, "did you slug her in the stomach?"

Mom just smiled and said, "No of course not.   But that old crone won't be poisoning any other kids tonight.   And by the way, which one of you brats put dog stuff in her mailbox?"

I could've lied and gotten away with it, but Pinky's just too little to get away with anything -- she started crying and said, "Liam and me did it."

I thought my mother was going to have a fit, but do you know what she did?   She said, "Good!"

I couldn't believe it!   My mother said "good" that we put a dogdoo in Old Lady Kroot's mailbox!   Isn't that amazing?   But then she said, "Never do it again, though."

There's always a catch, you know?

Anyhow, the rest of the night was pretty uneventful compared to that, but we got a lot more candy and stuff, and we walked all over the neighborhood til after 9:30 at night.   There were tons of other kids out, all dressed up, and whenever we bumped into any of them we warned them not to eat Old Lady Kroot's cookies.   But they all said when they went to Old Lady Kroot's she gave them all a Snickers, so I guess she made those cookies especially for us. Next year we'll have to have better costumes so Old Lady Kroot won't be able to tell who we are.

I wonder how she knew who put the dogdoo in her mailbox, anyways?   I mean, it's not like we left fingerprints on it.

November 2, 1960

Toren was back at school today, and Miss Kleinholz was right, they put her tooth back in, but now her jaw is all wrapped up and she has to eat through a straw for a whole week.   Mary-Ann Lindstrom says that's a good thing because now Toren can't whine at everything.

So today at recess, Scotty McDonald told me about the Dr. Evil show at the Royale Theater. He didn't go himself but his brother Jimmy did, and Jimmy told Scotty all about it.

It started with this Dr. Evil guy giving a lecture about the spirit world, then he did a bunch of magic tricks. Jimmy told Scotty it was the best magic he'd ever seen, and there was this one trick where Dr. Evil cut a girl's head off and it looked so real that somebody fainted!

Then there were live appearances by the Mummy and King Kong, and a Twist Contest, with the "real dead body free" as the prize. Shirley Moncrief and Mike Vecchio won the Twist Contest, so they blindfolded them and gave them their "real dead body" and guess what? It was a chicken! Just a chicken like you buy at the market! Jimmy said everybody booed at that one.

But after that there was a blackout where all the lights went out, and there were explosions and glow-in-the-dark monsters and skeletons and snakes, and Jimmy said that was totally cool. Then they showed three horror movies, 'Teenage Zombies,' 'Ghost of Dragstrip Hollow' and 'Invasion of the Saucer Men.' If Dr. Evil comes back in a few years when I'm too old to trick-or-treat, I'd like to go see that show.

November 3, 1960

Today Miss Kleinholz made me the Registrar. She said it was because I had "good reading and writing skills." I wonder where she got that idea? Maybe it's because she sees me sometimes talking to you in this Marty Graw Book? Anyway, now I have to keep track of who's at school and who's home sick and who's tardy and stuff like that.

It's pretty boring except that she gave me this big old notebook that lists not only all the kids in our class, but every kid in the whole entire school! It lists all the kid's names and birthdays and telephone numbers. I looked myself up and there I was: McAfee, Liam Freddy, 9-22-50, GLadstone 4-4701. And every other kid is there, too. So I got curious and guess what? I'm the only kid in the whole school named Liam and Colin is the only Colin, too. There's zillions of Johns and Billys and Bettys and Margarets and even two kids named Raju, but we're the only ones named Liam and Colin.

I went home after school and asked Mom why they named us Liam and Colin and she said they're Irish names. Liam is Irish for William. She said if I think about it, Liam is just the back half of William, and I guess it is. I'm happy it's pronounced "Lee-yum" and not "Ull-yum."

Anyhow, now I can be a spy! I'll know everybody's birthday and I've got everybody in the whole school's phone number! I can call them up and say funny stuff, or hang up on people I don't like. Or I could sell kids' phone numbers to other kids for a nickel and get rich! This'll be great!

November 4, 1960

So after school I was walking home with some kids and Duane Beedy came up to me and whispered, "Liam! If you want to hear the Monitors, meet me back here in 15 minutes."

I didn't know what to think, but Duane's an even littler kid than me, so if he's not scared I'm sure not going to chicken out. So I said, "OK," and I doubled back and met him.

We walked down to the corner where a big chunk of the curb is missing so that the rain water can drain down into the sewer. Duane said, "Stick your head down in there and listen," so I did.

"I can't hear anything," I said, but Duane said, "Shhh! Listen real close! Concentrate!" so I did. And after awhile I could hear all sorts of weird stuff like water dripping, and scraping noises, and funny echoes of talking and laughing and knocking.

"It's the *Monitors*," Duane said. "They're talking to each other. If you come back in a week it'll sound different, because the Monitors get younger and younger every day -- they only live for about a year, and they start out old until they become babies and die."

I don't know about Duane Beedy, do you know what I mean? Either he's really onto something big, or he's the craziest kid I ever met. When I got home I looked up "monitor" in the dictionary and the first definition said, "One that admonishes, cautions, or reminds, especially with respect to matters of conduct."

So maybe he really *is* right? I don't think so, though. If they're supposed to give out good advice, then I have some advice for them: "Hey Monitors? Move out of the sewer! It stinks in there!"

November 5, 1960

Aunt Gwen came over this afternoon and she was all dressed up to go to a wedding. She said, "I don't know why I go to these things, they never work out," and Mom said "Sometimes they do."

And Aunt Gwen said, "Yeah well, you can just tell I'm dying to tie myself to the stove, cranking out casseroles for Jim-Bob the pipe fitter."

Mom told her not to give up hope, and Aunt Gwen said, "You sound just like the old folks. Old folks, um, used to come up to me at weddings and poke me in the ribs and cackle and say, 'You're next.' They stopped after I started doing the same thing to them at funerals."

Just then the phone rang and guess what? Uncle Mick won the Irish Sweepstakes! No, not first prize or even second or third, but still he won some money. I'm not quite sure how it all works, but first your name has to be drawn and then your horse has to do good in this big race in Ireland. Anyhow, Uncle Mick got a telegram saying he won some money. When the kid delivering the telegram knocked on his door, Uncle Mick tried to refuse to take it. He said, "Only bad news comes by telegram," but this time he was wrong.

He won almost $2000! Isn't that great? He wants to go to Ireland to claim the prize because he says then he won't have to tell Uncle Sam about it, and he won't have to pay taxes. Dad says that's sort of crazy because it'll cost him maybe $800 to take a trip there which is more than the tax would be, but Uncle Mick says he's always wanted to go to Ireland anyways, so this is the perfect excuse. So it looks like he'll go in the spring when it gets warmer over there.

November 6, 1960

It's Sunday, which means no school which is great! I did nothing except goof off with Alex all day. Dad was reading the paper tonight and he said, "Hey Liam? You know that friend of your's, Nathan? The guy who shines shoes at the Mayfair? Well I don't want you hanging around him any more, you got that?"

I said, "How come?"

And Dad said, "Never you mind how come. Because I'm your father and I say so, that's how come!"

So I figured it must be something that was in the papers. I tried to get a peek, but Dad threw the papers in the trash real quick and when I tried to pull them out they were all covered with coffee goop and carrot peelings and ketchup, so I went next door to Pinky and Stinky's and read their paper, Here's what it said:

JUST TIDYING UP. Nathan Pierce Lamoreaux, 43, was arrested Friday night while drunkenly attempting to vacuum Sunset Boulevard. According to Lt. Robert Venable, "The Police Department received several phone calls reporting an intoxicated male stumbling down the center of Sunset with a vacuum cleaner, making 'vrroom vrroom' noises. So we investigated."

"Lamoreaux told us he'd been drinking gin and decided that 'the street was dirty,' so he broke the window at Michaels' Furniture Store, took a vacuum cleaner and proceeded to attempt to vacuum Sunset Boulevard," said Venable. Lamoreaux will be arraigned Monday on charges of breaking and entering, theft, drunk and disorderly and disturbing the peace.

Uh oh. Nathan's in some kind of deep dogdoo now! I bet Perry Mason could get him off, Perry Mason never loses. He always gets Della and Paul to help him, and he always beats that guy Hamilton Berger (and what kind of name is that? Who'd name their kid Ham Berger anyways?)

November 7, 1960

Today was Mary-Ann Lindstrom's birthday. How do I know? I saw it in the Registration Book: Lindstrom, Mary-Ann D., 11-7-50, EXbrook 3-0915. So when she came to school today I said, "Happy 10th Birthday, Mary-Ann D. Lindstrom," and her eyes got real big and she said, "Who told you?" and I said, "A little bird." Now she thinks I'm either a weirdo or a mind reader.

November 8, 1960

It's election day, so right now I'm watching TV to see who the next President will be. But the guys on TV are saying it's too close to call right now, and that we probably won't know for sure who won until tomorrow, which makes sense because there's millions and millions of ballots to count.

Colin got sent home from school by Nurse Norbitch today. I guess he got real sick and coughed a lot and had a sore throat and a fever too, so the Nurse called Mom, and Colin got sent home. Tomorrow he has to go get looked at by Dr. Dicksau.

November 9, 1960

According to the paper, Kennedy won! Mom and Dad are happy about that, but I guess a lot of other people aren't happy -- like

Vice President Nixon. But that's his problem. I think he should shave more often, don't you?

Guess what? Colin's got The Mumps! Dr. Dicksau said so. This is not supposed to be good for me either, because I've never had The Mumps before and I guess it's real catchy, so I have to be careful not to use his toothbrush or his fork or anything. I feel kind of sorry for the little guy -- he's coughing and his throat is all swollen, and he's got a bad fever. But at least now he'll get to stay home from school for awhile and watch Sheriff John.

November 29, 1960

Boy oh boy, here I am back again. Did you miss me? I didn't talk to you for almost three weeks! That's because of I got The Mumps from Colin and I got real sick too. I couldn't even get out of bed for Thanksgiving Dinner. Actually if you want to get technical, I only got The Mump. Dr. Dicksau said I got it only on the right side, which means I could get another Mump again sometime on the left side. Man, I hope not! The Mump is no fun at all!

Plus Dr. Dicksau said if I get it when I'm older it could be more serious because when you're older The Mump can settle in your testicles, which I'm pretty sure means your nuts. And one time in Little League Neil Barbutti threw a pitch and it hit me in the nuts and it hurt so bad it almost killed me, so I'd really rather not get a Mump there, y'know?

Anyhow, being sick wasn't much fun. Usually when you get sick you get to stay home and watch TV which is kind of cool, but this time both me and Colin were home and sick at the same time, so there was a lot of arguments over what to watch. I think we drove Mom crazy. One time I heard her answer the phone by saying, "International House of Mumps."

Have you ever watched Million Dollar Movie on Channel 9? They show a movie every weekday at noon, but the weird thing is they show the same movie every day for a week. That's not very smart is it? Anyhow one of the weeks we had The Mumps, the

Million Dollar Movie was 'The Mummy' starring Boris Karloff. We watched it five times, and now Colin is walking all over the neighborhood yelling, "Imm Ho Tep! Imm Ho Tep! Bring me Tana Leaves! Bring me Tana Leaves NOW!" He's doing it in school now, too -- holding one arm straight out in front of him, and trying to look like a Mummy. Colin can be pretty funny for a little kid.

Friday was my first day back at school in two weeks, and Miss Kleinholz gave me a hug when she saw me, which was cool except that I was scared I'd get stabbed by her big old pointy titties! Ha ha! And there was a lot of make-up homework that I had to take home with me and do over the weekend, which is why I couldn't talk to you sooner.

Nothing much else happened in school. James Watson moved away which is OK with me because I couldn't stand watching him eat his boogers. Toren and Scotty and Bobby and Mary-Ann and Alex and Rikki and Vicki and Betty Bachelis and everybody else is still there. Mary-Ann said one day while I was gone Toren stole a Chapstick from Betty, and Betty caught her with it red-handed, but Toren still denied it. And Bobby got in trouble one day because he was trying to do a loop-the-loop with his Duncan Yo-yo, and the string broke and the yo-yo went right through the window! Bobby broke the window! Isn't that great?

November 30, 1960

You know that TV commercial where the old guy says, "The little old winemaker -- me!" Well, that's us! Me and Scotty McDonald are making wine.

After school I was over at Scotty's and he showed me this book called 'The Home Vintner's Guide,' and it told all about how you can make wine out of grape juice and yeast and sugar. You just let it sit and ferment, which means you just sort of let it rot for awhile and it becomes wine. I've dranken wine before and it's a lot better than martinis, so we decided we'd make some.

We pooled our money and rode our bikes down to the Mayfair and bought a couple bunches of grapes, plus a can of Welch's frozen grape juice concentrate. Then we waited until Scotty's mom went out and we made the frozen stuff into juice, and squeezed the grapes. Scotty's mom had some yeast and sugar, so we dumped it in there and put it all in a big pail and covered it up and hid it in Scotty's garage. Now all we have to do is wait a month or so and we'll have wine.

December 1, 1960

Today I got this great idea and it worked, so I made a bunch of money without having to do anything. You might want to try this yourself, whoever you are. Here's how it works:

Every year we send out a bunch of Christmas cards to our relatives, and to Mom and Dad's friends. So after school today I asked Mom if she wanted some help addressing or mailing the cards.

She gave me kind of a suspicious look but then she shrugged and said, "OK, Liam, here's fifty Christmas cards, fifty return-address stickers, and two dollars. The envelopes are already addressed. If you really want to help, get on that bike of yours and ride it down to the Post Office. Buy fifty 4-cent stamps. Put one stamp in the upper right corner of each envelope and put a return-address sticker in the upper left corner, then mail them all off. Can you do all that?"

So I said, "Sure, Mom."

She stuck all the stuff into a bag and I headed off downtown on my bike. But I didn't go to the Post Office, I went to Chicken Delight and got one of Mom's dollars out and bought a big huge bag of Chicken Delight French fries for a quarter. Chicken Delight makes the best French fries in the world!

Then I asked the Chicken Delight Guy if I could borrow his pen, and I went around to the alley and went to work. In between French fries, I changed all the Christmas cards. First I threw away the return-address stickers. Then on each envelope I looked at the name and address and I copied it onto the upper left corner where the return address goes. Then I crossed out the main address. Then I just kept Mom's two dollars, and stuck all the cards into the mailbox.

Now the Mailman will see an envelope with a crossed-out address and no stamp. What will he say? He'll say, "Return to sender!" So they'll look at the return address, and they'll send the mail there -- which is exactly where I want it to go in the first place! This is like the very best idea I ever had! If everybody did it, nobody'd ever have to buy a stamp again, I bet! All the mail will get where it's supposed to go and I'd get to keep the money!

December 2, 1960

This was Music Day at school. Once every two weeks this special teacher comes to class and teaches us songs and music. Her name is Miss Purcell and she looks way too young to be a teacher -- she looks like a girl from the high school. She always brings an autoharp and a guitar, and she teaches us folk songs like 'This Land Is Your Land' and 'Drill Ye Tarriers, Drill' and '500 Miles.' She has real long hair that she flips around, and she says stuff like, "This song is the end! It's the ginchiest!"

So today she made me sing a solo during 'Tom Dooley,' and she said I had a "groovy" voice. I got kind of embarrassed. Then she said that people with groovy voices all have one thing in common: when they sing, their mouths are shaped like the letter 'A.' I'll have to look for that when I watch people sing.

Who do you think has a groovy voice? Miss Purcell likes this new folk singer named Joan Baez. I like the Coasters and the Drifters and Ray Charles. Lots of kids in class like Bobby Vee and Frankie Avalon, but I think those guys are a couple of numbnuts.

Bobby Del Valle just sings his own songs, like today at recess he sang: "Whistle while you work, Hitler is a jerk, Mussolini bit his weenie, now it doesn't work."

December 3, 1960

It's Saturday and Mom decided we'd go visit Aunt Gwen. Aunt Gwen lives in a real tiny apartment, but in a fancy part of town. There's trees all around, and she lives on the second floor of this old green building.

While we were there, this guy named Thad who lives next door came by in his bathrobe -- he said he accidentally left his toothbrush there, so he went into the bathroom to get it, then he left. Mom raised her eyebrows and Aunt Gwen smiled and shrugged. Then we all talked for awhile and Aunt Gwen made us a tuna fish sandwich.

Then this Thad guy came back over and said, "I thought it might be appropriate if we formally met. Greetings, my dear. I'm Thad." Mom shook his hand. Aunt Gwen said, "Thad is an extra in the movies," but he didn't look familiar to me. He had a tweed cap on, and one of those ascot thingies around his neck, and white buck shoes like Pat Boone wears.

Aunt Gwen said, "Thad, darling? Sis and I have some family business to discuss -- could you please be a dear and give the boys the grand tour of the neighborhood?" and Thad said, "I'd be my pleasure, Babycakes."

("Babycakes?" Barf-o-rama!)

So Thad said, "Come on, young fellows, Thad will show you around." We walked around the back of the apartment building and Thad pointed out some stuff. "See down that wide avenue there?" That's where none other than Mr. Cary Grant resides. And around that corner is the pastel hacienda of Miss Doris Day."

Colin said, "Who're they?"

"Why, they're movie stars," Thad said, "very famous stars, indeed."

Colin said, "Where does Gil Hodges live?" Then he made a big armpit fart, so I flipped his ear and we started wrestling on the grass and laughing. We got pretty loud and Colin yelled, "Hey! Let go you spaz!" and I was yelling back, and Colin yelled, "No fair! You cut one!" and we were rolling all around in the back yard.

Some of the neighbors started looking out their windows and Thad said, "Mercy! Will you two please stop being so childish?"

Colin looked up at him and said, "Of course we're childish, Mister. We're *children!*"

Then we went back to Aunt Gwen's and she gave us an Almond Joy. She's nice.

December 4, 1960

This afternoon I rode my bike down to the Mayfair and saw Nathan for the first time since he got arrested. He told me he couldn't remember anything about that night and that he was just going to admit he did it, and serve thirty days. Nathan said maybe he shouldn't have drunken so much gin.

I can't figure out why grownups drink so much gin and whiskey, can you? First of all it costs a fortune, and then it tastes like gasoline, and then people get really crazy after they drink it. Like Nathan tried to vacuum Sunset Boulevard, and Uncle Mick gets all sad and starts crying about Ireland, and Dad gets kind of mad, and Aunt Gwen gets funny and dances.

But then, grownups do a lot of things I don't think I'll do when I grow up. Like they smoke cigars and cigarettes, which stink. I'm going to smoke a pipe instead --they smell much better.

Grownups do all kinds of weird stuff -- like Scotty McDonald told me that his older brothers told him that teenage guys make sperms all the time, just for the fun of it. I asked him what they do with the sperms after they make them, and Scotty said he thinks they just flush them down the toilet. Why do they do that? Are they trying to make little toiletbabies? (Ha ha!)

Really though, why would you do that? Shouldn't you save them for when you'll really need them? What if you ran out of sperms? I don't get it.

December 5, 1960

From today's paper:

VACUUMER SENTENCED. *Nathan Pierce Lamoreaux, 43, was sentenced Friday to serve thirty days in the city jail after pleading guilty to reduced charges of destruction of property and drunk and disorderly, stemming from a Nov. 4th incident in which he allegedly stole a vacuum cleaner while intoxicated and attempted to vacuum Sunset Boulevard.*

So I wonder what'll happen to all of Nathan's pet shoes while he's away? I'll have to go down to the Mayfair and see.

December 6, 1960

Miss Kleinholz was sick today so we got a substitute named Mr. Cockfield. He's really skinny and bald, and has a way of scratching his left ear with his right hand where he sort of puts his whole arm over his head to do it. He looks like a monkey when he does it, so we named him Mr. Monkeyman. (Not so's he can hear it, of course.)

Anyways, Bobby Del Valle threw a huge spitwad at the blackboard while Mr. Monkeyman was writing a lesson on it, and the spitwad stuck to the board and spit started dripping down the board. Rikki Drinkwater yelled, "Eeeewww!" but nobody pays any attention to her because she's the girl I told you about who can't stop picking her nose, so her sense of grossness is out of whack.

Most of the kids just laughed, but then Toren Shumaker finked on Bobby and he got sent to Mrs. Palolozzi's office. I heard Mary-Ann Lindstrom whisper, "*Bitch!*" at Toren, and Toren turned white. I thought Toren would fink on Mary-Ann for swearing, but she didn't.

Actually Mr. Monkeyman was a pretty cool teacher... he let us do art almost all day long and I made a big watercolor of the

Sputnik. Mary-Ann worked really hard on a painting for about two hours -- I kept looking at it but I couldn't figure out what it was. Nobody could. Finally Mr. Monkeyman came over and looked at it.

"Hmmm, that's very interesting, Mary-Ann," Mr. Monkeyman said, "what exactly are you painting?"

Mary-Ann said, "God."

Mr. Monkeyman looked at her kind of funny and said, "But nobody knows what God looks like..."

And Mary-Ann said, "Well, they will in about an hour."

December 7, 1960

It's Pearl Harbor Day, so at school all the teachers were going around saying, "Pearl Harbor Day, Pearl Harbor Day, remember Pearl Harbor," which is kind of hard for us kids to do, since none of us was borned yet.

I went down to the Mayfair after school to see what would happen to all of Nathan's pet shoes, and there was this other guy there doing the work. I told him I was a friend of Nathan's and just wanted to check that everything was OK, and he invited me in and we talked for awhile.

His name is Archie, and he's Nathan's cousin. So that's why it's called 'Archie's Shine Parlor!' Archie said he actually owns two shine parlors (the other one is in Venice,) and he runs one and his cousin Nathan runs the other. I asked him who's running the other one now, and he said, "You sure ax a lot of questions, don't you, kid?" So I shut up. Anyhow I guess all the shoes will be fine.

December 8, 1960

So at recess a bunch of us were talking and Alex Eisenbaum said, "There is no Santa Claus," and I said, "That's easy for you to say because your family is Polish and Jewish and you don't even celebrate Christmas."

Alex said, "Just think about it, Liam. Tell me how one guy can get to every single house in the world in one night?"

Then Mary-Ann nodded and said, "Not only that, but did you ever see a flying deer?"

This made me think for a minute and I finally said, "I always wondered how a fat guy could fit down a skinny chimney..."

Bobby Del Valle said, "We always have a big fire on Christmas Eve, and so do lots of other people. Santa would burn his big fat butthole!" which made everybody laugh.

So I guess it's official: I no longer believe in Santa Claus. To tell you the truth, I've pretty much known it was a fake for the last four years. I figured out a long time ago that the Easter Bunny and the Tooth Fairy were fake, but somehow I liked thinking Santa was real....

When I told Mom I'd decided Santa wasn't real, she made a face and then we sat down and talked about it. She said I was right, but that "The spirit of Santa Claus is real." That's kind of a weird expression if you ask me, "the spirit of Santa Claus," like he's a ghost or something? But anyways she said, "Remember, Liam, Colin is only seven so he still thinks Santa is real. So even though you and I know better, let's just go on pretending for his sake, OK? Let's not rain on his parade?"

I said, "Sure." So that's that.

December 9, 1960

Colin gets kind of mixed up sometimes. Like this afternoon he was watching TV, and Mom said, "What are you watching?"

Colin said, "A science show."

So Mom said, "Learning anything?"

"Yeah!" Colin said. "The body consists of three parts – there's the Brainium and the Borax and the Abominable Cavity. The

Brainium contains the brain, the Borax contains the heart and lungs, and the Abominable Cavity contains the bowels."

Mom said, "There's more than one bowel? How many bowels are there?"

Colin said, "Five -- A, E, I, O, U."

December 10, 1960

When I walked into the house today after school, I could hear Mom on the phone in the kitchen. She was saying, "Uh huh.... oh really? The return address? You, too? Hmmm, that's very strange. Was it my handwriting? I see.... OK. Well it seems my eldest little darling has been up to something most interesting. I'll certainly be having a serious talk with him when he gets home..."

So I ducked outside real quick. Uh oh. I'm in some deep dogdoo now! What should I do? If I had about $100 I guess I could run away and get a job as a newspaper boy. I could get a sleeping bag and sleep in the vacant lot on Palomar Street, and take showers at the YMCA.

Or maybe I could be The Invisible Man in that old movie, and just move around wherever I wanted to and nobody could see me. They could never find me if I was The Invisible Man, I bet. Wouldn't it be cool to be invisible? You could sneak into movies without paying and you could look at Miss Kleinholz bare-naked and you could go anywhere you wanted to because nobody'd see you. Only problem is you'd get really cold because in order to be invisible you have to be naked, or else people would see your clothes walking by. How come that guy in the movie never mentioned that? Heck he was in England, too, where it's always cold....

December 13, 1960

Well I didn't get to talk to you for a couple days, because part of my being grounded was that I got grounded from the Marty Graw Book, too. I got yelled at pretty good for the Christmas cards thing. It looks like most of the people got their cards, but about 15 of them didn't, and a few of them had to pay "postage due." Maybe the Mailman figured out my plan and threw some of them out? I don't know…. But some of the people who got their cards thought it looked fishy, so they called Mom.

Actually I think Mom is madder at Dad than she is at me. After the whole story came out and Mom lectured me all about stealing and lying and how important it is to support our Government and the Post Office, then Dad said, "Oh Dearie, give the boy some credit for using his noodle. He thought he found a loophole in the system, and he went for it. What do you think guys like J. Paul Getty do every day?"

And yikes did Mom ever get steamed at that! She started yelling at Dad even worse than she yelled at me. And later I overheard Dad say we'll need to buy a big doghouse for the back yard, so I'm still hoping that maybe I'll get a dog for Christmas.

December 14, 1960

Frankie Dupoy has been waking up, isn't that cool? Oh, maybe I never told you about Frankie Dupoy? Well, Frankie is this boy from school who sleeps through recess every day. He never plays any games, he just sleeps in the sandbox. Sometimes he falls asleep in class too, and when that happens Miss Kleinholz sends him to Nurse Norbitch. Sometimes he comes back to class and sometimes he just goes home.

Anyways, lately he's been staying awake, and today he even played sockball with us. And guess what? He's an awful good sockball player, too, and he's not dumb like we thought. He just has some blood problem he says, but now he's taking pills for it and he feels much better. Every day he gets a little bit better. Isn't that great?

Can you burp whenever you want to? I can! Really, it's easy -- Frankie taught me how. You just swallow air and then you can burp whenever you want! He taught me how to even make Burp-talk, too, like say any words I want to say, but in a burp! Man, am I happy Frankie woked up!

December 15, 1960

We looked at our wine today over at Scotty's garage, but it doesn't look much like wine yet. It's pretty stinky actually, but the book said that's normal until it rots all the way and gets strained. The color was weird, though -- it's not dark enough. So Scotty said, "See those berries that grow on the hedge there? That's the color this wine should be. That's what wine looks like."

So I said, "Well, we could squeeze some hedgeberry juice and add it in?"

Scotty said, "Yeah!"

We picked a big bag of those dark purple hedgeberries and squeezed all the juice into the wine. It looks way better now. But then on the way home I noticed my hands were all purple, so I stopped at the Beedy's and used their hose to wash my hands but it wouldn't come off. Mom had a fit. She made me wash my hands with Boraxo until they were raw, but they're still purple.

After I got cleaned up, I noticed the Christmas tree was in the living room! It hadn't been decorated yet, but it was in the house and ready, so we strung some popcorn and some cranberries and we put up all the ornaments. Colin kept accidentally poking himself with the needle, so finally Mom told him to forget about stringing popcorn and just put up the balls and ornaments. The whole time we worked on the tree, Mom and Dad played this same album over and over again: 'The Norman Luboff Choir Sings Christmas Songs.' It sucks! I told them to play 'Yakety Yak' by the Coasters, but they wouldn't.

So this was my first real week back at school after The Mump, but tomorrow is the last day of school before Christmas Vacation. Wow, did I time that right! It would be terrible to have to get sick during vacation, wouldn't it?

December 16, 1960

We're off for Christmas Vacation! Yay! Today was the last day of school for two weeks. Awhile ago we all pitched in and bought Miss Kleinholz a Christmas present, so today we gave it to her. It was a bottle of Chanel No. 5, which Aunt Gwen says is the best perfume at the whole Rexall. Miss Kleinholz was really surprised and she almost started crying. I asked her why they named a perfume after a TV channel, but she thought I was kidding, but I'm not.

Since it was the last day of school, Miss Purcell the music teacher came in with her guitar and we all sang Christmas carols. She even let me play the autoharp, which is really easy once you get the hang of it. And Miss Purcell had black stockings on, and purple lipstick. She says when she comes back in January she's going to teach us some protest songs, which she says are groovy to sing because they make fun of the government.

Even Frankie Dupoy sang, and guess what? He has the lowest voice in class. Do you know that song called 'Get A Job' by the Silhouettes? The one that goes, "Yip yip yip yip, yip yip yip yip, mum mum, mum mum, mum mum, get a job, sha na na na, sha na na na na?" Well Frankie Dupoy can sing the bass part. In Burp-talk!

Oh, did you know that "I'm a lasagna hog" spelled backwards is "go hang a salami?"

December 17, 1960

Gramma came over today, and her face is much better now. She looks completely normal and I guess she's all over her stroke. The doctors tell her she should quit smoking, but she says the doctors can all go to hell. "I'll outlive all those sawbone sons of bitches!" she says.

I went down to the beach by myself this afternoon. I'm not supposed to do that but you only live once! It was all foggy and there was nobody there, which is nice -- I like to just sit in the sand and look at the waves and think about things. Like today I was thinking how terrible it would be to be a Mouseketeer on the Mickey Mouse Club. Seriously. I bet Annette and Cubby and Karen and those guys aren't allowed to get into any trouble at all, because if they did, it'd be in all the papers. What do you think? I mean, they probably make a lot of money being Professional Mouseketeers and all, but I don't think it'd be worth it. I'd rather just be a regular kid.

Oh I almost forgot: Mom scolded Colin tonight because he was sitting by the fireplace and singing along to the Christmas carol record, and he sang, "Chipmuuuuunks roasting on an open fire..." Mom didn't think that was funny, but I do.

December 18, 1960

It's the last Sunday before Christmas, so it's the day of the Christmas Parade. Every year they have a Christmas Parade down the main street and it's pretty neat -- not as big as the 4th of July Parade, but still OK. Dad says it's totally commercial and just a big ad for the local merchants, but I still like to look at it. Every float has a Santa and tons of elves, and there are horses dressed up like reindeers. This one reindeer-horse took a big ol' shit, and a Santa-on-Stilts slipped in the poop and fell off his stilts, but he didn't get hurt.

A bunch of kids from school were there, like I saw the Drinkwater twins, and Bobby Del Valle, and Mary-Ann and her mom. I think Mary-Ann's dad works somewhere far away like Arabia or something. One time she told me exactly where, but I forget now. She said he only comes home a few times a year. I hope he comes home for Christmas.

December 19, 1960

What's invisible and smells like carrots? Bunny farts. Ha ha!

December 20, 1960

Aunt Gwen came over for dinner tonight and she was in a good mood. She pointed out to Mom an article in the paper about this new pill called Enovid-10 that just became available today. Aunt Gwen says it's a Birth Control Pill, and that now women can finally gain control over their futures. Mom said, "Are you going to try it?"

Aunt Gwen said, "You bet your ass I am! I'm kissing this damn diafram goodbye! Of course, um, right now it doesn't matter too much..."

"Whatever happened to that guy we met at your place?" Mom asked. "You know, whassisname? Chad? Thad?"

Aunt Gwen said, "Thaddeus Himself? Umm, I had to let him go. Turns out he was hitting from both sides of the plate." (That surprised me -- I didn't think he looked like much of a ballplayer.)

Then Mom said, "I wish they'd made these pills available last month."

Aunt Gwen said, "You don't mean....?" and Mom nodded.

I missed most of what came after that because they kept their voices low, but I did hear Mom say, "Three weeks."

Aunt Gwen asked, "Does anybody know yet?" and Mom said, "No."

I went and got the Registration Book and I looked up Mary-Ann
Lindstrom's phone number, then I snuck the phone into the hall
where nobody could hear me and I called her up and I asked her
about the movie that Barbie Healthteacher showed the girls. I told
Mary-Ann what I heard and asked her whether or not she thought
this means Mom is expecting, and she said, "Sure sounds like it to
me, Liam." So I'm not 100% sure yet, but I think maybe Mom is
going to have a baby?

December 21, 1960

I hung out over at Scotty's for most of the day. He doesn't have
much to do on Christmas vacation because his mom goes to work.
Scotty's brother Jimmy is supposed to watch Scotty, but all Jimmy
does all day is work on this cool old motorcycle in the garage and
smoke cigarettes and drink Dad's Old Fashioned Root Beer with
salted peanuts in it. I haven't seen their mom much lately, but
Scotty says she's been kind of sad because Milo's in jail for
Christmas.

Anyhow we took a look at our wine again today and it's pretty
gross. Maybe that was a bad idea to put the purple hedgeberry
juice in there? It just didn't smell much like wine, so Scotty figured
the easiest way we could make it into wine would be to add wine.

So we looked all over the kitchen and under the sink there was
a great big bottle of Sauterne wine. I think Mrs. McDonald uses it
for cooking? Anyways, we took two or three cups of it and added it
to our wine, then we strained it through a cloth to get all the berry
parts and grape parts out. Now at least it kind of tastes like real
wine. Scotty says it should be ready to drink by New Year's Eve
and that we should celebrate New Year's by drinking our own
wine. Pretty cool, huh?

December 24, 1960

The last couple days I've been just plain too busy to talk to you -- I had to do all my Christmas shopping. I got some golf balls for Dad, and a calendar with pictures of Ireland on it for Uncle Mick, and a 45-record of The Twist by Chubby Checker for Aunt Gwen, and some football cards for Colin and some flowers for Mom.

Every year I always ask Mom what she wants for Christmas and she says, "Flowers, please," and I say, "Aw, c'mon Mom, flowers aren't a real present! They just grow everywhere!" And she says, "You asked me what I wanted, Liam, and that's what I want." So every year I get her flowers, and every year she seems happy about it. Sometimes I catch her sniffing them and smiling to herself about something.

Of course there'll be some other presents, too, like Dad will buy something for Mom but put "from the boys" on it, and Mom does the same thing for Dad, so Colin and I kind of get credit for stuff we didn't really buy -- I guess that's the "Christmas Spirit" or something. It seems like everybody's getting the Christmas Spirit -- like today through the window I saw Pinky actually put a flower in Old Lady Kroot's mailbox.

Colin wanted to sit on Santa's lap this year and tell him what he wanted, so I went along too. I wonder why I never noticed before that Santa is at five different department stores at the same time? This time I watched all the little kids real close, and some of them looked scared to death of Santa! Boy, I never was...

So anyways, today was Christmas Eve, and tonight was the big Christmas Dinner. Gramma was here, and Uncle Mick and Aunt Gwen, and Mom and Dad and Colin and me, and some of Mom and Dad's friends like Mr. and Mrs. Moffit from across the street, and two guys that Dad works with at Tri-Flex called Big Ed and Pete. Pete was a funny guy who told all kinds of jokes, and Mrs. Moffit was a real sweet lady who kissed me and Colin a lot. Dad says, "Theresa Moffit gets a bit sentimental after a martini."

Mom and Gramma made a big dinner, with turkey and stuffing and salad, and Aunt Gwen helped with cranberry sauce and smashed potatoes. And after dinner there was pumpkin pie! Colin stuck black olives on each of his fingers, then ran all over the house sticking out his black fingers at everybody and yelling "Tana Leaves! Bring me the Tana Leaves NOW!" After dinner all the grownups drank brandy and coffee, and me and Colin went out in the back yard and made up ghost stories.

Tomorrow is Christmas! How about that! I'm still hoping I'll get a dog or a BB gun, but I know I won't. What I want this year is a Flexy-Flyer! Do you have a Flexy? It's like a sled on wheels and they go really really fast! Dad says they're "dangerous as hell" though, and that "kids go hurtling down the street with their knuckles half an inch from being grated into Parmesan Cheese" so I'm pretty sure I won't get a Flexy. I wonder what I will get?

December 25, 1960

Uncle Mick once told me that some people don't do Christmas -- he says in places like South Korea and China nobody celebrates Christmas, and it's the same thing in India and also in all the Mohammed-type countries. Boy, those poor kids really get gypped, don't they? I wonder if you have Christmas wherever you are? I hope so, because it's just about the best day there is.

Colin woked me up at six in the morning, can you believe it? I thought he was going to pee in his pants! He kept saying, "Did Santa come? How do you know he came? Can we wake up Mom and Dad yet? Can't we go peek?"

Little kids sure are excitable, aren't they? He was bouncing up and down on the bed and I had to tell him to settle down. He said, "I'm not settling down. I'm Colin and someday I'm going to break my neck."

The rules are that we're not allowed to wake up Mom and Dad until eight o'clock, but we can open our stockings before that. Do you have stockings? Mom made these big stockings and she put our names on them, then she hangs them up next to the fireplace. On Christmas Eve, Santa's supposed to come down the chimney and fill up the stockings with little presents -- just small stuff like peanuts and candy and stuff that costs a dime or so, like a whistle or some baseball cards. Of course it's not really Santa who does this, it's Mom and Dad, but that's OK... it still tastes the same.

If you've been a bad boy, Santa supposedly fills your stocking with coal! (Or at least that's what they want you to believe.) They tell you this so you'll be good all year. Parents are sneaky!

Since it was too early to wake up Mom and Dad, I went and got the stockings and brought them back to our room, and we opened the stocking presents. That was fun, but it only took about five minutes and pretty soon Colin was going crazy to see the tree, and look at whatever might be underneath it. He was getting loud and I knew if he woked up Mom and Dad at 6:30 AM it wouldn't be a real good way to start Christmas, so I grabbed his shoulders and looked him in the eye and told him to shut up and calm down or else Santa would come back and take back all his presents and fill the stocking full of catdoo. That worked, because Colin has this crazy idea that catdoo is stinkier than dogdoo, even though I think they're about the same.

To keep him quiet I went into the kitchen to get him a glass of milk, only somebody stuck a mop in the way so I tripped and dropped the milk on the floor which made a big mess, and I couldn't find any paper towels so I mopped it up with toilet paper, which didn't work so good. But at least it didn't wake up Mom and Dad. And I got Colin to play Monopoly with me until eight o'clock, and by then I could hear Mom and Dad in the kitchen having coffee and talking about last night's dinner and how they hoped Theresa Moffit didn't have to be carried to her house across the street. She got sleepy while she was here.

At eight o'clock Dad came in our room and yelled, "Merry Christmas!" and then we got to go look at the tree and there was a trillion presents there.

Colin got real excited and started yelling, "Which ones are for me, which ones are for me?" and Dad told him to put a cork in his beak. So then all the presents got handed out.

I won't bore you with a big long list of who got what, because when kids do that at school it always sounds to me like they're bragging or something, and for all I know you just might be a Mohammed-type or a Buddha and I don't want to make you feel bad. But we got some good stuff, I can tell you that!

Later we went outside to play with the other kids and see what they got, and Stinky got a Flexy-Flyer, the lucky pup! I guess Mr. and Mrs. Vanderhoeven don't care if Stinky's knuckles get grated into Parmesan Cheese. Maybe after the newness wears off and he crashes it a few times, he'll let me ride it?

Then at about two o'clock, do you know what happened? It started to rain, so we had to come inside. That's when Mom suggested we all go to Father O'Dowd's special Christmas Mass, but Dad said it was really important that he listen a bunch of times to the records Mom gave him for Christmas -- Frank Sinatra and Julie London -- to make sure they weren't defective, because he'd have to return them real quick if they skipped. So he said he couldn't go to Mass. So that's that. Merry Christmas!

December 26, 1960

Not much happened today. I tried to get Stinky to let me try his Flexy, but he told me to go fly a kite. After I came inside, Mom sat me down and said, "Liam? Do you get along all right with Scotty McDonald?"

I said, "Sure. How come?"

Mom said, "Well... as you know, his mother works hard all day, and sometimes when she gets home there's no time for her to cook. Most nights Scotty has a boloney sandwich or a TV dinner for supper. Sometimes just a Bob's Big Boy and a Snickers..."

I said, "Cool!"

Mom frowned. She said, "I'd like to see that boy get a proper meal more often... How would you feel if he ate dinner over here sometimes? Like maybe two or three times a month?"

And I said, "Sure! That'd be fun." So that's that.

After that, Gramma and Aunt Gwen came over and they were all in the kitchen playing cards, and Colin was naked and he ran into the kitchen and yelled, "Look! Look!" Then he stuck a finger in his belly button and pulled his wiener and yelled, "Push the button, pull the chain, out comes a little doo-doo train!" Then he ran away laughing.

I thought Mom would get mad at him, but Aunt Gwen and Gramma started laughing, so Mom just rolled her eyes and said, "Good Lord, give me strength. Who made these kids, anyway?"

December 27, 1960

Me and Scotty decided we'd take the shortcut down to the beach today. Do you know the shortcut? First you have to sneak down through Eliot's back yard into the canyon, then you go down to the bottom where the creek is, and you follow the creek down to the beach. The last part of it cuts through this area that they're making into a big trailer park.

We hate the trailer park idea! First of all trailers are ugly, but besides that, once they turn it into a trailer park it'll be private and fenced off so we won't get to cut through there anymore to get to the beach. So every time we see stakes in the ground -- you know those pointy stakes with the red flags on them? -- we move them a couple feet one way or the other. Maybe now they'll build the trailer park all lopsided?

On the way through the canyon we went up to the cave. It used to be Stinky's Cave -- he discovered it but he's getting too old to care, so he gave it to us. Up in the cave we have an orange crate buried, and inside the orange crate is a bunch of stuff we'd get in trouble for if our parents found it. Stuff like these old Cavalier magazines we found in Dr. Dortmunder's garbage can, and some cigarettes and some firecrackers. So far we haven't smoked the cigarettes because they make you stink and I haven't figured out a way to disguise the smell from Mom and Dad. The magazines have pictures of ladies with their clothes off and they all have big bazoombas!

When we got to the trailer park area, some other kids were there and they threw some dirt clods at us, so we threw some back. It was a dirt clod war! Then they went away, so we snuck through the trailer park and went to the beach and guess what? Right near the jetty, Scotty found a five-dollar bill in the sand! What a lucky pup!

After that we spent about an hour looking for more money, but there wasn't any. Wouldn't it be cool if like some robber guys had hidden all their loot there from a bank robbery or something, and we found it? Like a million dollars? Anyways it got kind of cold at the beach so we walked back up the canyon into town, and Scotty bought us both some French fries at Chicken Delight.

Nothing much else happened today, except I heard that Kiki Dortmunder tried to climb her Christmas tree and she knocked the whole mess over, and shorted out all the lights and broke all the ornaments. Isn't that funny?

December 28, 1960

Mom did The Big Shopping today at the Mayfair and me and Colin had to go along. The Big Shopping is something she does about once a month and it takes forever! Dad says she buys one of everything in the store. All's I know is one shopping cart isn't enough, we have to have two, and Mom lets me drive the second one which is OK, except that she gets mad at me for riding on it and going too fast.

The only fun part about The Big Shopping is we get to pick out some of the stuff. Like Mom'll say, "Go get yourself some cereal, boys," so we get to see what the prize is, or if there's a baseball card on the back of the box. Colin likes Cocoa Puffs and Trix, and I like Kix and Corn Chex. Dad likes Grape Nuts, which taste like gravel. Mom likes Rice Chex which get all soggy and taste like slugboogers.

Sometimes if Mom's in a good mood she'll let us get some Van de Camp's Chocolate Chip Cookies, which is the best food ever invented in the history of the entire earth. Really! Have you ever had one? They're at the bakery part of the Mayfair, and there's a lady working there who wears a funny hat and an apron. Mom says she's supposed to be Dutch, but actually she's from Guadalajara and her name is Loopy.

Also there's a lunch counter at the Mayfair where you can get a Coke for a nickel (but a cherry Coke costs six cents.) They also sell hamburgers and hot dogs and French fries. The hamburgers are good but the French fries are way too oily. The waitress is this really funny lady named Rosie who sings and dances and tells jokes and smokes cigarettes and drinks coffee all day long. Whenever she sees me she says, "Heyo, Liam, c'mere and give ol' Rosie a hug, willya? Whatcha been doin' besides breakin' all them young girls' hearts?" She's a card.

Today I tried to get Mom to buy us some chocolate milk, but she said, "We have a big jar of Bosco at home. You can make some later," so I said "OK." You mix Bosco with milk, and stir and stir and stir it until your arm falls off, and then finally you get chocolate milk. It's pretty good, but not as good as Edgemar.

Do you have an Edgemar man? That's the milkman. Our Edgemar man is named Charley and he comes three times a week and drops off milk and orange juice and eggs and butter. If we're not home, he leaves it on the back porch with a bag of ice on it. Sometimes I can convince Mom to buy chocolate milk from Charley -- it's better than Bosco.

Anyhow the Big Shopping took all afternoon, and then after we got home it took another hour to put all the stuff where it goes. So pretty much the whole day was wasted.

December 30, 1960

I couldn't write yesterday because I didn't feel good -- I was sick in bed and so was Scotty. It started out when I rode my bike over to his place yesterday to see if he wanted to go downtown and watch all the weird old ladies return their Christmas presents for better stuff. When I got there, Mrs. McDonald was at work so I parked my bike on the driveway. Scotty's brother Jimmy stuck his head out from under his motorcycle and waved a wrench and said, "Yo, Microbe. The Punk is up in his room," so I went upstairs.

When I got to Scotty's room he said, "Liam, you gotta try it -- it got really good!" and he pulled out the bucket of wine. "I just wanted to make sure it was OK before New Year's Eve," he said, "so I tried it and it's pretty good! Here -- have some." So I drank some and it actually tasted OK. The hedgeberries made it tart but the sugar made it sweet again.

Scotty said, "Let's put it in the blender with some ice cream and make a malt!" So we got the blender and we looked through the freezer. They didn't have any Vanilla, but they had some Jamoca Almond Fudge so we put that in the blender with the wine and we mixed it all up, then we drank it.

After a couple glasses, Scotty said he didn't feel so good. Neither did I -- I thought I could feel the shits coming on so I rode my bike home as fast as I could, which wasn't very fast because I bumped into the curb twice and the bike fell over once. When I got home I didn't get the poops, but I barfed up some purple stuff and spent the rest of the day sleeping. I knew I'd get killed if I told about the wine, so I just said I'd been chewing lots of hedge-berries. And today I have a headache. I hope Scotty threw out the rest of it, because I'm sure not going to drink that crud again.

December 31, 1960

Tonight is New Year's Eve which I guess is supposed to be some kind of a big thing. All the grownups stay awake til midnight and drink champagne and sing songs, but the kids aren't allowed to, so it's no fun for us. At nine o'clock we get to watch TV and see all the people in New York City yelling and setting off fireworks and stuff. Big deal.

January 1, 1961

Happy New Year! It feels funny to write "1961," but I guess I'll get used to it. It rained all day today, so we had to stay inside and watch TV. They had this really cool parade on where everything was made out of flowers! How do they do that? They had people sitting on these cars made out of flowers (they're called "floats," but they don't float.) How come the flowers don't get squarshed? Then Dad and Uncle Mick sat around all afternoon and watched football, but me and Colin think football is stupid. We're baseball fans. I wish it would stop raining.

Scotty ate dinner over at our house tonight, and Mom asked him about his brother Milo. Scotty said Milo's still in jail and won't get out for about another year and a half. Mom looked sad when Scotty told her that. Then Dad tried to change the subject, He said, "So Scotty? How do you like school?"

Scotty said, "When it's closed."

January 2, 1961

It's Monday and we had to go back to school today. Ugh! It's still raining so we couldn't even go to recess. All the kids were bragging about the stuff they got for Christmas and Honica, but I think Betty Bachelis got the weirdest gift -- she got a step-dad. Her mom got married on Christmas Day to some guy named Jody Wharton, so I asked her if she was going to change her name but she said she likes Bachelis better because it sounds "exotic."

This new kid moved to town over Christmas Vacation, and he's in our class now. He has an exotic name too -- his name is Norman Giambalvo and he has eight brothers and sisters. I think he's going to be trouble. Uncle Mick always says that when a person's eyes are narrow it's a sign that they're mean, and Norman Giambalvo's eyes are so close together he looks like a possum. Plus he sneered at Miss Kleinholz when she introduced him to class, and he chews a toothpick and spits a lot. Even Bobby Del Valle seems a little bit scared of Norman Giambalvo.

January 3, 1961

Colin broke his arm! Colin broke his arm!

It happened at school today. He was playing at recess and he fell off the jungle gym. Usually when you fall you land in this barky kind of stuff so you can't get hurt, but Colin fell funny and he landed on a lower bar. I didn't see it happen because the little kids take recess at a different time than we do, but some of Colin's friends found me and told me about it. I asked Miss Kleinholz if I could call home, so they let me call Mom from Mrs. Palolozzi's office.

Mom said they took Colin to the Emergency Room and stuck his arm in a cast. She said it wasn't a real bad break -- just kind of a crack -- and that Colin hardly cried at all. Also it was his left arm which is good because he's right-handed. He'll have to wear a cast for six weeks, and Mom says he's already running all over the neighborhood showing it off, so I guess that means it isn't too bad. When I got back to class I tried to make myself look real sad because I thought maybe Miss Kleinholz might let me go home early, but she didn't fall for it.

By the time I got home, Colin's cast was already muddy and covered with grass stains and autographs and drawings in all different colored inks. He said he saw this movie once where this baseball player broke his leg, and all his teammates signed the cast. He's telling everybody how bad it hurts so they'll be nice to him, but Mom says he hardly cried at all when it happened. Still, I bet it hurts -- but then I wouldn't really know because I've never broken anything. Except Dad's windshield (Ha ha!)

January 4, 1961

Miss Purcell came into class today and told us that the whole 5th Grade is going to put on this big show in a few weeks, and she asked if anybody wanted to be in it. There's going to be singing and dancing and the School Orchestra is going to play.

Toren Shumaker said she wanted the starring role (of course,) and a bunch of other girls volunteered. The only boy who wanted to do it was Frankie Dupoy, and Miss Purcell was happy about that because he can sing low parts. Then she said she needed three more boys, and because I had a "groovy voice" she asked me to be one.

I wasn't really sure if I wanted to, but then Bobby said, "Go ahead, McAfee, you could be the next Pat Boone."

"Pat Boone's a spaz!" I said.

Scotty yelled, "Go ahead, do it, Liam!"

"Then why don't *you* guys do it?"

And they both said, "We will if you will."

So now we're all going to be in the show. That means every Friday from now on, we get to go to another room for a couple hours and learn songs with a bunch of other kids. Maybe it will be fun?

This Saturday January 7th is Colin's birthday -- he'll be eight. Mom and Dad decided that since he broke his arm, maybe Colin could use some cheering up with an official Birthday Party, so he gets to invite 14 of his friends over and there's going to be a real live magician and cake and ice cream. I overheard Mom and Dad making plans, and I heard Mom say, "You know, in some ways this isn't really fair to Liam. He didn't get to have a big Birthday Party."

And Dad said, "True, but then he didn't break his arm, either..." Then he said, "You're right, though. Why don't we let Liam invite a few of his friends, too? They'd probably like the magician."

Mom said, "Good idea."

So now I get to invite four kids to Colin's party. Who do you think I should invite? Colin has already asked Pinky and Stinky so I don't have to worry about them. I'm thinking I'll invite Alex

Eisenbaum and Bobby Del Valle and Scotty McDonald and Mary-
Ann Lindstrom. So Mom called their parents and officially invited
them, and that's that.

January 5, 1961

After school I went downtown with Mom so she could help me
pick out a birthday present for Colin. I didn't have too much
money, so Mom helped and I got him a Parcheesi game. I hope he
likes it, but Mom says even if he doesn't like it right away, he'll
grow into it.

So tonight Mom made it official: she sat me and Colin down
and told us that she was going to have a baby this coming summer.
I pretty much knew anyway, but Colin was surprised and happy.
He says he wants a little brother so he can boss him around the
same way I boss Colin around.

January 6, 1961

Today was the first rehearsal of the big school show. Miss Purcell
says the show will happen during the last week of the semester,
January 25, and that it's called 'Travel Dreams.' The Orchestra
has already been practicing for months because their stuff is
harder than singing. I guess how it works is I'm now in the 'Senior
Chorus.' There's about thirty of us, plus five autoharp players.
Then there's also a 'Junior Chorus' of littler kids. And then there's
the 'Mistress of Ceremonies' who introduces everything and
dances around and shows off -- that's Toren.

Miss Purcell listened to each one of us sing a little bit, then she
figured out who was a soprano and who was an alto, that kind of
stuff. (Most of the girls were soprano and most of the boys were
alto but a few were tenor.) Then she broke us all up into three
sections, and she taught each section a part. Then we all sang
together -- it was pretty fun.

It looks like the Orchestra will do six songs, the Senior Chorus (that's us) will do four, the Junior Chorus will do two and the Special Ensemble (which is three kids from the A6) will start the show with one song. Miss Purcell asked me if I wanted to sing a short solo on this really weird song called 'Arapaho Warriors,' but I said, "No, thank you." It's a hard song because it's in Arapaho, which is a foreign language. And besides I'd probably barf if I had to do a solo in front of all the teachers and parents and kids.

Do you remember that girl I told you about named Cookie Swansea who's a half-and-half and who's just about the best singer I ever heard? I said maybe she should sing the solo in 'Arapaho Warriors,' but Miss Purcell said Cookie was already doing a solo. Then Hermie Fleet volunteered to do it, but he sings like goosefarts. One thing Hermie can do really good, though, is play accordion, so Miss Purcell changed 'Arapaho Warriors' all around so that nobody has to sing a solo, and now there's an accordion solo in it for Hermie.

I guess I never told you about Hermie, did I? Well Hermie Fleet is this boy who's been in my grade for years. He wears a bow tie and a gray sweater to school every day, even when it's hot. He doesn't wear jeans or Keds -- instead he wears slacks and hard shoes, and he also wears glasses but I don't hold that against him because I do too.

Hermie gets straight A's and is always correcting other kids when they get questions wrong. Sometimes he even corrects the teachers! Hermie also knows how to tap dance and play the accordion. He doesn't get along with the other kids because he kind of thinks he's better than everyone else. Maybe Hermie Fleet will get married to Toren Shumaker and they'll make a bunch of shitburgerbabies?

January 7, 1961

It's Colin's Birthday and we had a great party. He got some good stuff from Mom and Dad: an L.A. Dodgers batting helmet and a new seat for his bike and tickets to Pacific Ocean Park. Also some clothes (ugh!) Aunt Gwen gave him a stuffed toy owl that says "Rexall" on it, and Uncle Mick gave him a book called 'Irish Proverbs.' I gave him the Parcheesi game, but he didn't seem too excited about that -- little kids are hard to predict.

At about noon all these kids came over, a ton of them! Mom and Dad had the party set up out in the back yard. I know a few of Colin's friends from the neighborhood (like Pinky and Stinky) but most of these kids I'd never seen before. There was this one boy from Mexico who ate so much ice cream I thought he was going to explode, and there was this really tall girl who laughed and laughed at everything anybody said, even if they were being serious. My friends also got here about noon, but we kind of hung out in a different spot, under the tree with Stinky and Uncle Mick and Aunt Gwen and the older people.

Colin got a lot of presents from the kids, and then everybody played Pin the Tail On The Donkey. Then there was a pinyata, which was completely crazy because Dad spun all the kids around blindfolded, so we got dizzy and nobody knew where the pinyata was. Then Colin blew out the candles and everybody sang "Happy Birthday" and Mom served the ice cream and cake. Little kids were chasing each other all over the yard and getting ice cream all over each other!

Aunt Gwen watched for awhile and said, "I think I've figured out the four rules of cake-eating for an eight-year-old: 1) Peel off frosting. 2) Eat frosting. 3) Throw away cake. 4) Ask for more cake."

About this time I went into the house to take a whiz, and I heard Mary-Ann and Mom talking. Mom was saying something about how pretty Mary-Ann's red checkered dress was, and what a nice girl she was. Mom said, "After two boys, I hope I get a girl next time...."

Mary-Ann said, "Well maybe you will, Mrs. McAfee. Liam told me that you're expecting."

Mom looked kind of surprised but happy, and she said, "Yes, dear, I am indeed. This summer there will be an addition to our family."

Mary-Ann said, "Does your vagina hurt when you have a baby?"

Mom waited a long time before she answered. She said, "Well, yes it does, Mary-Ann. Everything hurts. But it's well worth it, and it's a good kind of hurt."

Then Mary-Ann started waving her hands in circles and yelling, "OK! Thanks for the ice cream, Mrs. McAfee, but I have to go right now, because the magician is here!" and she ran out.

Then the magician came. His name was The Great Pepperoni and he wore a funny hat and did a lot of tricks with coins and rope. He made Colin volunteer to help with some magic stuff, and he told a lot of jokes like Steve Allen. At the end he juggled some stuff, and the last thing he juggled was a bowling ball and a knife and a chain saw, while he rode on a unicycle! Even Dad and Uncle Mick liked The Great Pepperoni.

There was only one fight the whole day and that was when one little kid was telling about his brother's wedding and talking about the wedding cake, and he shoved a big piece of cake into this girl's face and she started crying, and another boy punched the first boy. Bobby Del Valle jumped in and broke it up, and Mom cleaned up the little girl and everybody was friends again after that.

Colin got so much ice cream down inside his cast that Mom called him "a disgrace." Then she kissed him but he squirmed away.

January 8, 1961

We slept in late today because it's Sunday, and when we got up, Dad decided to make waffles. We hardly ever get waffles. Dad said to Mom, "Get out of the way, Dearie, ol' Pops is chef today!"

Mom always gets a little upset when Dad decides to cook, because he doesn't care how big a mess he makes. He's worse about messes in the kitchen than we are, he juggles eggs in the air and spills milk and goofs around a lot. Anyways I was a little bit worried when he said he was going to make waffles, because I wasn't sure if the waffle iron still worked.

You see, one day last year Stinky Vanderhoeven came home from Junior High with this wallet he made in Leathershop class. It was really neat looking -- it had designs on it, like a cowboy and a horse and a rope. Pinky and me thought it looked cool, so we decided to make wallets too. We walked down to the Thrift Store and bought a couple of old wallets for a dime each, then we brought them home and tried to burn patterns into them with some matches, but it didn't work. So we thought we could put checker marks on them if stuck them in the waffle iron for awhile, but they were plastic and they caught fire and melted.

We put out the fire with baking soda and cleaned the waffle iron as good as we could, but there was still a lot of melted goop we couldn't get out. And it stank too, so we sprayed some Right Guard in it, then we put it way back deep in the cupboard. I figured it'd be years before anybody tried to make waffles again, and by then I'd be too old to get the blame. But now Dad wanted to make waffles and I was worried, so I said, "Let's have pancakes instead! They're easier!"

But Dad said, "Nothing to it, boys, it's waffle time!"

He pulled out the waffle iron and opened it up, and it had all this black goo cooked into it, and it stunk awful. Dad said, "Goddamn! What happened to this thing?"

Mom looked at it and said, "Ew! That's disgusting!"

Dad said, "How old is this waffle iron, anyway?"

"I think we got it for a wedding present," Mom said.

So Dad shrugged and said, "Well, I guess nothing lasts forever," and he threw it out.

WHEW.

January 9, 1961

This dentist came to school today and taught us that a permanent set of teeth consists of eight canines, eight cuspids, eight molars, and eight cuspidors. Then he looked at everybody's teeth -- every kid in the whole school. Each of us got sent home with a Certificate of Dental Health. Here's what mine said:

CERTIFICATE OF DENTAL HEALTH
awarded to
LIAM McAFEE
In recognition of having a clean and healthy mouth as certified by a dentist.
Pacific Street Elementary, John B. Hopkins, D.D.S.
This certificate was issued without use of X-ray.
Note: better brushing needed.

January 10, 1961

Norman Giambalvo has only been here for a week and already he got benched. It happened today when Miss Kleinholz brought out a big globe of the Earth, and she talked about where all the continents were. She said, "Rikki? Come up here and show the class where North America is, please?" So Rikki Drinkwater took her finger out of her nose and showed us.

Then Miss Kleinholz said, "Thank you, Rikki, you may be seated. Now class? Can someone please tell me who discovered America?"

Norman said, "The nosepicker girl?"

Everybody laughed except Rikki -- she looked like she was going to cry -- so Norman got benched.

January 11, 1961

School was boring today. On the walk home I stopped by the Muraj Market and got some licorice. They sell licorice for two cents each, red and black. You know what I can't figure out? I can't figure out why some candy bars (like Hershey's and Snickers) cost a nickel and other candy bars (like Mounds and Almond Joy) cost a dime. Why is that? It's not like the dime ones are twice as big -- they're not. So why would anybody in their right mind buy a dime candy bar when they could get two nickel candy bars instead?

The people that run the Muraj Market are nice. Their names are Mr. and Mrs. Doha and they come from Alumnia. They talk a little bit funny and dress in the brightest colors, and they seem to know all the kids by name. And sometimes if a kid is broke, they'll slip him a free penny Tootsie Roll or an Abba Zabba. I've been going there every day for about two years because Mom gives me a nickel every day for milk, but I don't like milk as much as I like Snickers.

January 12, 1961

Today we learned all about the countries and their capitals. When we got to Finland, Miss Kleinholz said, "The capital is 'Helsinki,' and that's as close as you're ever going to get to swearing in this class."

After school there was a guy at the Mayfair handing out tickets to a Kid's Show at the Royale Theater -- free! It's a show for kids only, and it lasts from 1 until 5 this coming Saturday. They're going to show cartoons and some Three Stooges, then two movies, and it's FREE! Isn't that amazing? So I took a couple tickets for me and Colin.

Dad says the show is put on by the Chamber of Commerce and the whole idea is to get parents to bring their kids downtown to the theater, then the parents will have to hang around town and shop while their kids are at the show. Sure sounds like a good idea to me. Every kid I know is going to the Kid's Show. They're giving away prizes, too!

January 13, 1961

We had another rehearsal for 'Travel Dreams' this morning, and I got to hear Cookie sing her solo -- man is she good! I got goose bumps when she sang. I told her she sounded like that rock 'n' roll lady named Etta James, but Cookie made a face and said she didn't like rock 'n' roll, and she wanted to sound like this spiritual lady named Mahalia Somebody. I bet Cookie Swansea will be a big star someday.

Toren Shumaker tried to boss everybody around at rehearsal, but she stopped when Cookie walked over and reached behind Toren and snapped her bra strap. Cookie said, "Whatcha got this thing for, Twinkletoes?"

Toren said, "It's my training bra."

"Yeah?" Cookie said, "so whatcha training 'em to do? Speak? Roll over? Play dead?"

Toren didn't answer. Then the Junior Choir sang really off-key for awhile and Miss Purcell looked like she was going to tear her hair out, but she said she had "a couple more weeks to whip them into shape." I hope so.

January 14, 1961

It's Saturday night and we just got home from the Kid's Show at the Royale Theater. Mom gave us a ride there and she told me, "Keep an eye on your brother," but after we got there Colin said he'd rather sit with his friends, which was OK with me since I didn't want to get stuck with a little brother. So I told him to meet me by the drinking fountain as soon as the movies were over.

It seemed like every kid in the whole school was there, plus tons of other kids! Every seat in the theater was taken -- even the balcony where they don't usually let kids sit because we spit on people below and dump cokes on their heads. But this time I got to sit up there with Bobby and Alex and Scotty and Mary-Ann and Betty Bachelis and Frankie Dupoy.

I saw Hermie Fleet and Norman Giambalvo down in the second row, and lots of other kids -- in fact the only kids I didn't see at the Kids Show were Toren and Cookie. Probably Cookie was singing somewhere, and Toren was probably busy bossing her family around.

The Manager of the Royale Theater came out and gave a speech thanking the Chamber of Commerce for making the free show possible, and everybody booed him and screamed, "WE WANT THE SHOW! WE WANT THE SHOW!"

The Manager yelled, "Zettle down, kids, zettle down right now! HEY! SHADDAP!!"

Did I ever tell you about the Manager of the Royale Theater? Well, his name is Mr. Zupo and he's about ten feet tall and skinny, and has a real funny accent just like Bela Lugosy. I think he's from Europe somewhere. He doesn't like kids, and he's always kicking us out for talking or throwing popcorn boxes. He also kicks out teenagers when they're on dates and making out, or if they're smoking in the bathroom. Mr. Zupo likes to yell. I think if he had his way, all the movies at the Royale Theater would be those Adults Only movies that show titties -- that way he wouldn't have to mess around with us kids.

Anyhow, after Mr. Zupo made his speech they showed a dancing popcorn commercial, then a Flash Gordon and a Porky Pig and a Tom & Jerry. Then they showed two Three Stooges. The first real movie they showed was called 'The Lost World' and it had tons of dinosaurs that ate people. I liked it. All the kids were yelling and laughing and the girls were screaming, and every time a dinosaur ate a guy all the kids went nuts and yelled, "Yay! Yay! Eat him up, eat him up, mmm mmm good!"

About every 15 minutes there was a fight, and Mr. Zupo would run down the aisle and grab the fighting kids and kick them out, and all the other kids would yell, "Boo! Hiss!" at him. Most of the fights started because kids were throwing food and candy and coke at each other, or else flipping somebody's ears.

After 'The Lost World' there was an intermission, and Mr. Zupo came out and stood on the stage. He had a microphone and he said, "Now kids. QUIET!! If you take out your ticket stubs, ve'll be giving away zome prizes. SHADDAP, KIDS!! Look at ze numbers on your stubs, and if ve call your number, you vin a prize!"

So everybody sat down and paid attention, and Mr. Zupo started reading numbers. The first prize they gave away was five free passes to the movies, and some kid I never saw before won that. Then they gave away a five-dollar gift certificate to the Hamburger Hamlet, and this kid in third grade won that. Then Mr. Zupo said, "06589."

Well that was ME!! I couldn't believe it! I WON! So I ran up to the front of the theater and Mr. Zupo said "Congratulations," and he gave me my prize. And do you know what it was? It was a one-gallon bottle of Green Formula Grow-All Lawn Fertilizer, donated by Yoshida's Nursery. Can you believe it? All my friends laughed when I brought it back to my seat. What a gyp.

After that they showed a movie called 'The Seventh Voyage of Sinbad,' which is now my favorite movie of all time! This guy Sinbad has to battle this bad guy magician who shrinks Sinbad's girlfriend, and there was this duel with a skeleton, and a big cyclops and flying carpets and stuff. About halfway through the movie the picture got stuck, and it just stayed in the same place for a minute until this big hole happened in the picture, and it just sort of burned up! Everybody yelled "YAY! YAY! Do it again!" but the projection guy fixed it and the movie kept going. It was great! You have to go see it!

After that movie was over, they turned on the lights and it was the end of the show. You never saw so much popcorn on the floor -- I'm glad I didn't have to clean it up. When I got to the drinking fountain, Colin was there waiting for me and he was fine except somebody stuck a wad of bubble gum in his hair, so I had to borrow a pocket knife from Bobby Del Valle and fix it. Then we went outside and Mom picked us up and I gave her the fertilizer I won, and now we're home and that's that.

January 15, 1961

Why does it always rain on Sundays? It isn't fair, is it? There's nothing to do when it rains so Colin and me went over to Volker Dortmunder's house and played Chinese Checkers with him, but that was pretty boring. Dr. Dortmunder sat at the table and wrote checks all afternoon, and that made him even grumpier than usual.

I guess Mom felt sorry for us having to stay indoors all day so she made tacos for dinner tonight, which is my favorite dinner, and she let Scotty eat over too. When I was really little I didn't like the way tacos looked and I wouldn't try them -- boy was I a dumb little kid. Then Uncle Mick said, "Liam, it's just a Mexican cheeseburger," so I tried it and now it's my favorite. Scotty and me had to grate the cheese, but as a reward Mom cooked us some big Fritos. She calls them tostados but they're just big round Fritos.

January 16, 1961

Miss Kleinholz was crying in class today. Her Dad died on Friday and she was really sad, so all the kids tried to be extra specially nice to her, even Norman Giambalvo.

I was talking with Frankie Dupoy today and he told me a secret -- he said his real name is 'Francis,' but he says if I tell anybody, he'll pound me. I don't know if Frankie could pound me or not, maybe I could pound him? But I don't like fights so if you're reading this, don't tell anybody Frankie's real name, otherwise there'll be a fight and somebody will get pounded.

At lunchtime some old guy with a big camera came to school, and he took a picture of all us kids eating lunch. I wonder what that was for? Bobby said maybe he was a Russian spy, but Mary-Ann said that's too stupid to even consider.

January 17, 1961

It was Show And Tell Day at school, where each kid brings something into class and tells the rest of the class about it. Toren Shumaker brought her mom's wedding dress, and Miss Kleinholz let her go into the girl's bathroom and change into it and model it. I bet Toren's mom's going to get mad though, because the dress was way too long and the bottom got all muddy. Toren looked funny! And besides, who'd marry her, anyway?

Bobby brought a model car and Scotty brought a really old radio. Hermie Fleet brought an ant farm and gave a speech about ants. Norman Giambalvo brought a stuffed baby alligator and all the girls went, "Ewww," so he ran around sticking it in people's faces and yelling, "It's going to eat you! It's going to eat you!" until Miss Kleinholz made him stop.

Alex Eisenbaum brought an old newspaper from Poland and he read it in English -- it was all about Hitler and how he stole Poland. Mary-Ann brought a big thick book called a Thesaurus, where you can look up any word you want (even the dirty ones) and find other funny words that mean the same thing. I want one!

I brought an old baseball card of Jackie Robinson and talked about how he was the first Negro to play in the major leagues, and how the Dodgers are the best team. I wish I could play for the Dodgers, but I can hardly play for the Tocaloma Huskies.

January 18, 1961

Bobby Del Valle got benched today for bringing a picture of Veronica Lake in a bikini to school. She's this beautiful actress lady. All the boys were huddled together at recess and looking at it, and this teacher named Mrs. Blum walked up and saw it, so she took it away. She said, "This kind of picture is altogether inappropriate for school," and she tore it up and Bobby got benched, but only for a day. I wonder what would happen if you got caught with a bare-naked picture from Playboy? They'd probably send you to the electric chair, I bet.

After recess, Miss Kleinholz had art, and we all made collages. That's where you cut stuff out and then paste it all together, and guess what? Norman Giambalvo eats paste! He does! Betty Bachelis told him to stop it and that he was gross, but Norman just kept right on eating it and licking his lips. He likes it! What a weirdo.

January 19, 1961

My picture is in the paper! Well, not just *my* picture, but a picture of me and my friends. Underneath the picture here's what it says:

SANDWICHES FROM THE OL' LUNCH PAIL *are about all a fellow can get at lunch time nowadays at Pacific Street Elementary School. There's a fine cafeteria, but nobody to run it - and you'd be surprised how a shortage of cooks can thin out the broth. Miss Elizabeth Palolozzi, principal, says the city schools are hard put to it to find cafeteria personnel - and there'll be no hot lunches at Pacific Street until one is found. Putting on the feedbag here are, from left, Liam McAfee, Bobby Del Valle, Francis Dupoy, Mary-Ann Lindstrom, Betty Bachelis and Scott McDonald.*

We're famous!

January 20, 1961

Frankie Dupoy was really mad today, because the picture in the paper said "Francis," so now his secret is out and all the other kids are calling him "Francis," and he hates that.

We got to watch TV at school today. That's never happened before. It was because they made Kennedy the president, and Miss Kleinholz thought it would be good for the class to see how it works. He had to put his hand on a Bible and promise to be a good President. But what if he had his fingers crossed? Nobody even checked!

At ten o'clock Bobby and Scotty and me had to report to Room 13 to rehearse some more for the 'Travel Dreams' show. This time we all had to watch Toren do her dance and give her speech. She had those pointy shoes and a pink too-too, and she danced to 'Beautiful Dreamer' and some other song. Then she gave a talk about school spirit and how Pacific Street was the best elementary school in all of California, and about how lucky we all are to go there. Barf!

Then she said, "Miss Purcell? I can sing, too -- my dancing teacher says I'm a regular Shirley Temple!"

Bobby made a face and said, "Shirley Temple's not a real person, you dork! It's something you drink while your old man has a Manhattan."

After that we had to practice our four songs about a jillion more times. They sound a little better now than they used to, but I'm getting sick of them so I'll be glad when the show gets here.

January 21, 1961

Do you have S&H Green Stamps where you are? We do. Every time you buy something at the market or the gas station, they give you one stamp for every dime you spend. Mom saves all the stamps in a big box in the cupboard, and then every few months we have to stick them all in books. Then once you get enough filled up books, you can take them down to the S&H Green Stamp Redemption Center and trade them for all kinds of good stuff.

So today Mom made me and Colin stick stamps in the books. The stamps taste funny, so Mom gave us a couple of sponges and a bowl of water so we wouldn't have to lick them. We filled up two books with stamps today, so now we have eleven books. I wonder what we can get for that?

After we got done with the stamps I went down to the play-ground with Scotty and we played hit-the-bat. It's almost like baseball, except you don't need a full team. While we were there these two teenagers came up and said, "Hey, look, it's two baby girls with a bat. Whatcha doing with the bat, girls?" Then they took my bat away, and started banging the flagpole with it.

I thought they were going to break the bat so I told them to stop, but the fat one with the mustache said, "How'd you like me to use this bat on your skull, Four-eyes?" Then they laughed and banged the flagpole some more until the bat got big dents in it. Then they gave it back and left.

After they got pretty far away, Scotty screamed, *"Assholes!"* at them, and then we ran for our lives!

When I got home I overheard Dad talking to Mom. He was saying, "....And then the goddamn thing actually took a big nip at me! Can you figure that?"

Mom said, "Did it break the skin?"

Dad said, "Nope but it sure as hell tried -- it gave me a nice black and blue bruise. Somebody ought to have a nice, fat duck dinner for Easter, if you ask me..."

They were talking about Ducky next door. I don't know how other ducks act, but Ducky is not a nice duck. He bites everybody that comes near him except Pinky, and he honks all the time and wakes everybody up, and he smells bad and he poops all over the place.

January 23, 1961

I didn't talk to you yesterday because I got a cold and I had to stay home from school yesterday and today. Alls I did was sit around in my pajamas and watch TV, so it didn't seem worth talking about. Dad says I drove him crazy with all the sniffling. He kept saying, "Liam! Use a handkerchief, willya?" but I can't stand blowing my nose. First of all it feels funny to blow your nose, I think. I mean like all that wet junk in your nose shouldn't come out your nose, should it? It's sort of like barfing, you know? But also, how can people just blow snot out of their noses into a handkerchief, and then just fold up the boogery handkerchief and put it back in their pockets like nothing happened? That's disgusting if you ask me.

Anyhow tomorrow I have to go back to school, and the day after tomorrow is the big show. I'm glad my cold is going away. I'm not too crazy about the singing part, but I want to watch the rest of it. Maybe somebody will throw a tomato at Toren.

January 24, 1961

Miss Kleinholz had to go to her fathers' funeral, so we got this substitute named Mrs. Wolf. She was about 100 years old and wrinkly, and I don't think she had anything really ready to teach, so she just told us to be quiet and read. Jeez, what do I need to go to school for? I can read at home.

The Cafeteria reopened today because they found a new cook, a Chinese lady named Fritzi, isn't that funny? I never met anybody named Fritzi before, especially not a Chinalady. Today she served Penicillin Pizza and Boogers On A Stick.

I think Betty and Frankie like each other -- she hit him in the ear with a rock today, so he wrote her a note.

He whispered, "Psst! Liam! Pass this note on to Betty," so I passed it along, but then when it got to Toren she said, "Mrs.

Wolf? The boys are passing notes again," and she ran up and gave the note to Mrs. Wolf.

Mrs. Wolf read the note to herself, then she said, "Ordinarily I would read this note out loud, as punishment for note passing. But the nature of this note is rather personal, so I shall forego that this time, and this time only! No more note passing, class!" Frankie looked relieved.

So tomorrow is the big show. Miss Purcell came into each class and told all the kids who were performing that we have to meet in the Auditorium at nine o'clock to get ready. All the other kids and the parents arrive at 9:30, and the show starts at 9:45. Miss Purcell seemed really nervous about it even though she doesn't have to sing.

January 25, 1961

The big show happened today. Dad and Uncle Mick couldn't come because of work, but Dad said, "I'll be with you in spirit, Boyo. Break a leg!" (That's what people say when somebody's about to perform, they say "break a leg." How come they want you to break a leg?)

Aunt Gwen came with Mom. She said, "I wouldn't miss this for the world, Liam. This is your big break in show biz!"

So I walked to school with Pinky and we got to the Auditorium at nine o'clock, and Miss Purcell was running around acting crazy, trying to make sure everything was OK. She wanted all the chorus members to wear white shirts so I did, but some kids wore other stuff so Miss Purcell was trying to find white shirts they could borrow. Meanwhile the Orchestra was in another room and they were all arguing because some boy who played horn emptied his spit-valve into a girl's purse.

At about 9:35 I peeked out through the curtains and the Auditorium was almost full already! All the kids from the other grades were there, and all the teachers, too, and lots of parents --

mostly moms. It made me a little nervous -- not too bad, but I was sure glad I didn't have to sing a solo like Cookie.

There were kids standing at all the doors, and they gave everybody a program. I saved one. Here's what it said:

PACIFIC STREET ELEMENTARY SCHOOL
presents a
WINTER MUSIC PROGRAM
on
WEDNESDAY, JANUARY 25, 1961
9:45 A.M. in the AUDITORIUM

"TRAVEL DREAMS"

Toren Shumaker:
Dance and Introduction

Special Ensemble:
(Fred Castleman, Wendy Chalmers, Peter Le Boite)
Little Clock .... by F. Graichen

Junior Chorus:
Village Festival .... Czech Folk Song
Tyrolliene .... by E. Jurey

Orchestra:
At The Dance .... Folk Song
Angeline .... Folk Song
Magic Boat .... Brazilian Folk Song
Cape Cod Chantey .... American Sea Chantey

Senior Chorus:
Arapaho Warriors .... Indian Tune
Hawaiian Boat Song .... from Hawaii

Precious Lord Take My Hand ....,,.... Negro Spiritual
I've Got Sixpence, Jolly Jolly Sixpence .... English Song

Orchestra:
Skye Boat Song .... Old Scottish Song
Beautiful Dreamer .... by S. Foster

Miss Purcell - Music Teacher
Toren Shumaker - Mistress of Ceremonies
Hermie Fleet - accordion solo on Arapaho Warriors
Ernestine "Cookie" Swansea - vocal solo on
Precious Lord Take My Hand

The show started out with the Pledge of Allegiance, and Toren led that. The Orchestra played the National Anthem and every-body stood up, then the Orchestra played some song I didn't know and Toren did a ballet dance in her pink too-too. I was hoping she'd fall down, but she didn't. Then Toren gave her speech about how great our school was, and about how much we loved it and all that kind of gunk. What a kiss-ass!

After that, these two boys and one girl from the A6 played a special song called 'Little Clock.' They played piano and violin and cello, and were really good for kids. A cello is like a big violin with swollen glands.

Miss Purcell came out next and thanked everybody for coming (like we had a choice) and introduced the Junior Chorus, who all put their heads together like hound dogs and sang these two really dumb songs. There was this one kid in the Junior Chorus who cracked me up, though -- his name was Eddie and he kept going cross-eyed and rolling his eyes around, and on the last song he turned his eyelids inside out, which made all the girls squirm.

Then there was a five-minute break while the Orchestra brought out all their instruments. They got in tune, which took forever, and then they started playing. Miss Purcell got a big stick and acted real serious just like those guys on TV who flip their hair around. It was funny! I saw Aunt Gwen and Mom in the third row and they looked like they were trying to keep from laughing, too. I looked around for Colin, but he must have been sitting in the back because I couldn't find him.

The Orchestra played four songs, which seemed like it took forever. This guy named Jocko Collins played the drums -- he's a real juvenile delinquent. He chewed gum the whole time and looked like he was ready to beat anybody up who didn't like the music.

During the last song, all us Senior Chorus people had to line up by height and get ready to sing. Then it was time, so we went out and stood on these wooden planks and waited for Miss Purcell to wave her stick at us.

The first song was 'Arapaho Warriors,' which was the one Hermie was supposed to play an accordion solo on, except his accordion made a big fart noise and it wouldn't work! Hermie yelled, "Wait a minute, I'll fix it!" but the song kept going while Hermie fumbled around with his accordion, and by the time he got it fixed the song was almost over. Hermie looked like he was going to cry, but Miss Purcell gave him a hug and whispered something in his ear, and Hermie smiled and looked better.

Then we sang this real dumb Hawaiian song from Hawaii, and then Cookie sang her Spiritual song – everybody stood up after! Cookie can really sing.

Do you know the song called 'I've Got Sixpence, Jolly Jolly Sixpence?' It was the last song we did, and me and Scotty and Bobby decided we'd change it a little. We figured with thirty kids in the choir nobody would really notice if we sang some different words, so on the last verse here's what we sang:

I've got no pants, jolly jolly no pants,
I've got no pants to last me all my life.
I've got no pants to lend and, no pants to spend and,
No pants to bring home to my wife, (poor wife.)

No cares have I to grieve me,
No sexy little girls to deceive me,
I'm as happy as a fart, believe me,
As we go a rolling rolling home (dead drunk!)

Rolling home (dead drunk!) rolling home (dead drunk!)
By the light of the silvery mo-oo-oo-oon,
Happy is the day when the teachers go away,
And we go a rolling rolling home (dead drunk!)

Well, Miss Purcell was not happy with us afterward, and she told Miss Kleinholz to give all three of us a 'minus' behind our grades in music. I think I was going to get an A before this, so now I guess I'll get an A-. You know what? It was worth it.

Everybody seemed to like the Senior Chorus (especially they liked Cookie,) so when we left we were pretty happy. Even though we goofed off on the last song, Mom still tossed me a kiss from the third row -- I was glad none of the other kids saw.

Finally the Orchestra came back and did two more songs, and Toren did another dance to 'Beautiful Dreamer.' Bobby watched her and said, "Beautiful Dreamer? More like a nightmare if you ask me," but she danced good and that was the end of the show. Miss Purcell came out and thanked everybody and that was that.

After we all got home, Mom told Dad all about the show and said how proud she was of me. She never even mentioned that we goofed off on the last song.

January 26, 1961

Tomorrow is the last day of the semester and it'll only be a half-day, so today we kind of all said goodbye to each other, because we'll probably all be in different classes next year. I wonder what teacher I'll get in B6? Also, Report Cards come out tomorrow.

January 27, 1961

I did OK on my Report Card. I got 3 A's, 6 B's, 2 C's, and a D in arithmetic. I don't think I'll get too yelled at about the D because everything else was pretty good. In the 'Qualities of Citizenship' area, I got a 'outstanding' in enthusiasm, a 'unsatisfactory' in promptness, and all the rest 'satisfactory.'

Here's my grades:

Reading	A
Language	A
Handwriting	C
Spelling	B
Arithmetic	D
Geography	B
History	B
Science	B
Music	A-
Art	B
Practical Arts	C
Phys Ed	B

On the last page of the Report Card it says what teacher you get for next semester and I got somebody named Mrs. Wintering. I don't know who that is, but I'm sure she'll be better than Mrs. Blum. I asked around, and Bobby got her too and so did Mary-Ann and Betty, so at least I'll have a few friends in there. Scotty got Blum, though, and so did Frankie Dupoy and Alex Eisenbaum. Hermie Fleet and Toren and the Drinkwater twins got Wintering so I'm stuck with them again, and Norman Giambalvo got Blum. So I guess there'll be a bunch of new kids next week.

At the end of the day Miss Kleinholz came around and talked to each kid alone for a few minutes. When it was my turn she hugged me and told me she thought I should become a newspaper reporter. She said I was "curious" and "good at writing", and those were important qualities for a newspaper man. Miss Kleinholz was a pretty nice teacher. Plus I'm going to miss looking at her -- I bet the new teacher won't have big ol' pointy bazoombas to look at.

I had to turn in the Registration Book today, but before I did I copied down the phone numbers of lots of the kids -- I'm not sure what I'll do with that, but you never know. So I'm in sixth grade now, how about that?   I made it, I'm a Senior!   See you next semester!

January 28, 1961

Even though I did OK on the rest of my Report Card, I still got yelled at about the D I got in arithmetic.   Dad called me a "mathematical knothead," and now they're talking about getting me a tutor. Mom and Dad heard about some girl around the block who's supposedly a whiz at arithmetic, and now they want me to take a lesson from her once a week after school. They're going to pay her fifty cents an hour! The girl's name is Deedee Weever -- she's probably a big old scuzzy zitface who drools. Gee I can't wait.

At least they can't make me do arithmetic on the weekends, and it's Saturday so I walked downtown and goofed around.   First I went to Allegro Music.   They have all kinds of cool records at Allegro Music, but I hardly ever buy any because they're too expensive -- instead I buy the used ones at the Thrift Shop. Today there was an old guy at Allegro music who wore a top hat and played the harmonica. He said the harmonica was really easy to play and only costs $1.10, so I bought one. It's called an 'Atta Boy,' and it comes with instructions.

After the music store I went over to the Hobby Shop.   The Hobby Shop is this fantastic store where they sell electric trains and model cars, and magic tricks and baseball cards and gliders -- all the good stuff. It's my favorite store. They even have joke stuff like stink bombs, and they have this trick gum that turns your teeth black. One time when I was little I gave Colin some of that gum and he looked in the mirror and started screaming and having a cow, so I got spanked.

January 29, 1961

Duane Beedy got the Trenchmouth! I'm not exactly sure what the Trenchmouth is, but Mom says it's pretty nasty, and do you know how he got it? He got it from eating sawbugs! I'm not making this up!

Duane said that the Monitors told him to eat sawbugs because sawbugs are good for you, so he's been eating them for weeks and he got the Trenchmouth from it. Dad said, "That boy needs a Cyciatrist," which I think means maybe he's crazy. Mom and Dad told me to stay away from Duane for awhile, which isn't too hard because we're in different grades anyway -- I really never see him except walking home from school. He talks to himself, too.

Scotty came to dinner tonight, and so did Uncle Mick. Uncle Mick hasn't been around much lately because he got a new girl-friend, and Dad says he's been busy with indoor sports. We saw a picture of her and she looks just like a fashion model. Her name is Patrice and she's a nightclub dancer. Mom said that Uncle Mick could bring her to dinner next week if he wanted to, but he said he didn't want to send out any goddamn domestic signals.

After dinner Colin came running into the kitchen wearing Mom's robe and her high heel shoes, yelling, "IT'S STAR TIME!" His dirty old arm cast was poking out of the robe, and he did the Wah-Watusi and then sang 'Babaloo' by Ricky Ricardo. It was pretty funny -- Dad laughed so hard he farted! Sometimes I wonder about my little brother.

January 30, 1961

This was the first day of sixth grade and it's a lot different. First of all, now I'm in Room 4 which is a real room, not a bungalow. It's way better. The new teacher Mrs. Wintering is this skinny lady who comes from Mississippi. She talks even funnier than Mrs. Vanderhoeven -- like today we were talking about how Duane's trying to get rid of the Trenchmouth, and Mrs. Wintering said, "They'll give him peels."

I didn't get it, so I said "What?"

She said, "You know, peels? Aspirins, Vitamins, *peels!*"

She seems like she'll work out OK though, she tells little jokes and stuff. She's about 35 and wears her hair in a long braid, and she has a husband who's a fireman. They don't have any kids. She doesn't have any titties, but you can't have everything. There's about thirty kids in the class -- lots of them I knew from before, but some of them I don't know at all. Mom says that's OK, I'll get to know them soon enough.

Toren Shumaker might not be able to get away with much this semester, because first thing this morning a big girl named Robin Ward shoved her against the wall and said, "I've heard about you, Shumaker, and you can take your kiss-ass attitude and shove it right up your skinny butt!" Toren didn't say a word for the rest of the day.

January 31, 1961

Some of the new kids in my class are really good at sports. Like there's this one blond guy named Roger who's way taller than anybody else and he can play basketball like Wilt Chamberlain! Everybody wants to be on his team. Also there's the colored kid I told you about named Fred Brown, and he's a whiz at tether ball and sockball and kickball. Fred Brown is a real quiet kid. He doesn't goof around as much as we do, but he's nice. Mary-Ann says the big girl named Robin is good at sports too, but she's real loud and yells a lot.

We're still trying to get used to the way Mrs. Wintering talks. Like today she said, "Hey Bobby, shet that wender! Thanks, Hun, it's too col' in here." And later she told us "Here's where you line up when there's a fardrill." She seems nice, though, she doesn't yell much and she hasn't sent anybody to Mrs. Palolozzi's office. But then it's only the second day so she's still on her best behavior.

February 1, 1961

School was pretty routine today, except this painter guy came in and showed us some of these paintings he made. They were of houses and the beach and apples and junk. He was a very good painter! I don't get how he makes all that stuff look so real. I wish I could do that.

When I got home from school, Mom had an announcement for me. She told me it's official: I have to go to a tutor for arithmetic, starting right now, today! Disgustomatic! Every Wednesday at four o'clock for the next four weeks, I have to walk around the block to some pukeface girl Deedee's house, at 14710 Palomar Street. She's supposed to be some genius, and she's supposed to help get me caught up on arithmetic. Barf-o-rama! Mom gave me fifty cents to give her, then sent me off. I thought about keeping the fifty cents and just going to the beach, but I knew Mom would call later to make sure I showed up, so I walked over there as slow as I could and knocked on the door.

A real pretty girl opened the door. She had lipstick on, and shiny yellow hair that was pulled tight and went down to her waist. She was barefoot and she wore a short, pale dress. "Are you Liam?" she said.

My cheeks went all warm. I said, "Uh huh."

"Come in," she said, "I'm Deedee. How old are you, Liam?"

I walked into the house. "Ten and a third. How old are you?"

She said, "I'm fifteen. Quick: what's fifteen minus ten and a third?"

I said, "Umm.... four and something?"

She smiled and her blue eyes twinkled. She said, "Well, I'm going to help you figure out those kind of problems, Liam. Your mom says you're a very smart boy, you could just use a bit of a shove in arithmetic. Wouldn't you like to get a better grade on your next Report Card?"

She wore perfume and it smelled real nice. I barely even heard what she said, but I would've agreed with just about anything, so I said, "Sure!"

So I had my first lesson. Deedee brought me two homemade cookies and then she started talking to me about how if I was a baker and I baked 400 cookies, and I had to put them in boxes of a dozen each, how many boxes I'd have, and how many cookies would be left over. Stuff like that. She got out some paper and some pencils and we did some easy problems, and then they got a little harder and harder. When she smiled, I couldn't stop looking at her -- but the only way to get her to smile was to get a problem right.

When I got home I showed Mom the arithmetic papers we'd done. Deedee had written, "Making real progress!" on one. I think maybe I like getting tuted.

February 2, 1961

Lately Colin's arm has been itching him like crazy, but he can't scratch it because of his cast. So I got him a coat hanger and untangled it, so he can stick it down in there and scratch.

Colin is in a new class at school, too. He's in the A3 now and he got Mrs. Roberts, who's the meanest teacher in all of Pacific Street. I remember when I had her she used to give swats after school -- she'd wallop you really hard on the butt with a ping pong paddle. I hated her, she such a shitburger! So I told Colin about all the things not to do in her class. Like she especially gets mad about spitwads, so I told Colin to never throw a spitwad in Mrs. Roberts' class. I hope he believes me.

After school Colin and me watched Engineer Bill on TV for two hours. Engineer Bill is this guy who has a cartoon show, and he comes on and talks in between the cartoons. I guess you'd call him a 'host.' He's kind of a butt brain, but Colin likes him a lot. Engineer Bill wears an Engineer Suit and an Engineer Hat, and he plays Red Light, Green Light with you.

Do you know that game? That's where all the kids are supposed to go get a big glass of milk, and when Engineer Bill says, "Green light" you're supposed to drink it, and when he says, "red light" you're supposed to stop. But sometimes he says, "greenlightred-lightgreenlightredlight" real fast, and every kid in America ends up spilling milk all over themselves, or else they choke and the milk comes all shooting out their noses with boogers and stuff. I bet mothers all over the country hate Engineer Bill!

After awhile Uncle Mick came and sat with us and watched, and he showed us his ticket to Ireland -- he's leaving the first of next month to go get the money he won in the Irish Sweepstakes. I made him promise to send us some postcards.

Then this real old Felix The Cat cartoon came on, where Felix drinks a bunch of beer and starts seeing things and acting crazy and Uncle Mick said, "How about that? Damn! Felix The Cat is three sheets to the wind!"

Then Colin looked around to make sure Mom and Dad couldn't hear, and he started to sing the Felix The Cat Song. He sang:

Felix the Rat,
The wonderful, wonderful brat,
Whenever he gets in a fix,
He reaches into his bag of dicks.

You'll scratch your nuts,
You'll crap your butts,
Your farts will go rat-a-tat,
Watching Felix -- the wonderful cat!

February 3, 1961

Mom was really sick this morning. Colin and me could hear her in the bathroom barfing, and Dad was in there with her, telling her it would all be OK. Dad said Mom has "Morning Sickness." That's what ladies get when they're expecting, and they eat too many pickles. He said it's no fun for Mom, but that it's normal and it shouldn't last too long and that Mom will be fine in a few weeks. I sure hope so. I hate barfing.

Speaking of barfing, I wish they'd take the cast off Colin's arm. It stinks!

February 4, 1961

It's Saturday so I rode my bike over to Scotty's, then we went into town and snuck into the Royale Theater. I haven't seen as much of Scotty lately -- only at recess or after school -- because he got Blum and I got Wintering. He says Blum is terrible and that she's really strict, so I'm sure glad I didn't get her. Already she's sent Norman Giambalvo to the Principal's office three times, and even Alex Eisenbaum, who never gets in trouble, got yelled at. Scotty says the only kid in class she seems to like is Frankie Dupoy, who is doing real good now. He never falls asleep anymore, and he's kind of turned into this cool guy who everybody likes.

I guess we could've paid to get into the Royale Theater -- both of us had the fifty cents -- but it's a lot more fun to sneak in. The way we do it is so simple you'd think everybody would do it. Alls we do is go around the back and pound really hard on the back exit door, until some kid comes down and opens it and then we run in. It almost always works, although a couple of times Mr. Zupo opened the door and we had to run for our lives!

This time Betty Bachelis opened the door and she said, "I should've known it would be you two," and she let us in.

We saw this movie called 'Some Like It Hot,' which was really funny. These two guys accidentally see a big murder so they have to run away, so they dress up like girls and join this Girl's Band. Also it has Marilyn Monroe in it. Marilyn Monroe is even prettier than Marie Blessing. But not as pretty as Deedee Weever.

February 5, 1961

Last night about midnight, me and Colin got woked up by this terrible noise. At first we thought it was a dog fight, then we thought it was a cat fight, and then we couldn't tell *what* it was! It stopped after a minute or two, so we went back to sleep.

Then this morning after breakfast we went outside and talked to Pinky, and she said Ducky got ate by a fox last night! Wow! I didn't even know we had foxes around here. But that's what it was, all right -- there was even little pieces of fox fur laying around with the feathers. Mom said she's seen a small red fox in the neighborhood before, so I guess it ate up Ducky, beak and all. Pinky accidentally left the pen door open so she was real sad. But I'm not.

Aunt Gwen called Mom on the phone tonight and I didn't hear it all, but it sounded like maybe Gramma is sick again. I heard Mom say, "Jeez, Sis, I'm up to my ears right now -- I've been retching every morning and I feel like hell, and I've still got these three menfolk to take care of. I know it's asking a lot, but can you deal with it this time?" I guess Aunt Gwen must've said "OK." Mom didn't mention anything at dinner.

February 6, 1961

Somebody swiped Scotty's bike! He rode it to school and he locked the wheel to the rack just like always, but when school let out, the wheel was still locked to the rack but the rest of the bike was missing. Scotty was crying really hard. What a mess for poor old Scotty -- of all the kids I know, his family has the least money. I bet it'll be years before Mrs. McDonald can afford to get him another bike.

When I got home Mom was laying down in bed. I told her about Scotty's bike, and she said, "Liam? I'm sorry about your friend, but Mom doesn't feel well now and needs to take a nap, OK? Can you please go outside and play for an hour? And keep an eye on your brother?"

Gee, things aren't very good right now, are they?

February 7, 1961

Mom felt better today and she didn't get sick this morning. I'm glad of that because last night Dad had to cook dinner and he burnt everything, even though it was only Swanson's TV Dinners.

Today I told Mrs. Wintering about Scotty and his bike. She doesn't even know Scotty because he's in Blum's class, but she saw him sitting on the bench and sniffling during recess so she asked me about him. After I told her what happened, she said she'd talk to Mrs. Blum and maybe there was something that could be done, although she didn't know what.

I think maybe I like Mrs. Wintering. And she said some more funny stuff today in class: about two o'clock some clouds rolled in and it got real dark, so she told Robin Ward to "Turn on the lots." And then later, she said, "Hey, wake up, Bobby! What's wrong, you tarred?"

Lately at lunch Mary-Ann has been trading me her Hostess Cupcake for my Hostess Twinkie. Aunt Gwen sometimes says, "Variety is the spice of life." But Mary-Ann usually saves her dessert until after school anyway, and by then it's kind of crunchy.

February 8, 1961

Today was Wednesday, which meant I got to get tuted by Deedee again. School went by in a flash and I got to her house at five minutes to four. She said, "Hello young man, please come on in!" ("Young man!" Cool!)

She had on some really tight pants today -- I think they call them Capris? Her hair was down and all over her shoulders, and she wore a lacy shirt like the Mexican ladies wear, and she smelled even better than the Helms Truck. We did a couple of problems together and she sat right up close to me. I made her smile a lot. Four and two-thirds years isn't that many, is it?

I was feeling pretty happy when I got home, but the smell in the house made me even happier -- we had spaghetti for dinner tonight which is my favorite except for tacos. Mom cooks the sauce all day long and the house smells better than anything! And we also had garlic bread.

Scotty ate over (he's still real sad about his bike,) and so did Uncle Mick. Uncle Mick always manages to end up over here whenever we have spaghetti. After dinner I was outside watching him smoke a Tiparillo, and I asked him, "Uncle Mick? How old is Patrice? Your girlfriend?"

Uncle Mick squarshed up his forehead and said, "Damn, Liam, I don't really know... 'bout 26 or 27, maybe? I never asked her. Why?"

I said, "How come you never asked her?"

"Because it doesn't really matter, I guess," he said. "I can see she's close to my age -- I'm 32. Besides, when two people like each other, their ages don't matter, unless it's really far apart -- like 20 years or something."

I said, "Thanks, Uncle Mick."

February 9, 1961

When Dad got home from work tonight he opened the trunk of the car and pulled out a bicycle. It was a nice used Schwinn Continental 10-speed, maybe three or four years old but in really good shape. He said, "Your mother asked me to pick it up from the Cycle Shop. It's for your friend."

I ran inside and asked Mom what was happening and she sighed and said, "Liam, I've known Barbara McDonald off and on forever, and that family has had more than it's share of hardship. I talked to a couple of teachers from your school and to Father O'Dowd, and a couple of other moms, and between us all we came up with $55 so Scotty could have a bike -- a better one than he used to have. Who knows, the way things are going, he might need it to get a paper route soon."

I was excited! I said, "Does Scotty know?"

Mom said, "Not yet, and you better not tell him! Barbara's going to surprise him with it tomorrow." Then she whispered, "He needed it, Liam. It was all he had. So now he's got it."

February 10, 1961

Scotty rode his Schwinn Continental to school today, and all the kids were happy for him. He didn't mention how he got it, and nobody asked anyway -- everybody was just relieved to see him stop being so sad.

After school I had to get a haircut at Vince's. Mom had a doctor's appointment and couldn't give me a ride, so I had to walk there. Mary-Ann told me she'd never seen the inside of a barbershop and asked if she could watch me get my hairs cut, so I said, "OK," so we walked there together. I started playing my harmonica and Mary-Ann said she liked it. Cool.

I had to wait awhile for a barber, but luckily I got Cecil instead of Vince and he cut my hairs OK. There was a bunch of people getting their hairs cut, maybe because it's Friday and they wanted to look nice for the weekend? I don't know.

Anyhow, Mary-Ann was standing right next to the barber's chair and watching us real close and eating her leftover dessert. I think she made Cecil kind of nervous, just staring like that, so Cecil said, "Little girl? You're going to get hair on your Twinkie."

Mary-Ann said, "I know, I've seen my mom. I'm going to get boobs, too."

All the barbers and customers laughed real hard. I kind of got it and kind of didn't get it, so later I told Uncle Mick about it and after he explained it, I laughed too.

February 11, 1961

Aunt Gwen and Mom were talking tonight and Mom said, "It's been so long since I've been pregnant that I've forgotten a few things... Like I'm three months pregnant now, and I've forgotten when I can expect my baby to move."

Aunt Gwen said, "With any luck, the day he turns eighteen."

February 12, 1961

This morning I rode over to Scotty's but he wasn't there. His mom said he took off on his bike at about nine o'clock and she hadn't seen him since, so I rode into town and looked for him. He wasn't at the Hobby Shop and his bike wasn't parked at the Royale Theater, so I couldn't find him. But I ran into Bobby Del Valle outside the Mayfair.

Bobby looked around to make sure nobody was looking, the he said, "Liam! Looky what I got!" Then he reached up under his shirt and pulled out a Playboy fold-out. It was this beautiful blonde with huge bazoombas. She had tan lines that made it look almost like she was wearing a white bikini top with dark pink circles painted onto it -- but she wasn't. She was completely bare-naked!

"Wow!" I said, "where'd you get it?"

He said, "Swiped it out of a Playboy at the Pharmacy."

"What're you gonna do with it?" I asked.

He said, "Hide it in my closet, so my mom doesn't find it. Then I can take it out and look at it whenever I want."

Bobby's got plenty of guts if you ask me. I'm always too scared to even *look* at the Playboys when I'm in the Pharmacy, let alone swipe a fold-out.

Later when I got home I started looking around our room to try to find a hiding place, in case I ever have anything important like that to hide. There really isn't anywhere safe, though, so I guess if I get anything that good I'll just have to keep it in the cave with the other stuff.

February 13, 1961

Colin finally got his cast cut off today. Mom picked him up at
school and took him down to Dr. Dicksau's, and Dr. Dicksau cut it
off with a power saw! Colin was really brave, he said he wasn't
even afraid Dr. Dicksau would cut his arm off! I would've been.
Dr. Dicksau said that Colin's cast looked like it had been through
three World Wars. After they got the cast off, Colin's arm stunk so
bad they had to wash it with some real strong stuff that smelled
like when you get a shot. Colin said some of the skin on there
looked rotted.

Anyhow I guess his arm is still a little bit sore and stiff, but they
told him it'll be fine in a few days. Colin wanted to keep his cast
for a souvenir, but Mom said she wouldn't keep a disgusting thing
like that around the house, so it got thrown in the doctor's
garbage. Colin said he thought about going around the back and
looking through the doctor's garbage can, but he was afraid of
what he might find in there. Like what if maybe Dr. Dicksau had
to cut off somebody's leg or their appendix or something today?
Who knows what you might find in a doctor's garbage can? What
if there were eyeballs and stuff in there? In the movies, that's
where Dr. Frankenstein got all his body parts. At doctor's offices.

Since tomorrow is Valentine's Day, Mrs. Wintering let us do art
most of the day -- we made Valentine Cards. She said, "Y'all
should each make a card for your mommy, and also one for your
galfriend or fella."

But then most of the kids told her that they didn't have a
girlfriend or a boyfriend, so she said, "OK then. But it's s'posed to
be a romantic day, so just make one for your best buddy *of the
other sort.*" Lots of the kids groaned about that. For me, I guess
that means Mary-Ann -- she's my friend, so I made her a
Valentine. I gave it to her after school, and she turned red and
gave me one back, but the one she gave me wasn't the one she
made in school -- instead it was this one with a picture of a girl
playing the harmonica. It said, "Hope I'm not in a flat key, when I

play 'You Are The World To Me.'" It's a corny Valentine but I still liked it. Mary-Ann is pretty cool. For a girl.

February 14, 1961

I just gave Mom her Valentine Card and she liked it. I painted a heart on it and made up a poem:

"Roses are red, violets are blue,
You're the best mom, so don't get the flu."

February 15, 1961

Today Mrs. Wintering gave an arithmetic test. Ugh! It was a short test, only ten questions. If you got all ten right you got an A+. Nine right was an A, eight right was a B, seven right was a C, six right was a D, five or less right was an F. Hermie Fleet and Toren both got A+. I got a C, which is at least OK. After school it was my tutoring day at Deedee's, so I showed her the test and she said I was improving. Then we talked about what went wrong on the problems I messed up, and how to do them right.

I gave Deedee a Valentine Card, too. It said: "Happy Valentine's Day to a real groovy girl." She read it and said, "What a sweet kid you are, Liam! Thank you." Then she kissed me on the forehead, which made me dizzy.

She had on a yellow dress today, a short one so I could see almost all her legs. They're really tan -- how does she do that in the winter? I bet in the summer she spends lots of time at the beach. I wonder which beach she goes to? I wonder if she wears a bikini swimming suit? A little white one? I don't think I could concentrate on arithmetic at all if Deedee Weever sat close to me in a white bikini swimming suit.

February 16, 1961

Do you know what a 'summons' is? That's when a messenger kid comes into your class with a yellow piece of paper, and hands it to the teacher. The yellow paper is called a 'summons,' and it means somebody's been called down to the Principal's office. Whenever a kid comes into class with a yellow piece of paper and hands it to the teacher, all us other kids hold our breath because it means one of us is in some pretty deep dogdoo!

So today at about eleven o'clock this boy came into our class and handed a summons to Mrs. Wintering, and she said, "Liam McAfee? Please come up here?" My heart sank and all I could do was try to think of what it was I'd done bad in the last week or so, but I couldn't think of anything too bad. Mrs. Wintering handed me the summons and said, "Better go report over yonder to Mrs. Palolozzi's."

I walked there as slowly as I could, then finally I swallowed hard and went into the Principal's office. Mom was sitting in the waiting room and her eyes were red, and Colin was there, too. He looked just as confused as I was. I said, "Hi, Mom. Hi, Colin. What are you guys doing here?"

Mom said, "Sit down, Liam. We've been waiting for you. I didn't want to have to say this twice, so I made Colin wait until you got here." So I sat down and shut up. This looked important.

Mom talked real quiet like. She said, "Boys? There's no easy way to tell you this. I just got a phone call from Aunt Gwen. Your grandmother has died."

"Gramma? Died?" I felt kind of fuzzy. "What happened?"

"She had a heart attack. It was very quick. The doctors said she didn't suffer. I'm terribly sorry, guys."

Colin burst in to tears and Mom gathered his head in her arms and said, "It's OK, son, you just cry all you want to."

I didn't know what to do -- if I started crying too, Mom would really have her hands full, and besides I wanted to show her how grown up I was getting. Mom said, "We're all going home for the day. Neither of you has to go back to class. Let's just go on home, OK?" So we walked outside and got in the car and went home.

It was completely quiet in the car. I felt funny and mixed up -- my brain felt like your mouth does when you get a Novocain shot.

By the time we got home Colin had stopped crying, and Mom looked like she was feeling a little better. Dad was home from work and Aunt Gwen was there, too. Both of them looked kind of depressed, especially Aunt Gwen. She ran over to us and hugged us and told us to be strong, which made Colin start crying all over again, and then Mom saw Colin crying so she started bawling again. It was a mess. I went out to the garage to talk to Dad.

"It's a shame, isn't it? he said. "How ya holdin' up, Boyo?"

"OK, I guess," I said. "But I don't get it."

"Nobody gets it," he said. "This came as a shock to your mom and your aunt. Your grandmother was pretty young."

I said, "How old was she?"

"Fifty four," Dad said. That doesn't sound young to me.

So it's been a slow-moving and weird kind of night, like we're all living in the Twilight Zone or something. I think I'm going to bed now, even though it's only nine o'clock. I'll try to talk to you more tomorrow, but I don't quite know what's going to happen around here.

February 17, 1961

Me and Colin had to go back to school, but at least it's Friday so the weekend is coming. Mom says there's going to be a Funeral Mass for Gramma at Our Lady of Sorrows on Sunday, and that even Dad was coming. (Actually what she said was, "You still got that old Brownie box camera, Liam? Because if you do, you ought to get a picture of your old man sitting in church in a suit and tie. Might be the only time in your life you'll ever see it.")

Mrs. Wintering and Bobby and Mary-Ann and Scotty were all really nice to me when I came back to school today. None of them said anything directly about Gramma, but I noticed they were all just real friendly and helpful. It was kind of strange. Today in science we learned water is composed of two gins, oxygen and hydrogen. Oxygen is pure gin and hydrogen is gin and water.

After school there was a bunch of people at our house: men with suits on, and some neighbor ladies with food, and some other old people. The house had a funny feeling to it, like it wasn't quite home. I don't know how to explain it -- I wanted to go next door to Pinky and Stinky's, or better yet ride over to Scotty's, just so things would feel regular again. But Mom asked me to watch Colin, so I couldn't go anywhere. We tried to look at Dragnet on TV but there were all these people coming and going, so we couldn't watch too good.

And I miss Gramma -- she was nice to us.

February 18, 1961

I didn't have to go to school today -- it's Saturday -- but it wasn't quite a normal Saturday. Usually Mom and Dad sleep in on Saturday til at least eight o'clock, but today I could hear them rumbling around the kitchen at six. And Mom was on the phone with somebody at seven, talking about estates and insurance and legal junk like that. Then every so often, she'd cry a little.

I guess mothers hear their kids cry pretty often so maybe they get used to it, but kids almost never hear their mothers cry. I don't like this at all.

February 19, 1961

Mom woked us up at eight o'clock and put us into our best suits -- even Colin had to wear a tie. Mom wore a black dress with a veil in front of her face and Dad wore a suit, too. At about ten o'clock Aunt Gwen came over, and Mom and her sort of disappeared for about an hour, talking about the funeral. Dad sat on the couch and tried to watch a basketball game until 11, and then we all went down to the Church.

There were a lot of people in the parking lot waiting for the funeral to start -- lots of old people I didn't know, and some of them were telling stories about Gramma. This one old guy in a Army uniform looked drunk already, and just cried and cried to himself. I asked Mom who he was, and she said, "Oh, my God... I remember that man vaguely from when I was a kid. He looks different now of course, but I think he was one of your grandmother's old flames..."

The doors opened at noon and the first person I saw inside was a real tall lady, about twenty years old, and she was singing in Catholic, while an old lady with white hair played the organ. We all sat down and then Father O'Dowd got up and gave this long sermon about life and death, and rebirth with Jesus. Then he talked a lot about what a good Catholic Gramma had been, and how she was a great supporter of the Church. When he said that, Aunt Gwen whispered over to Mom, "Can you believe what an exaggerator that man is?" Then Colin said really loud, "Hey, who cut one?" and Mom shushed him.

There was a lot of singing and talking and kneeling and stuff, and then it was over and all the people at the funeral came over to our house. It was crazy -- there was like sixty people at our place. Somebody brought a box of See's candy and Colin locked himself in the bathroom and took little bites out of each candy until he found the ones he liked, then he put all the half eaten ones back in the box. Everybody was eating ham and celery and crackers and cheese, and drinking martinis and talking about Gramma. The old guy in the Army uniform never said a word to anybody, he just sat down in a folding chair in our back yard, all by himself, and silently cried all afternoon. Nobody seemed to know him.

I felt kind of sorry for him so I went out back and said, "Her, Mister? I'm Mrs. Owen's grandson. Would you like something to eat? We have all kinds of stuff..." But he just shook his head and kept on crying. He looked terrible -- his eyes were all swollen and his lower lip kept bouncing around. It was awful.

Finally it got dark, and little by little all the people slipped away. Mom and Aunt Gwen cleaned up the mess and that was that.

February 20, 1961

After lunch we were doing art and I learned an important lesson: never shake a bottle of paint without checking to see if the top is screwed on tight. I did, and my whole shirt got covered in orange poster paint. Mrs. Wintering said I looked like these two painters named Jacks and Pollack.

Scotty ate dinner over tonight -- we had beef stew -- and he said his brother Jimmy has finally got the motorcycle up and running. Did I ever tell you about the motorcycle?

Well, about six months ago Scotty's two brothers Jimmy and Milo pooled their money and bought this German Army Surplus motorcycle, left over from World War II. They saw an ad for it in some dirty magazine, so they sent off $299.99 plus tax, then they waited around for a month. (I'm not sure where they got all that money, but I bet they swiped it.)

Anyhow, the motorcycle finally got delivered in a big wooden crate, but it was in a jillion pieces and packed in this goopy stuff called 'creosote.' I guess Jimmy and Milo didn't read the ad very close, because they didn't realize they had to put the whole thing together themselves.

Milo decided it was too much trouble to clean the creosote goop off each part, so instead he stuck the parts in the oven and turned it up to 550 degrees for a few hours -- he figured the stuff would just kind of burn off. But instead it made all this terrible smelling smoke, and their oven burned up, and Scotty almost choked to death and their apartment stunk for a month.

Milo was doing most of the work putting the motorcycle together, but then he decided to become Milo The Moron Bank Robber. So now that he's stuck in jail, Jimmy took over. He's been at it for months, and now the thing is actually running and

Jimmy has been riding it around the neighborhood, but Scotty's a little worried because Jimmy likes to drive it 100 miles an hour and also he smokes that loco weed. I'm glad they finally got it put together, but I sure hope Jimmy doesn't crash it.

February 21, 1961

After school a guy in a white hat and a white suit came by the house and gave Mom a big vase. I asked what was in it and Mom said, "It's your grandmother's ashes, Liam."

I didn't really get what she meant and Colin must not have either, because he said, "You mean somebody went over to Gramma's and emptied out her ash trays? Like for a souvenir?"

Mom said, "No, not exactly. Now listen closely, boys, because this may be a bit difficult for you to understand... Your grandmother chose to be cremated. That was her wish. These are her ashes."

We both said, "What's 'cremated?'"

Mom sighed. She said, "Well, when people pass away, their spirits -- their souls -- go on up to heaven where it's lovely and peaceful. Gramma is there now. It's a much better place and she's happy."

Mom lit a cigarette and sat down. Then she said, "You see, the body doesn't matter anymore after we pass on, because no one lives there anymore. Some people want their bodies buried when they die, and other people donate their bodies to science. And many people prefer cremation. That's where the body is consumed and cleansed by flame."

Colin looked shocked. He said, "You mean they burned up our Gramma?!?"

"Well, it's not exactly like that," said Mom. "Your Gramma wasn't there anymore, son -- like I said, she's comfortable in heaven. After you pass on, the body is just an empty shell. She's happy about it -- this is the way she wanted it."

But Colin looked sick. "Who burnt her?" he said. "Where do they do it?"

"There a special place where they do it," Mom said. "Now please, Colin, please understand that many, many people do this. Millions of people, all over the world. It doesn't hurt her or anything, she was no longer there. It's like the final link in the cycle of life. Do you guys understand this at all?" She frowned. "You're all right, aren't you?"

I said, "Yeah, I think so," and Colin didn't answer. Then he said he just wanted to go out in the back yard by himself and look for four leaf clovers.

February 22, 1961

When Mom first signed me up with Deedee Weever, the deal was that I'd have to do four weeks of tuting. I hated the idea then, but now I'd kind of like to keep doing it. In class today I kept thinking, 'In a few more hours I get to see Deedee Weever's legs and smell her perfume,' but this is the fourth and last week. Maybe I should have did worse on purpose, so I could make the tuting go on longer? But then Mom and Dad would be mad. I don't know... kids just can't win.

Anyways, I went over to her house and there she was, looking like a movie star. She had a frilly pink dress on and white lipstick, and her teeth gleamed real white. We talked about my schoolwork, and then we did some more arithmetic. She tried to explain the "logic of math" to me, because she said instead of just teaching me how to do a problem, I'd be better off if she taught me how to think through a problem. I didn't really get it, but I acted like I did.

I tried to get a few facts out of her, like especially where she hangs out in the summer (State Beach,) and where she likes to eat (Ted's Grill,) and some other stuff like that. Who knows, maybe I'll bump into her once or twice this summer, accidentally-on-purpose? Also I asked her if she had a boyfriend, but she smiled and said, "A girl's got to keep some things secret, young man."

At five o'clock I gave her the fifty cents, and she wished me good luck and told me she hoped to see me again sometime. I liked that. I got halfway home, lost in a daydream of walking along the beach with Deedee Weever, when I heard a huge roar come down the street -- it was Jimmy McDonald on his motor-cycle. He drove right up Deedee's driveway and whistled, and Deedee ran out and jumped on the back of the bike and grabbed Jimmy around the stomach, and they rode off laughing.

I feel sick.

February 23, 1961

What do sea monsters eat? Fish and ships. Ha ha!

February 24, 1961

We had a Field Trip today, not just our class but Mrs. Blum's, too. Both classes got onto a big school bus and we went to the La Brea Tar Pits to look at the goo that killed the dinosaurs. It was pretty cool that both classes went together, because I got to hang out with Scotty and Alex.

Those guys have a lot of new kids in their class too, some groovy ones and some dorks. One cool guy is this kid named Nigel who comes from London, England. He has an accent and he says all kinds of funny things, like when the bus got in a traffic jam, he said, "Well, sod this for a lark!" And then he called underwears "underkecks," and when somebody got mad at somebody else, Nigel said, "Hey, don't throw a wobbly!" He cracked me up. Also he had ale in his thermos! I'm not making this up, his mother gave him something called Watney's Red Barrel Ale, and Nigel said his whole family puts it on their cornflakes in the morning instead of milk.

It took about 45 minutes to get to La Brea Tar Pits, and this girl named Lisa Chapps got carsick and barfed right out the window, but it only landed in the street and didn't hit anybody.

The La Brea Tar Pits are neat. They have all these fossils and things. A fossil is an exstink animal -- the older it is, the exstinkier it is. Also there are skeletons of dinosaurs there, and saber-tooth cats, horses, lions, mammoths and birds. The skeleton is what is left after the insides have been taken out and the outsides have been taken off. All these animals got stuck in the goo about a jillion years ago because they thought the tar was water. But they must've been pretty stupid to think that, because it smells just like tar.

February 25, 1961

Today Aunt Gwen and Mom and I had to go over to Gramma's apartment so they could go through her stuff, and it made both of them real sad. Most of Gramma's clothes were too small to fit anyone else, so Mom gave them to Catholic Charities.

Gramma had a lot of old pictures that were fun to look at -- pictures of Mom and Aunt Gwen and Uncle Jake when they were kids, but also some of when Gramma was a little girl over there in Ireland with Great-Grampa McLaughlin. Mom says that Great-Grampa McLaughlin fought in some war over there called the Easter War, and he was a friend of Michael Collins. (I know who that is, because we have a picture of him over our TV. He's Irish.)

But then Great-Grampa got in some kind of trouble and a bunch of other guys tried to shoot him, so they all ran away to America in 1918. Gramma was my age when they came here, almost eleven. There were pictures of her on a big boat -- she wore funny clothes!

I got to keep an old yo-yo and some other toys she saved, plus you'll never guess what Gramma had? She had a real old baseball card from about the 1920's, some guy named Henry Johns. Even though he was on the Yankees, I wanted the card so Mom let me keep it. Also Mom let me have a bunch of Gramma's jewelry -- it's real old and sparkly. Mom said, "You can give these to your wife someday when the time is right." Don't make me laugh.

March 9, 1961

I didn't talk to you for ten days or so, because nothing very interesting happened lately. In fact, just now as I opened up this book, Mom came in and I told her, "Things have sure been boring around here lately, haven't they?"

She said, "Thank God, Liam. After all that mess last month..."

Things at school are pretty much the same and nothing much has happened in the neighborhood either, except Stinky finally crashed his Flexy and bent the wheel and chipped a bunch of the paint off it, so I figure he'll let me borrow it soon. He also bled all over it and he hasn't washed the blood off yet. Mom has stopped getting sick and she says she's OK now. She eats lots of ice cream these days.

Last week Uncle Mick flew away to Ireland to get his money from the Irish Sweepstakes Place. He says they'll pay him in pounds instead of in money. That many pounds will weigh a lot, I bet. I looked at a map and Ireland is really far from here. Uncle Mick went on TWA and he had to fly first from Los Angeles to Chicago, then from Chicago to Maine, then from Maine over the ocean to Ireland. That's because the plane has to stop at the airplane gas stations. It takes more than a day and a half to get all the way to Ireland, but that's also because there's a time change.

I don't get why they do time changes, do you? I mean, if I'm going to meet Bobby at the Royale Theater at noon, what good is it if Bobby says, "Well, it may be noon where you are, but it's not noon where I am." How can that be? Shouldn't it be the same time everywhere? What kind of a moron thought that up?

March 10, 1961

When Dad got home from work today I followed him out to the back yard, and Colin was out there playing with a candle. He had a barbecue skewer with a big black bug stuck on it, and he was roasting the bug over the flame. Dad said, "Colin? What the hell are you up to?"

Colin said. "I'm cremating a bug."

Dad sighed. He said, "Don't you realize it's cruel to burn another living thing like that?"

"It's not cruel," Colin said. "This bug was already in heaven, so it can't feel anything now. It's OK -- Mom said so. It's like what they did to Gramma."

Dad frowned. "How can you be positive that bug was all the way dead before you started to cremate him?"

Colin said, "Because I made sure to stomp on him as hard as I could."

So Mom's birthday is coming up soon -- on March 21st. Tomorrow afternoon I'll have to ride my bike into town to look for something to get her. I have $1.55, but that might not be enough?

March 11, 1961

In order to get some more money I went to the Flying A Gas Station and when nobody was looking I took all the coke bottles from the side of the coke machine and rode over to the Hughes Market and got the 2 cent deposits, but that only made 44 more cents. So now I have $1.99 which doesn't buy a lot these days. What Mom likes best are roses, but the huge bouquet costs a fortune -- it's $3.00.

Then I rode over to the nurseries to see if I could swipe a flat, but they put all their flats inside because of the rain, so I rode home. I guess I might have to even mow some lawns or something to get some more money. Scotty says I could sit on the sidewalk and play my harmonica and people would give me coins, but I think you can go to jail for that, can't you?

March 12, 1961

I rode downtown again today to look for a present for Mom, but I forgot it's Sunday and most of the shops are closed. But then I saw Alex Eisenbaum walking down the street and he yelled, "Hey, Liam, look! The new cards are out!" So I stopped my bike and guess what? The new cards are out! Alex already had a big stack of them, the 1961 Topps Baseball Cards!

I said, "Where'd you get 'em?" and Alex said, "The Five And Dime," so I rode over to the Five And Dime as fast as I could.

Do you collect baseball cards? We do. Every year we wait around until April so we can get the new cards, but this year I guess they made them early. I ran into the store and they had a big display, but they only had the nickel packs. The nickel packs hold five cards and they're wrapped in wax paper with a piece of gum. We don't like the nickel packs very much because you can't see who's in there, and also the gum sometimes goes gooey and stains the cards.

But they also make a dime pack that holds ten cards, and it's wrapped in clear stuff so you can see who's on top and bottom, and it doesn't have gum. You might think us kids would like the gum, but it's this hard, flat bubble gum that tastes like balsa wood. And no matter how long you chew it, it won't make bubbles so we just throw it in the shitcan.

I went up to the counter and said, "Do you got any dime packs of the new cards?" and the lady said, "I think we have one box in back. I'll go look."

Oh boy! If it's in the back, that means the other kids haven't been able to go through it yet! This is the chance of a lifetime!

The lady came back with a box of the dime packs and I sat down in the corner and went through them all. There weren't any other kids around so I took my time, and can you believe what happened? I found one pack with a Don Drysdale on top, two packs with Gil Hodges on top, one pack with Sandy Koufax on the bottom and one pack with Mickey Mantle on the bottom! This is like a *gold mine! Think of the trades I could make! The other kids will be beating a path to my door!*

So I bought 19 packs of cards, then I went out into the parking lot and opened them all, and I still can't believe it! Besides all those other guys I just told you about, I also got another Mickey Mantle, a Roberto Clemente, a Willie Mays, two Dodger Team Cards, a Duke Snider, an Ernie Banks, an Al Kaline and a bunch of Dodgers like Charlie Neal and Jim Gilliam!

I also got two Yankees Team Cards, so I took them around the corner to the vacant lot where nobody could see, and then I tore them up into little pieces and spit on them and stepped on them and peed all over them. Then I ground them into the dirt until you could never even tell they'd been cardboard.

When I got home, I made Mom and Dad and Colin and Pinky and Stinky look at my new cards, and they were all really happy for me. This is like the greatest day of my life!

March 13, 1961

I took my new cards with me to school, and all the kids were jealous. They wanted to know where I got them, so I told them. It doesn't matter now if they know, because all that's left at the Five And Dime is the nickel packs. The only boy at school who doesn't care about baseball cards is Hermie Fleet, and he had a few problems of his own today.

We were making stuff out of wood, and Hermie had an accident -- he sawed his thumb. I think he was trying to make a covered wagon, but he ended up sawing his left thumb pretty bad, so he yelled and Mrs. Wintering took him to Nurse Norbitch's. A couple hours later he came back to school with a big Band Aid on his hand. He said he had to get four stitches.

I don't think I've ever gotten stitches before, but it sure seems like it'd hurt to have a sewing needle stuck through you, like you're a curtain or something.

March 14, 1961

This morning Mom didn't have time to make my lunch so she gave me 35 cents to eat at the cafeteria, but Fritzi was serving Diaper Dump Porridge and Sewer Soda, so I didn't eat anything. By the time dinner rolled around I was starved! Scotty ate over and we had ham and potatoes and peas. Then after dinner we all watched TV, and Elvis The Pelvis was on.

Dad doesn't like Elvis much but Colin and me and Scotty do, and Mom thinks he's cute. Scotty says Elvis would come in handy around the house because you could strap milk and ice cream to his hips, and then he could make you a milkshake whenever he sings.

March 15, 1961

Colin got grounded today because he pulled all the spikes out of Dad's golf shoes. He said he couldn't figure out why they had nails in them and he thought they should look like all of Dad's other shoes, so he got some pliers and yanked all the spikes out. Dad said those shoes cost him $24.50 and now they're useless, but Colin said, "You could still wear them to church..." Now Colin's grounded for a week.

March 16, 1961

We got a postcard from Uncle Mick. It had a cartoon on it of a guy drinking a black beer, and it had a stamp with a lady playing the harp. Mom read it to us:

3-5-61, Dublin. Arrived safely and all is well. I feel like I'm home! Raining but green - beautiful old city. Tomorrow I go to collect my funds, then to see Trinity College and St. Patrick's Cathedral. Tell Colin I saw a leprechaun. Love, Mick.

"Why'd he have to see a leprechaun?" Colin asked. "Ew, that's totally gross!"

Mom said, "Why, honey? Do you even know what a leprechaun is?"

"Sure," said Colin, "it's one of those guys with that horrible disease that makes your fingers fall off."

So tomorrow is St. Patrick's Day and Dad says Uncle Mick will drink so much whiskey in Ireland, they'll have to carry him home on a donkey cart.

March 17, 1961

Today Mom made me wear green socks to school, because she said all the other kids can pinch you if you don't wear green on St. Patrick's Day. I didn't know that. So I looked all around the class to see if there was anybody I could pinch, but the only kids who didn't wear green were Toren and Robin Ward and Hermie, and who'd want to pinch them?

Later an Audio-Visual kid came in and showed us a movie all about Civil Defense, called 'Fallout And You.' I guess it's supposed to help us be more prepared if Khrushchev decides to drop the H-bomb. Even if he did drop the H-bomb I don't think it would hit us here at the beach, but there's some people in town who are real scared and they've dug H-bomb shelters in their back yards.

Toren's family has one, even though according to Toren her dad is some famous five-star general in the Army and isn't afraid of anybody, which I think is BS. Also there's this kid around the corner named Eliot Somebody, and his parents have a H-bomb shelter. Eliot took me down in there once, and it's just an underground room with cots and a stove and lights -- it didn't look to me like it would save anybody from a H-bomb. Eliot's little brother said, "If the world could just stop war, then the world would be the best place in the world."

When I got home Dad had a glass of Jameson Whiskey in his hand and an LP by John McCormack on the record player, and Mom was making corned beef and cabbage. They said this is an important day to be Irish, but it looks to me like everybody thinks they're Irish on St. Patrick's Day, even the Mexican people and the Japanese and the Polish and the colored people. Maybe it's sort of like Christmas, where everybody gets a tree and gives presents, even if they're like Dad and don't go to Mass very often?

March 18, 1961

Last night I was laying in bed and a big Uh Oh Thought came into my head. You know how that feels, don't you? Like you're just laying there minding your own business, when suddenly you think 'Uh Oh!' and you remember something important? Well, that's what happened. Suddenly I remembered Mom's birthday is in three days, and I don't have a present for her yet, plus now I don't have any money because I spent it on the baseball cards.

So this morning Dad was out in the back yard practicing his golf swing and I went out there. I said, "Dad? Do you got any chores or anything around here that I could do? Maybe to make some money?"

He said, "No, I don't think so... do you need money?"

"$2.65," I said. "I have to get Mom a birthday present, but I don't have any money except the 35 cents you gave me last night for allowance."

Dad took a few more golf swings. Then he said, "Maybe you should have thought about that before you bought yourself all those baseball cards?"

So now I need to figure out how to get some money. I went inside and asked Colin if I could borrow some and he said, "Sure. For every dollar you borrow, you pay me back two dollars." What a shitburger. After lunch I rode over to Scotty's place to try to borrow some from him, but he didn't have any. Then I tried Alex, but he spent all his on cards too. Then I rode to the Rexall to see if Aunt Gwen would loan me some, but some other lady told me she doesn't work on weekends. At the nursery, all the flats were inside. So I gave up and went home. I think I'll go to sleep early tonight.

March 19, 1961

It's Sunday so I got to sleep in, and when I woked up, Mom was just getting back from the market. She did another Big Shopping, but this time she went real early so I didn't have to go. I helped her put away the groceries and she gave me a Milky Way. Mom was in a really good mood, and I almost came right out and told her that I couldn't get her a birthday present because I spent the money on cards, but then she pulled a big long roll of Green Stamps out of her purse and said, "Liam? Can you put these in the box in the cupboard for me?"

You know how in the cartoons when somebody gets an idea, a light bulb goes on right over their heads? That's the way I felt! Green Stamps! So after Mom went in her room to lay down, I looked in the box and there were eleven books of stamps plus a ton of loose ones, so I put one book down my pants and took off on my bike to the S&H Green Stamp Redemption Center.

A white haired old lady was there and I asked her what one book would buy, and she showed me. It was mostly little stuff for around the house, like a scissors. I asked her if she had roses and she said no. I told her I was trying to get roses for my Mom's birthday, and she said, "Well, why don't you just redeem the book for cash? Then you can buy the roses."

I said, "Cash?"

"Yes, cash," she said. "You can redeem a full book of stamps for $3.00 cash, if you wish."

So I said, "Yes, please!" and I got $3.00. Then I went to go get the roses, but the lady at the flower store said it would be better to buy them tomorrow so they'd be fresher, so that's what I'll do.

March 20, 1961

Mrs. Wintering just showed us a home movie of her and her husband, from when they went on a trip "over yonder to Hawaii." Her husband is a bald headed fireman and he's just as skinny as she is, and in the movie they were both wearing grass skirts and doing the Hulahula dance with flowers around their necks, and they were drinking big glasses of pink stuff with fruits and vegetables sticking out. Some of the Hulahula girls were pretty!

Toren Shumaker said, "Big deal! My mom can dance the Flamingo!" but then Robin Ward made a face at her and Toren shut up. Toren's been a lot easier to get along with lately -- I think she's afraid Robin will pound her. I bet Robin Ward could pound any of the girls and most of the boys too if she wanted to, but so far she hasn't.

After school I went and bought the huge bouquet of roses, and rode home with it and hid it in a bucket of water in the garage. Mom will be happy. Stinky saw me ride up with the flowers and said, "What's up, Loverboy, you getting married?" Stinky is so funny I forgot to laugh. But then he let me ride his Flexy for an hour and man, was it fun! If you take it down the Northfield Hill you can go a jillion miles an hour. It's pretty hard to stop it, though, once it gets going.

March 21, 1961

When Mom woked up we all sang Happy Birthday to her, and Dad made her breakfast in bed, and then we all gave her the presents. She liked her roses a lot. I thought Dad was going to ask me where I got the money, but he just looked at me and winked.

Colin gave her some bubble bath, and Dad gave her earrings and a new robe and some chocolates, and a gift certificate to Moms To Go, which is some kind of place for ladies who are having babies.

Mom has been getting a little bit fatter lately because of the baby, and she keeps asking us, "Does this dress make me look fat? What about this one? What about my butt -- does this make my butt look fat?" Dad told us to just say "of course not," even when it does.

Lately Mom and Dad have been trying out names for the baby, but they can't decide for sure until they know whether it's a boy baby or a girl baby. Mom wants to name a girl baby after Gramma, whose name was Brigid even though everybody called her Bridey. Dad says that's OK with him. He wants to name a boy baby Eamonn, but Mom likes Noel better. But Dad says he won't name a son after a Christmas song.

March 22, 1961

Postcard from Uncle Mick:

3-12-61, Galway. I love it here! Collected my cash from the Sweeps office, and the redhead who gave me my check had a celebratory pint with me afterwards. Took a side trip to the County of the Oulde Ones, what a beautiful spot. Slante, Mick.

I asked Dad what "slante" meant, and he said, "Goddamned if I know."

March 23, 1961

Betty Bachelis puked at school today, and I missed it. For three years I've been hoping for this, because maybe then she'd forgive me for barfing on her in the second grade. So she finally barfed but I missed it because I was playing dodgeball with the boys, and she barfed while she was playing hopscotch with the girls.

Isn't it kind of weird how there are "boy games" and "girl games?" Like sockball and dodgeball and four-square are boy games, but hopscotch and jacks and cat's cradle are girl games. What difference does it make, anyway? Girls are OK to play with. At everything except baseball, of course.

Anyhow, Betty barfed right after lunch and I think it was because she ate the cafeteria lunch today. Usually she brings her own, but today she ate the cafeteria lunch and Fritzi was serving Mystery Meat with Mucus Gravy. Anybody'd barf if they ate that. Luckily for me, Mom makes me a sack lunch every day.

Uncle Mick got home today from his trip. We haven't seen him yet because he was too tired to come over, but he called and said he brought me and Colin a present, so I hope we'll see him soon. Colin got ungrounded today.

Oh, I almost forgot: this afternoon I reached into the pocket of my jacket and found $2.65 in there! At first I couldn't figure out where it came from, but then I remembered the way Dad winked at me when I gave Mom her birthday roses.

March 24, 1961

After school Mom asked me to keep an eye on Colin while she went down to the store. So we were out in the back yard playing Gorgeous George (that's a wrestlerman,) and I was tickling Colin and he started laughing so hard he accidentally peed his pants. Not a great big pee, but there was a big yellow spot on his underwears. Eeww! He started crying because he thought Mom would yell at him, so I told him to just shut up and go change into some clean underwears.

For all I knew, though, Mom might be doing a laundry when she got back, and Colin didn't want to put his peed-on undies in the hamper because he was afraid she'd see it and he'd get in trouble. I figured we could dry out the underwears if we turned on the stove and dangled them over the burner, but I got too close to the flame and they caught on fire, and Colin started screaming and a bunch of pee-smoke filled up the kitchen.

So I threw the flaming underwears in the sink and put the fire out, then we picked up the ashes off the floor and sprayed the room with Right Guard. Then we rolled up the burnt underwears in some newspapers, and buried the wad deep in the trash can. Then we opened all the windows and doors and let the burnt-pee-smell out, and by the time Mom got back everything was OK, and that's that. As long as she doesn't know how many underwears he has.

March 25, 1961

Uncle Mick came over for dinner and had a bunch of stories to tell us about Ireland. He says it's real green and the people were friendly there, and there's lots of music and pretty girls with red hair, but it rains too much. He brought Mom some junky old tablecloth that looked like it came out of a garbage can, but Mom went all goo-goo and said it was the most beautiful antique Irish linen she'd ever seen. I wonder if all pregnant ladies get crazy like that? Then he gave Dad a bottle of whiskey and gave me and Colin each a sweater. We were hoping for something better, but that's life.

After dinner I asked Uncle Mick if he was going outside as usual to smoke his Tiparillo, but he said he decided to give up smoking since he couldn't find any Tiparillos in Ireland anyway. He said, "Now I feel better and I have more wind and I smell better, and it's a whole lot safer to drink out of old beer cans lying around the apartment."

So now Uncle Mick is all crazy about travel and he says he wants to go to Tahiti and Bora Bora and Fugi, but first he wants to take us all down to Tijuana Mexico for a day. He says it only takes about three hours to drive there, and that it's a really fun place. He told Dad, "If you'd be willing to drive, I'll use the sweepstakes winnings to pay for everything for all of us. Gas, food, gambling, drinks, souvenirs for the boyos, everything!"

Mom shrugged and said, "Sounds like fun, but I'd be too out-numbered. Unless Sis came too...." and Uncle Mick said, "Gwen? Well, I guess she could come." So now it looks like we all get to go to Mexico, two weeks from today. Colin wants to break the World Record for Taco Eating, but we're not sure how many the record is.

March 26, 1961

Me and Scotty rode our bikes to the park today, and we played tether ball and climbed on the monkey bars. All the kids who play basketball were locked out of the gym today, because somebody flushed a baseball mitt down the toilet and it overflowed and the gym floor got all flooded with shitwater. The park director was really mad because the gym floor is made out of wood and it's not supposed to get wet.

Some kids at the park were playing poker for pennies and they asked if we wanted to play. Scotty didn't have any money but I played for awhile and won a nickel so I bought some Red Hots.

March 27, 1961

In class today Mary-Ann passed me a note that said, "Quick! Look at Rikki," so I looked at Rikki Drinkwater and she had a ball-point pen stuck up her nose. I guess she figured out a better way to pick her nose? She was just kind of fishing around in there with her pen. Then she'd pull it out and look at it, and if there was a booger in it, she'd just flick the pen and the booger would get pushed out. A couple of times the booger got stuck in the pen though, and she had to flick it and flick it a bunch of times to push the booger out.

Mary-Ann was laughing so hard she turned all red in the face and I was afraid she'd have to go to Nurse Norbitch's. Mrs. Wintering said, "I reckon the rest of the class would like to know what's so funny, Mary-Ann?" but Mary-Ann couldn't even answer because she was laughing too hard, so Mrs. Wintering told her to go outside and said, "Don't come back until you get over your case of the giggles."

This is the last week of school before we get a whole week off for Easter Vacation. Mrs. Wintering says if we're a really well behaved class for the rest of the week, she won't give us any homework during Easter break -- but if we're bad, she'll give us so much homework we won't have any time to play. So we're all trying to be good.

March 28, 1961

We were having a dirt clod war after school and I threw a dirt clod at Pinky and it hit her in the face and cut her cheek. I didn't mean to do it, but it just happened. Mr. Vanderhoeven came over and talked to Mom and now I can't play with those guys for a week, and my allowance got suspended for two weeks. I'm broke!

March 29, 1961

At recess we were playing dodgeball and that Nigel guy from England starting kicking the ball real fancy-like with his feet. He says over there in England everybody plays a game they call football but we call it soccer, and you have to learn all kinds of fancy kicking. He tried to teach it to us, but I guess it takes awhile because we were lousy at it. Nigel said, "It's a skoosh, spud!" (That means "It's easy, pal," but we didn't think so.)

Nigel knows how to play golf too. He asked if there was any golfing courses around, but the only one is real far away and you have to be a member. Nigel says a good way to make money is to sneak onto a golfing course and look in the woods and in the lakes for golf balls that guys lost. Then you can hang out in the parking lot, and sell the golf balls to other guys. Nigel said, "You can get half a bob each for them." I wonder how much that is in money?

After school I went and visited Nathan at the Shine Parlor, and he told me Mr. Harrington's wife found out about his other wife and family, and now she wants a divorce and all his money.

Did I ever tell you about Mr. Harrington? He's the President of Harbor Federal Savings and he lives in the rich part of town with his family. They have two kids. But Nathan says he also had another secret wife and family over in Culver City, and that neither family knew about each other until last week when Mr. Harrington sort of got his kids mixed up somehow, and one of his wives got suspicious and had him followed by a private detective. I wonder if it was a private detective like Edd "Kookie" Byrnes on 77 Sunset Strip? Anyways, nobody on 77 Sunset Strip would be able to say what Nathan said, because if they said it on TV they'd get fired. Nathan said, "It just goes to show you, even them rich white Republican motherfuckers has got to reap just what they sow."

March 30, 1961

Bobby Del Valle brought this little tape recorder to school today -- he got it from Blue Chip Stamps. (Blue Chip Stamps are sort of like Green Stamps, except they're blue instead of green – duh.) Anyways, it's like a spy tape recorder and you can just put it anywheres and turn it on, and everything gets recorded! Isn't that cool? I bet we could make a rock and roll record and make a jillion dollars, but Bobby doesn't think so.

He took it outside during recess and hid it in a bush near the hopscotch and we tape recorded all the girls playing. After school we listened to it and it was funny! Robin Ward was trying to boss everybody, but then Mary-Ann said, "Why don't you go sit on a ice cube?"

I figured Robin would pound her, but she didn't. Then Mary-Ann said real calmly, "You don't need to be that pushy, Robin. You're the best athlete in school, the girls will already listen to you without you yelling." And Robin didn't pound her or anything, she just got quiet. Uncle Mick once told me if he lived to be a hundred, he'd never understand women.

March 31, 1961

It's the last day of school for a week, because this Sunday it's Easter. Mrs. Wintering came to class today wearing a big wide hat that she called an Easter Bonnet -- I never saw a hat that big before, but Mrs. Wintering says they're the latest rage down in Mississippi.

So Mom thinks we should go to Sunrise Services at Our Lady of Sorrows on Sunday, but Dad says it's important to hang around the house and wait for the Easter Bunny to arrive, but that's just an excuse because Dad doesn't like Mass. Even Colin knows the Easter Bunny is a fake.

One cool thing about Easter is that the Mayfair Market is going to have a huge Easter Egg Hunt on Sunday, and it's free for all us kids. They're going to close down the market at noon and hide candy eggs all over the market, and then at one o'clock all the kids get to run around and look for the candy, and we get to keep whatever we find. I bet that'll be fun, unless some big kids beat up everybody.

April 1, 1961

Scotty and me decided we needed to make money, so we got a shirt cardboard and we cut it into little squares, then we got a pen and we made some business cards. They said, "McAfee and McDonald, Hedge Trimmers Supreme." (He wanted to put his name first, but I told him it was alphabetical.) Then we got two of those clipper thingies out of his garage, and went off riding our bikes around the neighborhood and knocking on doors.

Every time we saw a house with a hedge, we knocked on the door and said, "Good afternoon, Ma'am, we were just passing through the neighborhood and we noticed that your hedge is badly in need of trimming. Haven't your neighbors mentioned that it looks unruly?" (I like that word "unruly." That was Scotty's idea.)

After about twenty houses we finally got some lady who asked, "How much do you charge?" and Scotty said, "We'll do the whole hedge for $2.50." The lady said "OK," so we went to work.

It was one of those hedges that runs down the side of a house, kind of like a fence between two houses. Since half the hedge was in the neighbor's yard we didn't have to do that side, so we just did the one side. It took us two hours and it was hard work, but it came out OK except in a couple spots where it was uneven. The lady didn't mind that too much, but then she came out and said, "What about the top?"

We looked at the top and said, "We can't reach up there," and she said, "You can use my stepladder, boys." So we had to spend another hour trimming the top, and then we said, "All done, Ma'am," but the lady said, "What about the cleanup? You don't expect to leave all this mess laying around on the ground, do you?" So we had a spend another hour raking up the leaves and stuff and putting it all in the trash.

Then we said, "All done, Ma'am," but the lady said, "What about the other side? Did you boys think you could just trim half a hedge?"

Scotty and me looked at each other, and I said, "But lady, the other side isn't even your hedge, is it? That side is your neighbor's hedge, isn't it?" and the lady laughed and said, "April Fools! I was just kidding, boys. You did a good job -- here you are," and she gave us $3.00 and two Cokes. We're in business!

April 2, 1961

Happy Easter! Even though we didn't have to get up for Sunrise Services, Mom still made Colin and me go to regular Mass this morning. It was pretty crowded in church and Father O'Dowd told the story of Easter, but he had a sore throat so he had to cut it short. Aunt Gwen called it the "Reader's Digest Condensed Version of The Resurrection."

After church we came home and changed clothes and then Mom took us down to the Mayfair for the kid's Easter Egg Hunt. We got there about 12:30 and the parking lot was already filled up with kids. Some kids were there with their moms, and some were there on bikes and hanging out together. I saw a bunch of kids from my school: Bobby was there and Scotty and Norman and Toren and Hermie Fleet. Also there were lots of kids from other schools there, kids from about five years old up to about twelve. They wouldn't let any teenagers in to the kid's Easter Egg Hunt.

At about ten minutes to one, a guy with a green apron and a bow tie came out of the market and yelled, "Hey kids, gather around and I'll explain how the Easter Egg Hunt works," so we did.

He said, "The Easter Egg Hunt will last for exactly 15 minutes. Candy eggs have been hidden all over the store, some in clearly visible places and others in not so visible places. Before we start, we'll give out an empty bag to every child. Please allow the younger children to have the candy that's easier to find. Once your bag is full, simply come back up to the front of the store and you will be allowed to keep what you've found. We hope you all have lots of fun, and Happy Easter!"

Then they divided us into groups of about ten kids each, at the head of each aisle. I guess they figured if they did that, it would kind of split things up so there wouldn't be too many of us trying to get the same candy eggs? At one o'clock, another guy blew a whistle and we all took off running and looking for the candy Easter eggs.

Some of them were pretty easy to find, just little piles of Easter eggs sitting on the floor. The guy with the green apron and the bow tie kept saying, "Let the little folks have a chance! Please have regard for the younger kids!" but nobody paid attention -- everybody just grabbed up all the candy eggs they could. I found a big pile right away which filled up my little bag, so after that I just watched the other kids. Some kids starting looking on the shelves and there were some eggs hidden there, like behind the Ajax and the Clorox and stuff. Once the kids figured that out, they started pulling boxes and cans off the shelves, and a few kids just started knocking stuff onto the floor in order to look behind it.

Hermie Fleet found a bunch of eggs in the freezer department and when the other kids saw that, they all ran to the freezer and started pulling out TV dinners and boxes of macaroni and tossing them on the floor to look for the candy. Then somebody yelled, "Hey, does chocolate milk count?" and before you knew it, kids were pulling milk and butter and cheese out of the refrigerators and throwing it all on the floor.

Bobby Del Valle slipped in some milk and fell down. He got mad at some other kid and said, "You put that there on purpose just to trip me," and the other kid said, "No I didn't," and they yelled about it for awhile, and then Bobby threw a orange at the other kid.

The other kid said, "Hey, knock it off!" and Bobby said, "Make me!" and then they started throwing orange and lemons and grapefruits at each other. Some of the grapefruits got thrown pretty hard and knocked down some big stacks of Rice-A-Roni and Kraft Parmesan Cheese.

Meanwhile Norman Giambalvo found some Reddi-Wip and started spraying some kids with it, and Colin helped himself to some Hawaiian Punch, and Toren decided the regular candy bars were better than the candy eggs, so she just started eating the

Snickers bars. Then a big kid found some eggs and asked if they were candy eggs and he ate one, but it was a real raw egg. He said, "Eeww!" and threw it on the floor, which made some other kids want to throw eggs, and pretty soon lots of kids were throwing eggs at each other and sliding around in egg-goo.

The guy with the green apron and the bow tie was going nuts, running around and yelling and also some of the parents were screaming at their kids to stop it, and then somebody came on over the speakers and yelled, "THAT'S ENOUGH, KIDS! The Easter Egg Hunt is over!" Most of the kids yelled, "Boo! Boo!" and a lot of kids just kept on eating stuff and pulling junk off the shelves and throwing it at each other and laughing. It was a real mess.

After awhile they herded us all up and we had to leave the Mayfair. Mom said we all "behaved like monkeys in the zoo," but she didn't really scream at me or Colin too bad -- she didn't see him drink the Hawaiian Punch. She also said it was a stupid idea in the first place, and if the Mayfair was smart they would've had the Easter Egg Hunt outdoors in the parking lot. She's probably right. But it wouldn't have been near as much fun that way.

April 3, 1961

Mom had to go into Santa Monica today so I went with her. I guess there's some kind of shirts Dad needs, and the only place that has them is a store called Campbell's. We parked the car in a parking lot and I got to see Roberta the blind lady.

Did I ever tell you about the blind lady? Across the street from Campbell's in the parking lot there a little wooden shack that sells candy and popcorn and cigarettes and newspapers, and it's run by this blind lady named Roberta.

People come up and ask for a newspaper or a Milky Way, and she knows exactly where each newspaper is, and each kind of candy. She recognizes people's voices and seems to know everybody. When people pay her, she knows what each coin feels like and she makes change. I can't figure out how she knows the difference between a one-dollar-bill and a five-dollar-bill, but she does. And even though I've only met her three times, I went up and said, "Hi, Roberta," and she said, "Hello, Liam. How is your family?" I think Roberta the blind lady is amazing and should be in Ripley's Believe It Or Not.

April 4, 1961

I went downtown with Alex Eisenbaum today and we bought some rolls of caps at the Hobby Shop. Then we were standing in front of the Royale Theater and popping caps with our feet. You know how to do that, don't you? You just tear off about ten inches of caps from the roll, then put them on the ground, and then slide your foot over them real fast, and they go off: pop, pop, pop, pop, pop!

Mr. Zupo heard the caps going off and he called the police on the phone and complained. A cop car pulled up and Mr. Zupo ran outside and yelled, "I vant zese boys arrested! Zey're playing vis dangerous explosives!"

One of the cops looked at him like he was crazy and said, "'Dangerous explosives, huh?' You mean a goddamn *roll of caps?* Look here, Zupo..."

But Mr. Zupo interrupted him and said, "I demand you arrest zese boys!"

So the cop winked at us and whispered, "Just get in the cars, guys, and don't worry..." So we did, and the cop drove us about two blocks and let us go. He said, "Listen, fellas, I know it's tempting to bait that fool, but why don't you just stay away from the Royale for a week or two?"

We said, "OK. Thanks, Mister Policeman!"

Uncle Mick would say, "That Zupo guy ain't exactly got both his chop sticks in the chow mein."

April 5, 1961

Scotty and I played Chicken If You Don't this afternoon, and I lost. That meant I had to do whatever Scotty wanted me to, so he told me to get a big dogdoo and put it in a paper bag, then set it on fire and leave it on Mrs. Kroot's porch and ring the doorbell and run away. The idea is that Mrs. Kroot would answer the door, see the burning bag and step on it to put out the fire. Then she'd get dogshit all over her shoes.

So we found a big old black dogdoo and Scotty used a stick to shove it in a bag. Then we stuck it on her porch and I used some matches to set the bag on fire, then I rang her bell and ran across the street. We hid behind Stinky's hedge so we could see Mrs. Kroot's porch without her seeing us.

But nobody answered -- there was nobody home. The bag burned for a minute or two, then it went out. I thought we should go get it, but Scotty said, "You want to risk getting caught just to get a burnt bag of dogdoo off Mrs. Kroot's porch?"

I said, "Scotty, she'll know who left it there because we stuck dogdoo in her mailbox last Halloween." So I went over there with a wad of newspaper and picked up the burnt dogdoobag and threw it in the garbage. At least Scotty can't say I'm a chicken.

April 6, 1961

Uncle Mick stopped by our house today and he asked Mom how she was feeling. Mom said, "Ever since I've been pregnant, I haven't been able to go to bed at night without celery. That can't be normal, can it?"

Uncle Mick said, "Depends on what you're doing with it." Mom threw the celery at him.

April 7, 1961

Today was pretty boring. None of my friends were around, so I just practiced my harmonica and watched Bozo The Clown on TV and listened to Mom and Dad argue about tomorrow. We all get to go to Tijuana tomorrow -- I bet it will be fun. Dad wants to take us to the horse races while we're there, and also he says the grownups should drink tequila and eat tacos, but Mom says that'd be crazy for a lady who's five months pregnant. Anyhow me and Colin are looking forward to going -- we've never been to a foreign country before.

April 8, 1961

Mom came in and woked us up at six o'clock so that we could get an early start on our day in Mexico. An hour later Uncle Mick and Aunt Gwen came over, and we all piled into Dad's Buick and took off driving. It was a little bit crowded in the car: Mom and Dad and Uncle Mick sat in front, and me and Colin and Aunt Gwen sat in back. Aunt Gwen brought some comic books so that me and Colin would have something to read while we drove there. I guess it took about four hours until we got to the border. Some Mexican guys in uniforms waved us through and then we were in Mexico! Yay!

"The first place we have to go is the Long Bar," Uncle Mick said. "Even the boys will like that." So we drove a few blocks and then parked the car.

As we were getting out of the car, these two kids who were about my age came over and said, "Hey Mister? For a quarter we watch your car -- make sure nothing bad happens to it."

Mom reached into her purse, but Uncle Mick tried to stop her. "Don't give these little hoodlums anything," he said.

But Dad said, "That's easy for you to say, Mick. It ain't *your* car." Mom gave the kids the quarter, and we went into the Long Bar.

Boy, was it a long bar! It went almost a whole block! Me and Colin had a lemonade, and the grownups had tequila with salt and limes, all except Mom who said it wouldn't be good for the baby. Outside there was a guy with a cart screaming, "Tacos, tacos," and Colin yelled, "I'm hungry!" so Mom went outside with us and looked at the guy's taco cart. I think she was trying to make sure his tacos weren't made out of gopher dicks or something. I guess they passed Mom's inspection, because she got us each two tacos and they were the best tacos I ever ate in my life! I could've eaten ten of them, but Mom said, "We're going to be down here all day, boys, save some room for other stuff."

Back at the Long Bar there was a bunch of fat guys playing music. They had horns and guitars and one real big guitar, and they sang pretty songs in Mexican. Uncle Mick and Aunt Gwen sat in a corner and drank Tequila and talked. I overheard a little of it, and Uncle Mick is sad because his girlfriend Patrice left him for some rich Hollywood guy with a long car. Aunt Gwen told him to buck up, he'd find another love. Gee, she should talk!

After awhile Uncle Mick said, "Well, folks, what do you want to do now? Should we go to the horse races or the bullfights? Or maybe you just want to go shopping? Or some of us might want to go see a hoochie coochie show... what do you think?"

Mom said, "I want to get some of those pretty baskets, and I think Gwen wants to pick up a couple dresses. The bullfights are too bloody for the boys, and I'm afraid you're on your own for a hoochie coochie show -- my husband won't be going with you if he knows what's good for him."

Dad turned to the bartender and said, "Another round," and they all had another Tequila. Meanwhile Colin found a slot machine in the corner and put a slug in it and he won a jackpot, but it was Mexican money so he couldn't figure out how much he won. The bartender said it was about two dollars worth, so Colin stuck it in his pocket -- he was real happy.

Next door to the Long Bar there was a big store where they sold pottery and guitars, and baskets and clothes, so Mom and Aunt Gwen and Colin and me went over there. Dad and Uncle Mick stayed at the Long Bar for awhile, but after about half an hour Dad came and joined us. He said Uncle Mick went out exploring and we'd meet him in an hour at the Casino down the street.

It's fun they way they sell stuff in Mexico: the man at the store would say, "That dress is only five dollars," and Aunt Gwen would say, "Oh, that's far too much. I'll pay two dollars." Then everybody argues about it for 15 minutes, and finally the dress costs $3.50. I wish it was like that at the Mayfair Market.

Outside the store there was a guy with a cart pulled by a zebra! He tried to get Mom and Dad to sit on the cart and get their pictures taken, but Dad said, "No, thanks." I looked real close at the zebra and guess what? It was just a old broken-down donkey with stripes painted on him. What a fake! Next to the zebra man there was a different taco stand, so Mom got us another taco. That taco was really good too, but it wasn't crunchy like the first guy's.

Across the street I saw Uncle Mick drinking a bottle of Tequila and going into some place called Furryland. I figured maybe Furryland was like Frontierland or Fantasyland on Walt Disney's Wonderful World of Color, so I walked across the street and peeked inside, and you'll never guess what I saw in there! Are you ready? There was a woman dancing around and she was completely bare-naked! I only got to see it for about ten seconds because this fat guy started yelling in Mexican and shoved me outside, but the woman was real old -- like around 40 -- and she had hair between her legs! Isn't that amazing? I'd heard about that before, but I'd never actually seen it.

Anyhow we all had a great day and the grownups played some games at the Casino and they all lost money, but not very much. Mom got some pottery and baskets and Aunt Gwen got some dresses. Uncle Mick was real nice and paid for everything, but then he drank a whole bottle of Tequila and started crying about the little poor Mexican orphan kids, and finally he fell asleep in the back seat.

Colin and me ate five tacos each and we got to buy some firecrackers. Dad smuggled two bottles of Kahlua over the border

-- all I could think about was when Brian Evans's family smuggled their dead gramma across the border in their trunk. Eeww!

By the time we got home it was almost ten o'clock and every-body was tired. Anyhow, I liked Mexico. And I wonder if Deedee Weever has hair between her legs?

April 9, 1961

Mom and Dad were all pooped out from our trip yesterday, so they just took naps all day while me and Colin watched cartoons. For dinner we had two pizzas delivered, one with pepperoni for me and Colin, and one with pineapple for Mom and Dad. *Pineapple!* Disgustomatic!

April 10, 1961

School started up again today, and Toren showed up with all her hair cut off. She used to have real long curly blond hair, but now it's cut really short. She wouldn't tell why she did it, but at recess Hermie Fleet told me that Toren saw some fashion model on TV who ironed her hair to make it straight, so she tried it too. But I guess you're supposed to put a towel in between your hair and the iron, and Toren didn't know that, so she ended up burning off half her hair. So she had to cut the rest of it off. Isn't that funny?

April 11, 1961

Today was opening day for the Dodgers, and Mrs. Wintering let Bobby Del Valle bring his transistor radio to class so we could listen. All winter long we wait to hear Vin Scully's voice. That other guy Jerry Doggett is OK too, but we like Vinny better.

I think it's funny how grownups always tell kids not to smoke or drink because it's supposed to be so unhealthy, but then on the radio they say, "The Dodger games are brought to you by Blatz Beer and Roi Tan Cigars." Anyhow the Dodgers won. I'm going to ask Dad if he'll take me and Colin to a game soon.

April 12, 1961

It's been freezing around here lately, which is pretty rare. Dad calls it a "cold snap." This morning Mom sent me off to school in a big coat and some gloves she called "mittens," which made me feel silly, so I took them off as soon as I got around the corner. She tried to get Colin to bundle up too, but he said, "I'm not gonna wear those ear muffins."

Anyhow it was cold. At recess I felt a rumbling in my stomach, so I looked around to make sure nobody could hear, then I cut a fart and do you know what happened? *Steam* came out my butt! I didn't know butts could do that, did you?

So today this Russian Communist guy named Yuri Gagarin became the first guy to make an orbit around the earth in a spaceship. Pretty cool, huh?

April 13, 1961

At school Mrs. Wintering made each of us stand up and tell what we wanted to be when we grew up, and who we wanted to get married to, and why. I thought about telling the truth and saying I want to marry Deedee Weever, but I figured somebody would tell her, and that'd make me feel like a dork. So I said, "I want to play baseball for the Dodgers and marry Sophia Loren. She's beautiful and she probably makes good spaghetti." (This is pretty much true. Also she has big tits, but I didn't say that in class.)

Toren said, "I want to be first lady and marry President Kennedy because he's the most powerful man in the world, and then I could get him to drop bombs on people I don't like." Bobby Del Valle said, "I want to be a cop and marry Marilyn Monroe, because she's rich and I bet she's a good kisser." Mary-Ann said, "I'm going to write books and marry John Steinbeck. Even though he's an old man, I like his books and he has a cute beard and he's nice to dogs." Robin Ward said, "I'm never going to have a job and I'm never getting married. I'm going to move to Tahiti and live with a pelican in a grass shack!" Robin is a strange girl.

April 14, 1961

Mrs. Wintering got mad at Bobby Del Valle today because of something he said to Toren Shumaker. We were all on the playground and Bobby said, "Hey, Toren, look down in your shirt and spell 'attic.'" So Toren looked down into her shirt and said, "A - T - T - I - C," and all the other kids started laughing except for Norman Giambalvo who kept saying, "I don't get it, I don't get it."

Toren didn't even have to fink on Bobby, because Mrs. Wintering overheard the whole thing and she didn't think it was funny. She said, "You boys are fixin' to drive me nuts! Bobby? You know better than that -- you're on the bench the rest of recess. Tell Toren you're sorry, then don't say another word -- now *sit!*"

April 15, 1961

At dinner tonight Colin said, "Pass the salt, will you?" But he didn't say "please," so Mom said, "What's the magic word?" Colin thought for a second and said, "Abracadabra?"

A few minutes later, Dad asked him what he learned in school last week, so Colin wiped his mouth and stood up and said:

Mary, Mary, quite contrary,
How does your garden grow?

With silver bells and cockle shells,
And one goddamned petunia.

I thought Mom was going to choke. Dad ordered Colin into our room without any more dinner and no TV tonight, but I don't think Colin minded too much about the dinner because he was done eating anyway, and besides he doesn't much like tonight's dessert which was Lime Jello with Reddi-Wip.

April 16, 1961

It's Sunday and I played baseball all day with Scotty and Stinky and Alex and some other kids. When I got home Dad said, "You really like baseball, don't you Liam?"

I said, "Heck, yeah!" and he said, "Well looky here," and he pulled two tickets out of his shirt pocket. "They're for tomorrow night's game," he said, "the Cardinals are in town. Bob Gibson's pitching. Just me and you, boyo. You want to go?"

YAY!!!!

April 17, 1961

I just got home from the baseball game and man, was it cool! The Dodgers lost 9 to 5, but I still thought it was the greatest. They play the games in this big place called 'The Coliseum,' and there was a jillion people there. Duke Snider knocked a homer and that made Bob Gibson mad, so later in the game Gibson hit Snider with a pitch and broke his elbow, and everybody booed.

We sat next to some nice people from The Valley. They laughed when I asked Dad if I could have some money for the "Concussion Stand," so I guess I said it wrong? Anyhow I got to eat two hot-dogs and some peanuts and help Dad drink a Blatz Beer. Jim Gilliam hit a foul ball right near us but I didn't have my mitt, and besides these two big guys got in a fight over it, so I'm glad I wasn't too close or I would have gotten squarshed.

April 24, 1961

Last Tuesday I started to feel a little bit funny, and I had the poops real bad. Mom took my temperature and it was 102, so I got to stay home from school Wednesday, Thursday and Friday. I guess it was some sort of a bug? Usually if I get sick it's kind of fun because I can just lay around in my pajamas and watch TV, but this time I kept getting dizzy every time I stood up. I don't know what I had, but I'm glad I didn't barf.

April 25, 1961

I went back to school today, and it wasn't so bad. After recess Mrs. Wintering showed us five short movies. The first one was called 'Paper and I,' and it was about a talking bag. The talking bag wants to teach Billy the history of paper making, so it tells him about papyrus and printing presses and stuff, until at the end Billy finally takes the bag to school and eats his lunch.

Then we saw 'The School Bus And You,' which was a safety film. It told us to get in the bus, get off the bus, and try not to get runned over.

After that there was 'The Goof.' This was about two kids named Ted and Pam who raise cute little hamsters and sell them to labs for medical research. They're especially proud of this one big daddy stud hamster named Mr. Brown. Also Ted and Pam don't like this loudmouthed little redheaded brat kid named Henry. They call Henry "The Goof." But then Mr. Brown The Hamster escapes, and The Goof finds him, so now they're all friends.

The next film was 'Timothy the Turtle,' where Betty, Jack, and Timothy the Turtle all go to a toy store and Timothy gets really excited by a bunch of toy turtles. But then Betty runs over him with a toy car.

After that we saw 'Judy's Smile,' which is about these two talking toothbrushes named Mr. Morning Toothbrush and Mrs. Evening Toothbrush. All they do all day long is worry about Judy taking care of her teeth. Mr. Morning Toothbrush told us to never put money or marbles in our mouths, and Mrs. Evening Toothbrush told us not to stand behind the batter at a baseball game.

April 26, 1961

Lately Mom's been on this big vitamin kick. She says she has to take lots of vitamins for the baby, and now that she's read about vitamins she thinks me and Colin should take them too, so she got a big bottle of vitamins that are shaped like the Flintstones. They have pills of Fred and Barney and Wilma and Betty, but they still stink like vitamins.

Also every day now we have to eat this big flat pill shaped like a Necco Wafer. It's a pill that keeps us from getting this poison called Strontium-90, which is supposed to be in the milk because of all the H-bomb testing. But we still have to drink the milk. I don't get it.

April 27, 1961

Scotty got suspended from school! He got kicked out for three whole days by Mrs. Blum, and do you know what for? Because he was pitching pennies at the wall with another kid, and Mrs. Blum called it "gambling." Can you believe that? I guess technically they're right, but it was only a penny. He showed me the letter he had to bring home to his mother. Here's what it said:

Los Angeles City School Districts
PACIFIC STREET ELEMENTARY SCHOOL
Jack P. Crowther, Superintendent of Schools
Elizabeth Palolozzi, Principal

Dear Mrs. McDonald,

Because your son Scott was reported to this office for gambling, it is necessary to suspend him from school. Before Scott will be readmitted to school it will be necessary for us to meet to discuss this matter further. We have reserved eight a.m. on Wednesday, May 3, for this conference. Please being Scott to school with you at this time.

While suspended, Scott should remain at home under the supervision of a responsible adult during school hours. If for any reason the above time is inconvenient please call GLadstone 4-5639 to arrange a more suitable time.

Sincerely,
Elizabeth Palolozzi, Principal.

Boy, Scotty's in some deep dogdoo now! What I don't get is how come when they're real mad at you, they tell you to stay home? That's not a punishment. It's like a holiday.

April 28, 1961

Today after school I went over to Scotty's to see what he was doing during his suspension. His mom was at work, but him and his brother Jimmy were out in the garage. Jimmy was wrapping some rags around some arrows and soaking the rags with gasoline. He said, "Hiya, Microbe. Hey, my girlfriend tells me you can add and subtract now -- you must be a regular Einstein."

I almost said something smart-alecky but I figured I'd get pounded, so I just said, "What's with the arrows?"

Scotty said, "Wasps." He pointed to this huge, football-shaped nest in one of the trees in their front yard. "We're gonna get 'em with flaming arrows like the Indians do in the movies! You wanna help?"

"Sure!" I said. So we all took turns shooting flaming arrows at the wasp's nest with a toy bow. Scotty shot some arrows but mostly the flames went out before the arrows got there. The ones I shot either bounced off the tree or missed and landed in the grass.

Jimmy said, "Gimme that bow and get outta my way, you worthless pussies," and he shot better -- a couple of his arrows actually hit the wasp's nest, but it didn't fall apart and it wouldn't burn. A few wasps came out to see what was happening, and I didn't like the way they looked.

Pretty soon we ran out of arrows. Jimmy was daring enough to run up to the tree and get the arrows back so we tried again, and on the second round we did a little better -- a few more arrows stuck into the nest. Some white smoke curled up from one arrow, but the nest still wouldn't catch. By then a bunch of mad looking black-and-yellow-striped wasps were flying around between us and the tree, and we ran out of arrows again. It seemed kind of dangerous to go and get the arrows back.

I said, "Now what?" and nobody answered. Then Jimmy disappeared into the apartment and came back with a coffee can. He said, "The hell with this William Tell shit, I'm smokin' these bastids out!" So he filled up the coffee can with gasoline and ran right at the tree.

Scotty yelled, "Stay low so you don't get stung!"

Jimmy ran past the tree and tossed the gasoline at the ground where a couple of burning arrows were, and the gas flamed up with a big *whoosh!* and a fireball raced up the tree, and some leaves and branches caught fire.

All of the sudden the wasps decided to ditch. Thousands of them poured out of the nest. Scotty and me ran as hard as we could for the garage. The air was full of smoke and wasps, and I could hear them buzzing all around us as we ran. Jimmy ran for the garage too, and he was yelling, "Shit! Fuck!" so I figured he was getting stung. It was scary!

We got into the garage and slammed the door shut and wasps were smacking against the garage windows with little *dink! dink!* sounds. Through the window we could see that the tree was kind of wrecked; it was black and a lot of the leaves were gone, and there was patches of burnt grass around it.

There was a freezer in the garage, so Jimmy stuck some ice on his face where he got stung -- somehow me and Scotty didn't get stung at all. After about an hour we all came out, and I guess the wasps must have moved away to build a new home somewhere else. When Jimmy took the ice pack away from his face he had all these lumpy bumps on his cheeks and nose and neck. Even though I guess I should've felt sorry for him, all I could think was, 'Good -- now maybe Deedee Weever will think you look like a fat, dickless, booger-headed Frankenstein from Mars, I hope.'

April 29, 1961

Lately on the TV News all they ever talk about is Cuba, and some place called the Bay Of Pigs and some guy named Castro. Do you know what language they speak in Cuba? I do. Cubic. Ha ha!

April 30, 1961

Me and Stinky got in trouble today because we decided to kidnap Pinky's Barbie Doll. We held it for ransom but Pinky didn't have any money to pay, so we just kept it for awhile and then we gave Barbie a mohawk haircut and gave it back. Pinky threw a fit, so we got yelled at.

May 1, 1961

The most amazing thing happened yesterday: Willie Mays hit four home runs in a game against Braves! Four homers in one game! Man!

So today is something called May Day, because it's May 1st. When I got to school I saw Mrs. Blum and I said, "Happy May Day, Mrs. Blum," and she said, "We don't celebrate any Communist holidays at this school, young man."

I'm not sure what she's talking about but I guess I won't wish anybody else a happy May Day.

May 2, 1961

My assignment for school is to invent something. Mrs. Wintering says we can invent anything we want and we don't have to actually build the invention, just draw pictures of it and describe it.

So I wanted to invent a shoe-tying machine. That would be pretty cool, wouldn't it? You just stick your shoes in there and they'd come out all tied! I figure some people are so lazy they don't even want to brush their teeths themselves so they buy electrical toothbrushes, and some people are so lazy they don't want to dry their hairs with a towel so they buy electrical hair dryers -- well then, why not make a shoe-tying machine? Plus, then fat people like Mom wouldn't have to bend over. But I couldn't figure out how to make it work, so I gave up.

But then I got another idea because I was looking at Fred Brown today and he had a band aid on his face and it looked funny because band aids are pink, and Fred is much darker because he's a Negro person. So I figured that people who are different colors ought to have their own band-aids, too. I mean, some people are sort of brown like Cookie Swansea and some people are sort of reddish and some people are sort of yellow and some people (like Mary-Ann) have lots of freckles -- hardly anybody is pink, you know? So I got a box of band-aids out of the medicine cabinet and painted them with poster paint and that's my invention.

May 3, 1961

Mrs. Wintering gave me an A for my invention -- she said it was one of the only ones that would really work. Most of the other kids made up impossible ones like Time Machines and Invisible Rays and stuff like that. Hermie Fleet made a Bird Diaper so his pet bird wouldn't poop all over the cage. What a dork.

Scotty ate dinner over tonight, and he told me all about Mrs. Blum's class. Man, am I lucky I got Mrs. Wintering instead -- Mrs. Blum is a witch! Almost everybody in their class has gotten in trouble, even the kiss-asses, and Scotty has spent almost as much time on the bench as he has at recess. Norman Giambalvo has already been suspended twice, and Mrs. Blum yells so much she made some of the girls cry. Scotty says he'll sure be happy when summer comes. Duh!

After dinner we had a pogo-stick contest. Scotty pogoed 224 times without falling off and Colin got to 209 but then he said he felt sick. Mom was watching and she said, "Don't toss your cookies, boys." I pogoed 614 straight times. I'm the pogo champ!

May 4, 1961

Miss Purcell is back. She went away for a few months to visit her family in Brooklyn, but now she's back and she came to our class today wearing black tights and white lipstick. She played guitar for us, and we learned some folk songs by this guy named Woody Somebody.

Miss Purcell said this Woody guy also played harmonica, so I showed her mine and she said, "Play something, Liam!" So I played 'Oh Susanna,' and Miss Purcell made everybody clap, which embarrassed me. Then Miss Purcell said it would be OK if people wanted to dance to the music, but the only person who got up and danced was Toren. She did this thing she called "interpretive dance," but it just looked spazzy to me.

Have you ever eaten cornbread? I didn't know they could make bread out of corn, but Fritzi served it in the cafeteria today, and I got Bobby to let me try some of his, and it's great! Fred Brown laughed really hard when he heard I'd never had cornbread -- he said, "Where you been all your life, Leon?" (He calls me "Leon" instead of "Liam," but I don't mind.)

May 5, 1961

We had another arithmetic test today, and this time I got a B! Mrs. Wintering said it must have paid off for me to have a tutor after all, which made me wonder what Deedee Weever has been doing lately? I forgot to ask Scotty whether Jimmy got over his wasp stings.

At recess we played kickball and that Nigel guy can kick the ball wherever he wants to -- it's amazing. He says almost everybody in England can do it and that we should all go to England on vacation some year, but I don't want to go because it's foggy and they don't have baseball there. Also Uncle Mick says it was the goddamn English who made it so tough on us Irish-Americans, so I bet he'd hate me forever if I went to England on vacation -- or even if I brought Nigel home for dinner. Like it's Nigel's fault?

May 6, 1961

We just had a big game of War -- do you play War? It only works good when you can get at least ten kids, because then you can have the Good Guys against the Bad Guys. Nobody wants to be a Bad Guy for very long though, so we switch sides every half an hour or so.

Everybody has a toy gun, and if you get shot you have to lay down and count to twenty before you can get up again. If you don't have a toy gun that's OK too. Heck, Pinky usually just points a hammer and yells, "*Dow dow dow dow dow! You're had!*"

Usually the Bad Guys are Nazis so we can yell things like, "Die, Kraut Shitbrain, die!" but then it gets weird if Volker Dortmunder or his little sister Kiki are playing, because they're Germans. So if we're playing with them, then the Bad Guys become Japanese and we all make fake slant eyes and say, "Hey, I went to school at UCRA." If a Japanese kid ever moves into the neighborhood, then I guess the Bad Guys will have to become Russians.

Anyways, today there were twelve of us so we had a good game. It lasted all afternoon and it moved all over the neighborhood, except when we got too close to Old Lady Kroot's she turned on her sprinklers. For awhile me and Colin and Stinky and Alex and Scotty were the Good Guys, and we captured Kiki Dortmunder as a prisoner of war. Kiki is only five so it wasn't like we got their General or anything like that, but still it was OK. We put her in the POW Jail, which is the pen where Ducky used to live. Kiki didn't seem to mind -- she just played with her dolly and fell asleep.

But then the Bad Guys were closing in on us, so we had to retreat. We needed to move the prisoner, so we put her in Stinky's wagon. We didn't want her to escape and we didn't have any rope, so Colin got some duct-tape out of our garage and we duct-taped Kiki to the wagon. Then we ran off with her but the wagon went off the curb and flipped into a muddy ditch, and Kiki was all duct-taped to the wagon so she bonked her head on the curb and got real muddy, and she couldn't get out and it was a big mess. Then Dr. Dortmunder came outside and had a cow and started swearing in German, so that was the end of the game, and that's that.

May 7, 1961

It's Sunday so we got to sleep late -- it was nice. Then Colin decided he wanted to cook breakfast. Sometimes Mom lets him make scrambled eggs all by himself, but today he wanted to make fried eggs but he wasn't sure how, so he asked Mom, "How do you make the kind of eggs with the target in the middle?"

Personally I hate fried eggs so I just had cereal. Fried eggs are goopy and I can't stand poking the yellow part and popping it like an eyeball, and watching all that gunk drool out.

May 11, 1961

Well, I couldn't talk to you for three days because Dad made me go three days without TV or the Marty Graw Book. I guess it's sort of stupid to carve your name into a table with a nail and then blame it on your brother.

May 12, 1961

This coming Sunday is Mother's Day, so today Mrs. Wintering had us all make something nice for our mothers. She said we could make anything we wanted to, like art or a card, or build something out of wood, just anything. I asked Mary-Ann what she was going to make, and she said a collage -- that's one of those things where you cut stuff out and then paste it all together again. It seemed like a pretty good idea to me, so I did one too.

Mrs. Wintering pulled out a big stack of old magazines, so we looked through them and cut out lots of pictures we thought our moms would like, then we pasted them all down on another piece of paper. My collage came out all right -- it had lots of pictures of babies and roses on it. I hope Mom will like it.

May 13, 1961

I'm not supposed to go down to the beach all by myself, but sometimes I do it anyway. Today all my friends were busy and Colin was driving me nuts, and it was overcast and kind of cold -- those are my favorite days to go down to the beach, so I walked through the canyon and ended up at State Beach.

There's a long wooden bench there, right on the sand, and in the summer it's filled with older kids who tell us to go away, but today it was empty so I sat down. Nobody was there except the seagulls and a couple of dogs. It was real quiet and nice.

After awhile this old wino-looking guy sat down on the bench next to me. Usually those guys act weird and make me nervous, but for some reason this guy seemed OK and I didn't feel funny with him sitting next to me. He didn't talk, he just watched the waves roll in and drank from a bottle of Ripple. Then after about ten minutes he cleared his throat and said, "Your name is Liam, isn't it?"

I was surprised. I said, "Who are you? How come you know my name?"

He smiled and said, "I met you at your grandmother's funeral."

I looked at him real hard and then it hit me: he was the guy in the back yard who couldn't stop crying. The guy Mom said she recognized from somewhere.

I said, "You wore an Army uniform, didn't you?"

He grinned and said, "Yes. It was the only thing I had that looked halfway respectable."

I looked at him closer and he seemed pretty old. He had gray whiskers and blue eyes. He didn't seem dangerous or anything, so I said, "What's your name?"

"Well," he said, "I used to be Major Henry Johnstone but you can just call me Major Hank, even though I haven't been in the Army for ten years now."

I didn't say anything so he went on, "Your parents have probably told you not to talk to strange old men, especially if they're drinking, and I don't blame them for that. That's generally a fairly intelligent approach. In this case, however, you and I have already met -- and as you've no doubt ascertained, I am not a threat." He looked at me and smiled.

I said, "Mom kind of remembered you, but kind of didn't. But you knew Gramma, didn't you?"

He sighed and said, "Liam? You may be a little too young to understand this fully, but your grandmother was the love of my life."

He ran his fingers through his hair, then opened up a piece of Fan Tan Gum and popped it in his mouth. "She was the one thing about this existence that kept me sane," he said. "It is my only great regret that Bridey and I never had our time together, because you see, she loved me as well. But somehow we were never available to one another at the same time." He stopped and took a drink from his Ripple.

After that, we were both silent for a long time. I wasn't scared of him -- he didn't seem crazy and he was real polite. Then he got up and said, "Young Liam? These are the nicest days at the beach, aren't they? The foggy days when it's quiet? I can see that you appreciate them, too."

He walked a few steps toward the water, then turned and said, "I'm afraid now I must be off. I hope I'll see you here again one day, and if you speak to your mother of me, please allow her my kindest regards? I recall her as a youngster, Liam, and she was a gem. You're a lucky boy. I'll be seeing you another day, I hope."

Then he walked down to the water and stared at the sea. After awhile Major Hank threw the Ripple bottle far out into the surf, and disappeared up the beach.

May 14, 1961

Last night the Dodgers won their sixth game in a row, so today I was in a pretty good mood from the start. It's Mother's Day, so I gave Mom her collage and Colin gave her a used Hula Hoop he got at the Thrift Store for a dime. Mom told him thanks, even though

I heard her ask Dad, "What the heck is a pregnant lady supposed to do with this thing?" We got to go out to dinner anywhere Mom wanted, so she picked this place in Santa Monica Canyon called Ted's Grill. They make the best onion rings in the entire universe.

May 15, 1961

Today at recess Mary-Ann and me and some other kids decided to go to the Auditorium and jump around on the stage and pretend we were on Broadway, which was fun for awhile but then it got boring. Then Mary-Ann found this big black umbrella and decided that we all should jump off the stage and pretend that the umbrella was a parachute, but nobody was brave enough to try it. I didn't want to do it because I remembered when I was eight I jumped off the side of a construction sight into a pile of sand and sprained my ankle, and had to use crutches for a week. And then Stinky Vanderhoeven loosened the screws on my crutches, so that when I leaned on them I went crashing down and got a bloody nose.

When I got home from school, Aunt Gwen was there and she was talking to Mom. I heard her say, "Y'know, I always thought he was just a fool, but, um, now I think maybe he's sort of a kind-hearted fool?"

Mom laughed and said, "He's a challenge all right, that Mick."

Hmmm....

June 1, 1961

In school they taught us a new word, 'doldrums.' It means sort of a dull, calm time where nothing really happens. So I guess you could say things have been in the doldrums around here lately, which is why I haven't talked to you for awhile.

The only interesting thing that happened recently was this one terrible thing: Kiki Dortmunder came home from kindergarten last week and went into their garage and Dr. Dortmunder was hanging there -- he hanged himself!

Kiki screamed and their mom came out and called the police, and a bunch of cops and fire trucks came. Everybody was crying and screaming and it was just awful. I felt really bad for poor Kiki.

The paper said that Dr. Dortmunder left a note why he did it, and that it has something to do with some guy's trial happening over in Israel. I'm not quite sure of all the details, but I think Dr. Dortmunder was afraid he'd get caught for some stuff he did during the war. Dad said, "I just *knew* that man was a Nazi!" but Mom said, "Stop gloating and take out the trash."

Bobby Del Valle says when people get hung, they take a shit in their pants. I wonder if that's true? Mrs. Dortmunder took Volker and Kiki out of school and they moved away, so I guess I won't see them anymore. Their house has a 'For Sale' sign in front of it, but I don't think anybody will buy it. How much would *you* pay for a house if it had a dead Nazi ghost hanging in the garage, with a big bunch of sauerkrautshit in it's pants?

June 2, 1961

Tonight Mom made tacos again. Yay! She had to make a ton of them, though, because Scotty and Uncle Mick and Aunt Gwen all ate over. Mom was cooking for hours. I heard her say, "I feel like a coolie. This is no way for a pregnant lady to work!" And do you know what's weird? Aunt Gwen and Uncle Mick are being real nice to each other lately. I don't get it.

June 3, 1961

Uncle Mick got thrown in jail last night! Aunt Gwen told us all about it. What happened was after they ate dinner over here they went to this nightclub called Finnegan's Wake, and they stayed real late and Uncle Mick drank a lot of beer. Then he tried to drive them home, but a cop pulled him over and made him blow into this little thingamajig, and then the cop took Uncle Mick away. Aunt Gwen said to Mom, "They might have even let us go, but Mick got a little bit mouthy with them..."

"Did he now? Not our Mick?" Mom said. "What did he say?"

"One cop told him, 'According to this gauge, you're legally drunk.' Mick said, 'Well, if it's legal, than what the hell's the big deal?! Leave me alone, officer, I'm legally drunk!'"

Mom started laughing. "He didn't?"

"He sure as hell did," said Aunt Gwen, "but he probably won't remember. The cop said Mick was a smartass, so they cuffed him. But they're letting him out later tonight."

Uh oh! Uncle Mick is in some deep dogdoo!

June 4, 1961

During dinner Colin reached over to get some salt and he said, "Some firemen came to my class today, Dad. They taught us First Aid."

Dad asked, "Really? What did they teach you?"

"Lotsa stuff!" Colin said. "Like before giving a blood transfusion, find out if the blood is affirmative or negative. Also, to remove dust from the eye, pull the eye down over the nose."

Dad smiled. "That sounds like it would hurt."

"Yeah!" said Colin, "it does. And for a nosebleed, put the nose much lower then the body until the heart stops."

Mom raised her eyebrows. "Are you sure you've got that right?"

"Yeah!" said Colin. "And for fainting, you rub the person's chest, or if it's a lady, rub her arm above the hand instead. Or put the head between the knees of the nearest medical doctor. For a dog bite, put the dog away for several days. If he hasn't recovered, then kill it."

Dad says we should trade in Colin on a used Pontiac.

June 5, 1961

At lunchtime Mrs. Wintering announced we were going on a field trip for the rest of the day. Everybody cheered because usually field trips are lots of fun and we get to go to interesting places like museums or concerts. You'll never guess where we went today, though -- we went to the Hyperion Sewage Disposal Plant in Playa Del Rey. I'm not making this up, we really did! It's this big huge place where all the pee and turd-water from the whole city of Los Angeles comes. You can smell this place from half a mile away.

When we got there, the driver parked the bus and we walked a long ways, and then a funny looking lady named Maxine came out and gave us a guided tour. She had a nose like Captain Hook.

Maxine told us that 300 million gallons of sewer water come there every day, and that they treat it and then dump it in the ocean. The first place she showed us was this gigantic room about the size of a baseball park, where jillions of gallons come in. Then we went to another building that had a big spinning thing called a 'centrifuge,' which is where they separate the liquids from the solids. Do you realize what that means? There was *millions and millions* of turds in there -- it was so gross Rikki Drinkwater stopped picking her nose, and we were all hoping Toren Shumaker would barf, but she didn't.

Bobby Del Valle said, "How come they call it raw sewage? Does anybody actually cook it?"

After they separate it, they put chemicals on it and they save all the solid parts to make fertilizer out of it, then they pump the liquid stuff through five miles of pipe. Then, at someplace way out in the ocean and 200 feet under water, they let it all go. Maxine said that the Hyperion Plant has been there since 1894, but in the old days they didn't separate the stuff or put any chemicals in it, they just dumped the poop straight into the ocean. Mary-Ann said she's never going to eat a tuna sandwich again.

So then when I got home from school, Pinky told me that Duane Beedy's mom and dad are going to send Duane to a head shrinker now. After Dr. Dortmunder hung himself, Duane was going around school telling everybody that Dr. Dortmunder had the right idea and that it was much better to be dead than alive, because then you could come back as a Monitor. I guess that scared his parents, so now Duane has to go talk to a doctor once a week. I told Dad about it, and he shook his head and said, "That poor little mixed up bastard..."

June 6, 1961

In school today we saw this movie called 'Down In The Mines.' It was all about minerals and gold and 'smelting,' so Scotty got this idea that we could make our own gold coins if we only had some gold to melt.

So after school we went over to his place and heated up his mom's iron skillet until it was almost white, then we put her gold pen and pencil in there and melted them for awhile so we could make a coin. Only it didn't work and they just got kind of gooey, and when they cooled off they wouldn't write anymore. It sounded like a good idea, but I'm glad I didn't think of it.

June 7, 1961

Over in Mrs. Blum's class they held a Spelling Bee, and Frankie Dupoy won it. Scotty says Frankie has turned into a real nice guy and he gets along with everybody, and all the girls like him, too. That's weird because back when he was sleeping all the time, everybody thought he was a retard.

After school I went over to Alex Eisenbaum's house and visited his mom and dad Feigl and Wlodzimierz. (I like to write those names -- it's fun.) I asked Alex what his parents thought about Dr. Dortmunder being a real Nazi, but Alex just said, "Shh, Liam! They don't even want to *think* about it."

June 8, 1961

When I was borned my parents planted a little tree out in the back yard, the kind they call an Evergreen Elm. It grew real fast and now it's 35 feet tall and there's a family of raccoons that live in it. Mom feels sorry for the raccoons and she leaves piles of dog biscuits under the tree for them, but Dad thinks the raccoons are a nuisance because they knock over the garbage cans.

So last night the garbage cans were all knocked over and Dad got mad and chased all the raccoons up the tree and yelled at them. Then this morning when Dad went out to get the paper, right in the center of the newspaper there was a big raccoondoo! Isn't that funny? A raccoon took a steamer on Dad's L.A. Times!

June 9, 1961

Today we had our Final Exams -- all day long we got tests in everything: arithmetic, spelling, reading, handwriting, everything! It sucked. But I think I did pretty OK this year. Mrs. Wintering said she grades "on the curve," which means the more stupid people you have in your class, the better it is for you. We have a bunch of dumb kids, so I guess I'll do OK.

Bobby Del Valle got in trouble for peeking. Mrs. Wintering said, "Bobby? I shore hope I didn't see you lookin' at Mary-Ann's paper," and Bobby said, "I hope you didn't either." So now he gets lowered a whole grade in citizenship. I peeked too, but I didn't get caught.

When I got home I noticed Mom sure is getting fat. I asked her when the baby was coming and she said, "Not for two more months, Liam. Why? Do you want it to come sooner?"

I said, "I don't know..."

"Well, it'll come in it's own time," Mom said. "Before you know it, you'll have a little sister." Mom seems sure the baby is a girl, and Dad wants a girl, too. I guess they think girls are easier to have than boys, but when I look at some of the girls in school I'm not convinced at all.

June 10, 1961

It's Saturday and me and Scotty decided we should make some money, so we tried to get some hedge trimming jobs again. But this time nobody wanted their hedge trimmed, so then Scotty said, "Hey! I've got it! Let's sell lemonade!"

So we pooled our money and rode our bikes to the Mayfair and bought two cans of that frozen lemonade gunk for 15 cents a can, then we went back to Scotty's place and mixed with it water and sugar, and made it into lemonade. Then we got a folding table from his garage, and we made this big sign that said, "Lemonade - two cents a glass." We're in business!

We sat outside his apartment and said to everybody who walked by, "Hey mister! You want some delicious lemonade? Only two cents a glass!" but hardly anybody wanted any, so we drank most of it ourselves. We sold ten glasses so we each got a dime back.

I guess we lost money, but at least we got to drink a heck of a lot of lemonade for a nickel each.

June 11, 1961

I walked down to the beach again today, and that old Army guy Major Hank was down there again, Gramma's friend, but this time he didn't have any Ripple with him. He came up to me and said hello and we talked for awhile. He's a pretty nice guy for a wino. I asked him when he met my Gramma, and he said he'd known her since the Great Depression, so then we talked about the Great Depression for awhile. He asked me, "Have you ever been hungry, Liam?"

"Sure," I said, "who hasn't?"

"*You* haven't, that's who!" he said. "When you have to make soup out of sawgrass and ragweed, *that's* hungry, son."

I didn't say anything back.

He went on, "I knew guys who lived in rusted out car bodies. I once knew a whole family that lived in a piano box."

I couldn't tell if he was pulling my leg or not, but either way it sure made me feel lucky.

June 12, 1961

Uncle Mick came over for dinner tonight, and he told us he had to pay $125 for when he got caught driving after drinking lots of beer. He told me not to drink beer and drive, which is a pretty safe bet since I'm only ten.

Also at dinner we were talking about the universe and Colin said something funny. He said, "Mrs. Roberts told us the moon is a planet just like earth, only even deader. And she says for hundreds of years people thought the moon was made out of green cheese -- but then the scientists found out it's really just a big hard rock."

Uncle Mick said, "Oh?" and Colin said, "Yeah, that's what happens to cheese when you leave it out."

June 13, 1961

Miss Purcell came around to all the classes today and tried to talk us all into performing at the 6th Grade Talent Show on Thursday. She said, "Liam, you could play something on your harmonica!" She said anybody who did it would get a better grade in music, but I still told her I didn't want to, and neither did Bobby or Mary-Ann. I think she's mad at us now.

After school I went down to the Thrift Store and I found a whole bunch of cool record albums for only a dime each. I got a Coasters record and a Drifters record and one by the Clovers, too!

Mom says all I ever spend money on is either books or records or baseball cards, which is pretty much true. I have a lot of records for a kid.

I used to have a lot more records last year, but I had to give them back. There was this ad in the Saturday Evening Post that said you could get twelve different record albums for free if you joined this thing called a Record Club, so I signed up and got all these free albums... it was great! But then they started sending more records every three weeks, whether I wanted them or not -- corny stuff like Ray Conniff and Johnny Mattress.

I thought they were free too so I kept them, but the records just kept coming and then they started sending me bills and saying they were going to put me in jail. Finally Dad got curious and read some of the letters, and it turned out I was supposed to pay for those records. They never told me that! So I had to send them all back, even though by then the good ones were all scratchy, and Liberatchy and Doris Day had mustaches and beards drawn on them.

June 14, 1961

In a few more days school gets out for the summer, and the last thing they do before Summer Vacation is pick next year's Marty Graw King and Queen. Here's how that works:

Marty Graw doesn't happen until September, just before school starts again, and every year they have a Marty Graw King and Queen. The King and Queen are always 6th graders (which means us.) So each 6th grade class nominates two possible Kings and two possible Queens. There are four 6th grade classes, so that means there are eight possible Kings and eight possible Queens. Today they had the nominations, and I got nominated! Cool, huh?

Maybe I'll get to be King but I doubt it because there are some A students up for it like Hermie Fleet, and some tough guys who'd probably try to beat people up if they don't vote for them, like Norman Giambalvo. For Queen I'm happy Mary-Ann got nominated, but she probably won't win because Toren is also nominated, and Toren'll probably pay all the kids a nickel each to vote for her.

Anyhow, today was the nominations and tomorrow is the voting. Kids get to vote, but so do teachers -- and the teacher's votes count for more. Then they keep the winners names a secret all summer long until Marty Graw. All the nominees come to the Marty Graw and then Mrs. Palolozzi crowns the King and Queen.

June 15, 1961

Today was the big 6th Grade Talent Show, so Mrs. Wintering marched us all down to the Auditorium at one o'clock. All the other kids in the whole school were there, but no parents -- just kids. I knew almost all the performers in the show, so it was kind of fun even though it was dopey.

First a girl named Lisa Chapps came out and sang 'Blue Moon,' but she looked kind of sick -- Mary-Ann said she ate something for lunch that disagreed with her, which doesn't surprise me because Fritzi was serving Dead Sea Soup and Wormburgers in the cafeteria today. Then Betty Bachelis played 'Heart And Soul' on the piano. Then these two boys I never saw before came out dressed like horses, and they sang, 'A Horse is a Horse, of Course of Course.' That's from Mr. Ed on TV.

After that, Hermie came out and tap-danced, and then he played 'Lady Of Spain' on the accordion. Then Fred Brown came out and played a crazy drum solo, and after that Toren did some ballet dancing. (Barf!) Then Robin Ward twirled a baton -- she was really good, she threw it way up in the air and caught it behind her back and between her legs! Then Nigel came out and did tricks kicking a ball around, and then a boy I never saw before tried to play an electric guitar, but every time he turned it on, it squealed real loud and hurt everybody's ears. Then it was over.

Tomorrow is the last day of school! I can hardly wait -- we get the whole summer off to sleep late and goof around and go to the beach and play! Maybe I'll see Deedee Weever at the beach, who knows? I bet if I had X-Ray Vision like Superman, I could see right through her bikini bathing suit!

But then when you stop and think about it, maybe if you had X-Ray Vision, you'd also see right through her skin too, and alls you would see is bones? I don't know...

June 16, 1961

Except for Christmas, the last day of school before summer vacation is the best day of the whole year! All the kids were really happy today, even the kids who got bad report cards or who got Blum again next semester. Pretty much everybody stayed with the same teacher -- I got Wintering again which is a lot better than Blum. My report card was about the same as last semester, except my grades in spelling and history went up and my grades in science and music went down. But the best part is I got a C+ in arithmetic. Mom and Dad will be happy, I hope. Here's what I got:

Reading	A
Language	A
Handwriting	C
Spelling	B+
Arithmetic	C+
Geography	B
History	B+
Science	C
Music	B
Art	B
Practical Arts	C
Phys Ed	B

And I still don't know what practical arts means. Mary-Ann showed me her report card and guess what? She got straight A's! She never got that before, so she was really happy. At lunch time all the kids were saying goodbye to each other and wishing each other a happy summer and stuff. Everybody said, "See ya at the beach, Liam" except for Fred Brown, who said, "See ya at the park, Leon." So I asked Fred why he never goes to the beach and he said, "What for, man? In case you haven't noticed, Fred Brown already got himself a tan."

Fred told me he was going to take drum lessons all summer long -- his dad is a musician who plays drums at a place in Santa Monica called The Zanzibar. They have a band called 'Dr. Rhythm and his Nightcrawlers.' I told Fred I'd like to see his dad's band sometime this summer, so Fred wrote his phone number down and said, "That would be cool. Just pick up the phone and dial, Leon."

Hermie and Toren got straight A's again -- it figures. Bobby Del Valle did real good, for him: he got all B's and C's but he also got a lot of "unsatisfactories" in citizenship and stuff like that.

Some kids brought autograph books with them and some had cameras, too. I didn't bring a camera, because during the summer I'll be seeing anyone I'd want to take a picture of, and why would I want a picture of somebody I don't want to see?

At one minute to three all the kids started counting down with the clock, yelling "60, 59, 58, 57," all the way down to when the bell rang, and then everybody cheered and threw their notebooks into the air! WE'RE FREE! Free for the whole summer! Mrs. Wintering yelled, "Y'all have a safe summer, kids, and y'all have loads of fun!" Outside the school all the kids were laughing and making plans. Mary-Ann told me she's going to be hanging out at Bel Air Beach and said she hoped she'd bump into me -- I'd like that, too.

June 17, 1961

Colin got an F! Mom and Dad are really mad because neither him or me has ever got an F before, but Colin got an F in (what else?) arithmetic. So now Mom and Dad are going to send him to Deedee over the summer. What a lucky pup! Dad was mad. He said, "Why'd you get an F, son? What happened?"

"Mrs. Roberts asked, 'How much is 12 times 3?' And I said '36'" said Colin.

"But that's right," Dad said.

"Yeah, but then she asked me, 'How much is 3 times 12?'"

"So? What the hell's the goddamn difference?" asked Dad.

"That's exactly what *I* said!"

So I went downtown to the Hobby Shop today and bought Dad some golf balls for Father's Day tomorrow. When I got home, Mom didn't feel like cooking so we got to eat at The Hot Dog Show, which is like my favorite restaurant. Have you ever been there? On the sign out front there's a huge hot dog with a halo, and the place is painted pink on the outside, with white wooden posts. They have seven different kids of hot dogs -- like the basic hot dog is called 'The Mutt' and it's just mustard, relish and onions. But then there's all these fancy kinds of hot dogs, like 'The Huskie' which has chili and cheese and Parmesan cheese -- it's really good! They also have a hamburger they call 'The Show-burger,' plus malts and shakes and fries and onion rings and cokes. Inside, all the booths are red and there's an electric train that runs all around the whole restaurant, up near the ceiling. All us kids like The Hot Dog Show.

June 18, 1961

It's Father's Day today so Mom asked Dad what he wanted, and Dad said he'd like to play golf. Boy it's a good thing I got him some golf balls, huh? Dad has a bunch of funny old golf clubs he carries around with him, like a 'mashie' and a 'spoon' and a 'dingle,' but he still doesn't golf very good. He says his best hole is the 19th hole.

For dinner Dad barbecued some chicken, and Scotty ate over and he said he'd never had barbecue before, can you imagine? Maybe that's because he doesn't have a dad. Mothers never barbecue because they don't like to cram all their hair into that tall white barbecuer's hat.

June 19, 1961

Boy, does it feel nice to wake up on a Monday and not have to go to school! This is the life.

One of the best things about summer is that you never have to wear shoes if you don't want. I don't know about you, but I like that. A lot. Also it stays light real late and we don't have to come inside until about nine o'clock.

Mom had a doctor's appointment today and Aunt Gwen had the day off, so she took me and Colin down to the County Fair. It's this big deal they have every summer, with rides and games and food and stuff. At the penny toss I won a baby rattle, which is kind of convenient since Mom's going to have a baby soon. Maybe the baby would like the rattle?

So on the way home I was sitting in the back seat of the car playing with the rattle. It has one of those suction cup thingies on the bottom so you can stick it on a tabletop, and I was messing around sticking it on parts of me to see how good it would stick. I tried it on my leg and my arm and my cheeks. Finally I thought I'd try sticking on my eye, just to see how it felt, so I took off my glasses and stuck it there.

It didn't hurt or anything so I sort of left it on there for awhile and pretended I was a monster with a bug eye. But then I tried to take it off and guess what? It wouldn't come off.

No matter which way I pulled, I couldn't get that thing off my eye. I tried to lift it gently and I tried to yank it, but it just would not come off. For a few minutes I was sure I'd have to go to the

Emergency Room and have an operation -- everybody at school would laugh at the moron who had to have an operation to get a baby rattle off his eye. It would hurt terrible! I might go blind! It would cost a fortune! Dad would kill me! So I messed and messed with it until finally I pried the corner of it off my eye, and the thing went *pop!* and off it came. Whew.

I figured nobody would be the wiser about how dumb I was, but then Aunt Gwen turned around to ask me something and she said, "Oh My God, Liam! What in the world did you do to your eye?"

So I looked in the mirror and my whole eye had this huge black and blue circle around it, kind of like Pete the Pup on The Little Rascals. Then about five minutes later I got this big black eye. When we got home Mom and Dad weren't happy, but Uncle Mick said it looked cool and Colin said I should make up a story about how I got in a fight with the Strong Man at the Fair (like anybody'd believe that!)

June 20, 1961

How can you tell when a moth farts? He suddenly flies in a straight line. Ha ha!

June 21, 1961

I had to go to the Eye Doctor today, partly because Mom and Dad are worried about my shiner from the rattle, but mostly just because it's time for my yearly checkup. The Eye Doctor is named Dr. Gilroy and he's a cool guy who likes baseball and fishing and tell lots of jokes.

He pointed flashlights in my eyes and then put drops in them, and made me look into all kinds of weird machines like they have on the Twilight Zone. Then he gave me some crappy cardboard sunglasses and sent me home. I couldn't go outside for the rest of the day and I wasn't allowed to watch TV for a couple hours, but at least it didn't hurt or anything. I like Dr. Gilroy.

June 22, 1961

Stinky got in some bad trouble today because he dumped a whole bag of marbles into the gas tank of his dad's car, and now Mr. Vanderhoeven has to take the car to a special mechanic to get them out of there. Stinky said he did it because he wanted to see if the car would make cool noises if there were marbles rattling around in there. I wonder if it did?

Stinky gets some pretty weird ideas. Like one time last year we saw this movie on TV where Jesus walked on water, so Stinky figured if he put enough Jello in a swimming pool, probably *anybody* could walk on water. So he put 48 boxes of Jello into the Dortmunder's pool, but it didn't work and it messed up the filters and Dr. Dortmunder had a fit.

And then another time Stinky tried to put his sister into the clothes dryer to see if she would get dizzy and barf, but Pinky ran away and hid in the duck pen.

June 23, 1961

Colin went to Deedee's today to get tuted in arithmetic. When he got home I asked him how she was, and he said, "She's stupid and old and ugly!" I guess it's funny how two people can see the same things so differently, isn't it?

June 24, 1961

Dr. Gilroy called my parents today and he said I had a serious problem with my eyes. Duh! Like I've been wearing glasses since I was two years old because it's fun looking like a dork?

But this time I guess it's different -- he said the shiner from the rattle wasn't a problem, but for some other reason my retinas are starting to get detached. I'm not sure exactly what that means, but now I have to go get an operation. Tomorrow morning! Also Dr. Gilroy says that while I'm asleep they might as well fix this other eye problem I have, which is that my right eye drifts outward.

Mom says I had an eye operation once before when I was only two, but I don't remember it. She says I'll have to go into the hospital, but the operation won't hurt, and the only bad part is that I'll have to wear patches over my eyes for a few days. That won't be fun because I won't get to watch TV or write in the Marty Graw Book, but at least I'll be able to practice my harmonica and listen to Vin Scully and the Dodger games.

So tomorrow morning Mom takes me to St. John's Hospital. She says she'll stay with me all the first day and night. After that she'll be coming home to sleep, but she says there will be a bunch of other kids in the Children's Ward so I'll have people to talk to. I have to stay there for two nights, so wish me luck!

June 29, 1961

Well, I'm back -- did you miss me? I couldn't talk to you til now because first I was in the hospital, and then after I got home I had to lay around the house with some patches on my eyes for a couple days.

Anyhow, here's what happened. On Sunday morning, Mom took me in to St. Johns. We had to sit in the waiting room for an hour because a nurse told us they didn't have very many people in Admissions on Sunday. Then Mom had to sign a whole bunch of papers that said she promised not to sue the hospital if I came out of there with two wieners and Miss Kleinholz's bazoombas or something.

A real pretty nurse came in after awhile. Her name was Cindy, and she took us to a room where they made me change into a girl's nightgown with a big hole in the butt. Mom made me wear my mucklucks. Then they gave me a little blue pill. I said, "Is this pill going to knock me out?" and Cindy said, "No. That pill is going to make you so that you don't *care* when you get knocked out."

After that I got kind of dizzy and silly. Mom said I was singing the Bosco song and giggling, but I don't remember very much. I do remember they put me on a table with wheels, and pushed me all around the hospital. That was fun. Then they put this mask over my face and told me to breathe deep. The stuff was real cold and it made my nose tingle. They said, "Count backwards from 100," so I tried, but I think I only got to about 95.

About five seconds later I woked up in another room and I couldn't see anything because I had patches over my eyes. They told me whole operation was already done! I was really thirsty so I asked for some water, and they gave it to me in a bottle with a straw. Mom was waiting there and she asked me if I was OK. I don't remember much after that because I think I fell asleep again.

So anyway I had my operation and was in the hospital for two days. There was a bunch of other kids there, but it was kind of hard to play with them because I couldn't see. But Mom brought me a transistor radio so I got to listen to the Dodger games, and I met this other kid named Roosevelt who also had patches on his eyes, so we told jokes and ghost stories. I tried to practice my harmonica but it drove some of the other kids crazy, so they made me stop. It wasn't so bad at the hospital except that the food was even crummier than Fritzi the Chinalady's.

On Tuesday I came home, but then I just laid around in bed for a couple days. It's boring when you can't do anything and you can't watch TV. Mom made me some chocolate chip cookies though, and Colin didn't bug me too much.

Mom finally took me in to Dr. Gilroy's today and he took the patches off my eyes. Then he shined a flashlight at them for about

20 minutes. He said, "Can you see all right, Liam?" and I said, "No because you're shining a flashlight in my eyes."

Then he said the operation was a success but I have to be a little bit careful for the next few days, like I'm not supposed to jump on a pogo stick or ride a Flexy or do anything that might undo the operation. But that's OK because Stinky won't let me ride his Flexy anyway. Plus tonight we're having tacos so I wouldn't want to pogo anyhow, because everybody knows if you pogo after tacos you'll poop in your undies.

June 30, 1961

I was playing around this afternoon in the back yard, and the phone rang. Mom said, "Hey, Liam? It's for you -- it's Coach Cunningham. He wants to know if you're planning to play Little League for the Huskies again this year?"

Ugh. I knew Coach Cunningham was going to call sometime soon -- I've been sort of dreading it, to tell you the truth. I mean baseball is like my favorite thing in the whole world, but I guess I'm pretty bad at it. And plus, I think I've finally figured out Coach Cunningham is a royal shitburger. He's kind of like what Mrs. Wintering says they have a lot of in Mississippi -- what do you call it? A racist. So I asked Mom to tell him, "No, thank you."

Mom seemed a little bit surprised at that, but she didn't push it.

July 1, 1961

Alex Eisenbaum asked me if I could spend the night at his place tonight, but Mom wouldn't let me. She says I need at least one more night at home since I'm supposedly still healing from my operation.

Today was Saturday so Colin and me got to watch baseball on TV -- the Dodgers beat the Phillies 5 to 2. It would sure be great if someday we could get a colored-TV like the Vanderhoeven's have, but Dad says with the baby coming and all, not to even think about anything like that unless he can get a big raise from Tri-Flex.

Uncle Mick came over for awhile this afternoon. He says he wants to go back to Ireland soon, and this time he wants to take Aunt Gwen with him. It's weird now with those two, they hang out a lot together.

Mom said to Dad, "I wonder if Gwen realizes what a lunatic of a sot your brother is?" and Dad said, "Well, I wonder if Mick realizes what a neurotic mess your sister is?" After that, Mom and Dad didn't talk to each other for awhile.

July 2, 1961

Right now it's about five o'clock and Mom says I can sleep over at Alex's tonight. Alex made this big tent in their back yard, so we get to go camping! (Actually it's just a bunch of blankets clothes-pinned to the clothes line, but it seems like a tent.) It'll be fun, I hope? Right now I'm just about to walk over there with Mom, so I'll tell you all about it tomorrow.

July 3, 1961

So last night me and Alex went camping in the Eisenbaum's back yard. We had air mattresses and sleeping bags, and we just hung out in the tent and played with our Pez dispensers and listened to the Dodgers until about ten o'clock. Then we got into our sleeping bags and read Mad Magazines and comic books with flashlights.

Alex has these great dirty comic books -- he calls them "Tijuana Bibles," but I never saw one in Tijuana. They all have drawings of regular comic book people like Superman and Popeye and Olive Oyl and Dagwood and Blondie, only they're all bare-naked and doing nasty stuff with each other!

In the morning Mr. Eisenbaum woked us up, and we went inside and ate some breakfast called "locks." It smelled like catfood! Then we got to eat this really hard doughnut called a "bagel," which was good except it was so chewy it took about half an hour to eat it.

Anyhow it was fun over at the Eisenbaum's place, and I got home about noon. Then Scotty came over, and we went out in our back yard and played with model planes. I had some firecrackers left over from Tijuana, so we put some in a plane, then we poured glue all over the plane and set it on fire and watched it blow up. *Ka-blooey!*

It was neat except we almost set the fence on fire, and Mr. Vanderhoeven yelled at us because he was trying to take a nap. Scotty said, "Hey, it's Monday! Shouldn't you be at work?"

Mr. Vanderhoeven didn't like that very much -- he called Scotty a bunch of names I bet he can't say at their Holy Roller Church.

July 4, 1961

Happy Fourth of July! Today they had a big parade downtown, so I rode my bike down there and checked it out. Basically it was just like the Christmas Parade except instead of dressing up like Santa, all the people dressed like Uncle Sam. There were the same horses and floats and junk like that.

I saw some of my friends there, and a few kids from school. Mary-Ann was there. She said, "That fat ass Norman Giambalvo has a slingshot -- he says he's going to shoot horses in the butt so they'll throw off their riders."

I kind of wanted to see that, but she didn't, so we went over to Chicken Delight and ate French fries instead.

July 5, 1961

Mom made pancakes for breakfast, and me and Colin were arguing over who would get the first pancake. Mom said, "If Jesus were sitting here, He would say, 'Let my brother have the first pancake. I can wait.'"

Colin said, "Liam, you be Jesus."

After breakfast I had to go see Dr. Gilroy again. He looked at my eyes and said they were all healed up, and that I could go back to being a 10 3/4-year-old boy again, whatever that's supposed to mean.

July 6, 1961

Today Pinky and Stinky and Colin and me played Cowboys and Indians all day. Colin and me were the Indians, so we decided to tie Pinky to a lamppost and burn her at the stake, but she fell asleep which sort of ruined the whole mood.

Mom made spaghetti tonight -- yum! She says the reason her spaghetti sauce is so good is because she uses plenty of mushrooms. Mushrooms are these vegetables that always grow in damp places, so they make them look like little umbrellas.

July 7, 1961

I went bowling today with Mary-Ann. Mom said it would be OK if we took the bus to Llo-Da-Mar Lanes, so Mary-Ann and me got on the Blue Bus. It costs a quarter. Guess who was on the bus? Father O'Dowd. He was reading a newspaper, but he saw me and he said, "Hello, Liam. We haven't seen your family much at Mass lately, although your mother came by last week. How are your eyes?"

I said, "Much better, Father."

Mary-Ann whispered in my ear, "Why do you call him 'father?'"

I whispered back, "Because he's a priest."

"Why does he wear his collar backwards?" she said.

"I don't know."

So she asked him, "Mr. Priest? Why do you wear your collar backwards?"

Father O'Dowd looked surprised. "Because I'm a Father," he said.

Mary-Ann said, "My dad is a father too, and he doesn't wear his collar backwards."

Father O'Dowd smiled. "He is your father. I am a Father to many."

Mary-Ann said, "How many, Mr. Priest? 'Cause there's this kid at school named Norman Giambalvo who has eight brothers and sisters, and his dad doesn't wear his collar backwards either."

"Child, I am Father to all who wish it," Father O'Dowd said. Then he went back to reading his newspaper.

It took about ten more minutes to get to Llo-Da-Mar Lanes and just as we were getting off the bus, Mary-Ann whispered something to Father O'Dowd. So a couple minutes later I asked her what she whispered, and she said, "I told him maybe he should wear his pants backwards, too."

At the bowling alley you have to pay a quarter to rent bowling shoes. Isn't that a gyp? Why can't you use your own shoes? So we got our shoes and then we picked out our bowling balls and we bowled three games. I bowled a 65 and a 74 and a 80, and Mary-Ann bowled a 88 and a 43 and a 70. So I guess we're both pretty lousy bowlers. After we paid for the bowling we played pinball for awhile, then we took the Blue Bus home but we didn't see Father O'Dowd.

July 8, 1961

It's Saturday so Dad didn't have to work. This new restaurant opened in town called Whipple's House of Waffles, and Dad decided we should all go out to breakfast and try it out. Yay! Me and Colin both got a Belgium Waffle with strawberries on top, and Dad let me drink a cup of coffee with milk in it.

July 9, 1961

There's this new movie called 'Guns Of Navaronne' playing at the Royale. Me and Scotty and Bobby heard it was good, so we decided we'd go down there this afternoon and sneak in. We went around to the back door and banged on it real hard and guess who opened the door? Mr. Zupo!

He grabbed Bobby by the shirt collar and said, "You again! I'm going to call your fazzer. Right now! And if you don't tell me your name zis instant, I'm going to call ze police. Now, vot is your name?"

Bobby squirmed around but he couldn't get loose. He said, "Saul."

Mr. Zupo said, "Saul vot?"

"SAUL T. PETER!" Bobby yelled. Scotty and me started laughing, and then Bobby broke away from Mr. Zupo and ran down the street towards the Bay Car Wash.

Mr. Zupo ran after him, so me and Scotty took off in the other direction, over the fence and down into the canyon behind the library. We slid down this big hillside and landed in the creek and ran through a bunch of brambles until we got all out of breath, then we sat down and laughed until our stomachs hurt. I hope Bobby got away too, but he probably did -- Bobby's real fast and I don't think Mr. Zupo could keep up with him for too long.

July 10, 1961

Mom and me and Colin were at the Mayfair this afternoon, and we bumped into Mrs. McDonald, Scotty's mother. She and Mom talked for a few minutes, mostly about the baby. After awhile Mrs. McDonald said to Colin, "Well, Colin? Are you excited about the new baby?"

Colin said, "Sure, and I know what we're going to name it, too. If it's a girl we're going to call it Brigid, and if it's another boy we're going to call it quits."

July 11, 1961

Every summer since I was a little kid, Mom and Dad have taken us up to the High Sierras to go camping and fishing for a week. It's always pretty fun up there -- we catch these fish called trouts and we eat them. Every year Colin manages to stick a hook through his finger, and Mom always makes Dad handle the worms. Dad just fishes by himself and drinks cold beer and looks at the pine trees.

This year Mom decided since she's going to have a baby in a few weeks she'd be too uncomfortable to sleep on the ground, so we're still going to go to the High Sierras, but instead of camping we're going to stay at some place called Curley's Cabins. Dad got two cabins that are connected to each other -- one for me and Colin, and one for him and Mom.

Anyhow we're leaving in the morning -- at 4 AM! Dad figures it's a good idea to leave real early like that, since we have to drive all the way across this terrible place called the Mojave Desert. It gets about a hundred and fifty degrees in the desert, so it's better to leave before it gets hot.

So for the next week I'll be writing to you from up in the High Sierras. I wonder if my handwriting will look the same?

July 21, 1961

Well, here I am back again -- I didn't get to talk to you up in the High Sierras after all, because Mom forgot to pack the Marty Graw Book. So now that I'm home again, I'll just tell you about the trip.

First we drove across the desert which took all day. The desert is really boring and hot, and all full of cactus. Colin had to stop about every hour to pee on a Yucca tree, which drove Dad crazy. Mom hooked wet towels up to the windows to keep the car cool, and mostly we just read comic books and looked out the window at the desert going by. We also played a game of who could spot the most out-of-state license plates on the other cars.

They say a lot of gold mines are hidden away in the desert, and if you're lucky maybe you'd find the Lost Dutchman's Mine? That would be great I guess, but you could also die in about ten minutes out there. It's so hot I bet you'd die and your tongue would get all swollen, and a bunch of frothy white goop would come gushing out your nose and your eyes. No wonder all those old prospectors in the movies always have a mule with a bunch of water bags.

Finally we got out of the desert and we drove up this skinny road into the mountains. Higher and higher we went until there were big trees everywhere and snow on top of the mountains.

By the afternoon we got to Curley's Cabins and this old white-haired guy called Curley came out and showed us around. But there's nothing to see around Curley's except for a couple of horses and a real skinny cow. I was hoping Curley would turn out to be Curley Joe from the Three Stooges, but he wasn't -- he was just another old guy with the same name.

Dad wanted to go fishing at sunset but Mom and me and Colin were tired so we stayed in one of the cabins and played Rummy while Dad fished. They didn't have TVs in the cabins, but at least they had a radio so we could hear Vin Scully.

Then the next day we all went fishing in the morning. Dad says the best times to fish are at sunrise and sunset. He caught a few trouts the first day, but nobody else did. Catching trouts is hard because lots of times they're too smart to get hooked -- they just steal your bait and run away.

In order to catch trouts you have to stick some bait on your hook, mostly worms or salmon eggs. A couple times Dad used grasshoppers or pieces of cheese, but mostly it was worms. Have you ever poked a worm with a hook before? It's kind of disgusting because you have to stick him a whole bunch of times, and some-times the worm just breaks into two worms! Mom won't touch the worms and Colin always hooks himself, so Dad has to do a lot of work for everybody, but he says he doesn't mind as long as he doesn't run out of ice cold Olympia Beer.

So pretty much every day up there in the High Sierras was the same -- we'd go fishing in the morning and then do something different every afternoon. Like one day we went to the really cool ghost town named Bodie. It had an old haunted graveyard! Then another time we went to see the Mammoth Lakes and they were pretty. Mom and Dad took lots of pictures there.

On our fourth day up there, Colin slipped in some shale and slid halfway down a mountainside and skinned himself up something awful! Mom had to put iodine all over his legs and butt. Then after that he got sunburnt, then he got stung by a bee and bitten by mosquitos. Plus he didn't catch a single trout and every time he tried to fish, his line got caught in a tree or on some rocks. And then he got poison oak on his hand, and he must have scratched his dick after that because the poison oak got there, too. I'm not sure Colin likes the High Sierras very much.

I didn't catch very many trouts either, but at least I caught a few. So did Mom. When we caught them, Mom cooked them and they were really good. She soaks them in milk and then puts flour and egg and bread crumbs on them, then she fries them in butter so they get real crispy! But trouts have a lot of bones so you have to be careful when you eat them because you could choke, or poke a hole in your throat and croak.

So anyways, then the trip was over and we said goodbye to Curley and we drove back across the desert again. I guess we had a good time up there in the High Sierras.

July 22, 1961

Pinky got in trouble today -- she found some of her mother's lipstick so she put it on. Then she kissed all the walls a bunch of times, and then wrote her name about a million times on the wall with the lipstick. Stinky says they can't paint over that stuff, either -- so Pinky wrecked their house. Isn't that funny?

July 23, 1961

It's Sunday and Mom decided we hadn't been to Mass in a long time, so she took Colin and me to Our Lady of Sorrows. I felt bad for Mom because she's just about to have the baby any day now, and those pews are uncomfortable enough to begin with.

Anyhow, Father O'Dowd was reading some Bible stories, and he read, "The man named Lot was warned to take his wife and flee out of the city, but his wife looked back and was turned to salt."

Colin asked Mom, "What happened to the flea?"

July 24, 1961

I feel pretty terrible today. I decided to cut through the canyon and go down to State Beach, and when I got there I saw a bunch of beautiful girls in bikini bathing suits, and one of them was Deedee Weever. She was sitting with a group of about eight teenagers, so I sat down in the sand about 100 feet away and just watched.

After awhile Deedee and this other girl got up to walk over to Neeny's Weenies to get some lunch I guess. They were coming right towards me, so I stood up and said, "Hi, Deedee. Isn't it a nice day for the beach?" Deedee waved at me but she didn't say anything, she just walked on by. Then I heard the other girl say, "Who's the kid?" and Deedee said, "Oh, just some little neighborhood retard I had to teach how to add."

July 25, 1961

Today I was reading the Santa Monica paper -- it's called the Evening Outlook (but Dad calls it the Evening Outrage.) There were two things in there that caught my eye. The first thing was that Roger Maris already has 40 home runs and it's only July! I wonder if he'll break the record?

The other cool thing was an ad for a place called the Zanzibar. It said, "Appearing Saturday: Dr. Rhythm and his Nightcrawlers." That's Fred Brown's dad's band. Maybe I'll call Fred Brown on Saturday -- I'd like to see his dad's band.

July 26, 1961

Jimmy McDonald taught me and Scotty how to light farts today. Did you know you could light farts? I didn't. Me and Scotty didn't actually do it, but Jimmy did and it sure was funny. He was laying on his back on the couch and then when he had to cut one, he just rolled up his legs so that his butt was sticking out, then he lit a match and put it right near his butt and then *whoosh!* This blue-green flame shot right out his butt!

Scotty and me laughed until our ribs hurt! We keep saying, "Do it again! Do it again!" but after a few times Jimmy's blue jeans got a burn mark on them, so he quit.

Later I told Uncle Mick about it and he said, "You have to be really careful, Liam. Sometimes when you do that, your ass can make sort of a hiccup, and the flame can get sucked back up inside you, and you explode! You don't want your asshole to explode, do you?"

Wow! I wonder if that's true?

July 27, 1961

Colin went swimming this afternoon. He wasn't supposed to get home until about four o'clock, but he came home at about 3 and said he got banned from the Tocaloma Municipal Swimming Pool for peeing in the pool. I knew Mom and Dad would get mad if they found out, so I rode my bike over there and tried to talk the pool people out of it.

I said, "Come on, can't you give him another chance? Lots of little boys pee in the pool," and they said, "Yes, but not from the diving board."

July 28, 1961

Dad was in a terrible mood when he got home from work tonight. He told Mom there was a letter in his pay packet saying that everybody has to work less hours for a couple months, because Tri-Flex lost some contract with Buick or somebody. Dad said, "Goddamn it all to hell! We're expecting another baby and the bastards are cutting my pay?" Then he went into the kitchen and poured a big martini. Colin and me stayed away from him for a couple hours until he got in a better mood.

July 29, 1961

So I called Fred Brown this morning and asked him if his dad's band was playing tonight at the Zanzibar, and he said, "Yeah, but the Zanzibar is a *bar*, man! You got to be 21-years-old to go in there."

We talked about it for awhile and then Fred said, "Listen, Leon, I'll tell you what. The bar'll be closed this afternoon, but the band will be setting up and rehearsing, so if you want to hear Dr. Rhythm we could go in then. I done it before -- it's cool." So we made a plan to meet there at two o'clock, and I took a Blue Bus into Santa Monica.

The Zanzibar is a little old run-down looking place, next door to a bunch of pawn shops. I was early and nobody was there yet, so I walked over to Zucky's and tried to order a hamburger, but they wouldn't let me in. This wrinkly old sourpuss lady pointed to a sign in the window that said, "Barefoot? No service," and I was barefoot so I couldn't get in. So I walked down the street to Arsenio's Market and asked the grocer for a couple of paper bags, then I put them on my feet and went back to Zucky's and said, "I'm not barefoot anymore."

The lady said, "Those aren't shoes," so I said, "The sign doesn't say you have to wear shoes, it just says you can't be barefoot."

So she went and got the manager, and he came outside and looked at my feet and started laughing. He said I wasn't barefoot, so they had to let me in, and I got my hamburger. The prune-face lady was my waitress. Can you guess how big a tip I left?

By then it was after two o'clock so I went back to the Zanzibar and there was a truck parked outside. Five or six colored men were unloading the truck and bringing stuff into the bar -- drums and big amplifiers and guitars and stuff. Fred Brown was helping too. He said, "Hey, Leon! You want to meet Dr. Rhythm and the Nightcrawlers?" and I nodded so he introduced me to the guys. They all shook my hand and said, "Nice to meetcha, Leon," so I helped them move their stuff into the bar.

The Zanzibar has two rooms -- the Zanzibar Room and the Congo Room, and Dr. Rhythm was setting up in the Congo Room. It took a long time to put the drums up, and plug in all the stuff. The Congo Room was falling apart, with tape on the windows and big stains on the wallpaper, and it was hot in there so the guys were all taking bottles of beer out of the fridge and drinking them. They didn't pay much attention to Fred or me -- we just watched. After awhile they all started yelling, "*Testing! Testing, one, two, three, four,*" and then they started playing.

Dr. Rhythm is the bestest band! They have a guitar, a bass, a saxophone, a piano and drums, and they all sing. They do songs like "What'd I Say" and "Roll Over Beethoven" and "Yakety Yak" -- all my favorite songs, and the guitar player plays the guitar with his teeth, and behind his back! If Dr. Rhythm ever makes a record, I want to buy it.

Fred's dad played the drums and he did a long drum solo, and then the rehearsal was over and that was that. Fred seemed really proud of his dad, and I would have been too, if it was my dad. So anyways I got to see Dr. Rhythm and his Nightcrawlers. If they ever come to your town, don't miss them.

July 30, 1961

Today me and Scotty figured out a cool new way to make some money. We rode our bikes to the Mayfair and we used the pay-phone there, and we called up the Operator and we faked like we were crying. We told the Operator, "My brother and I are trying to call our mother to come pick us up, but the payphone ate up our dime!"

The Operator said, "What number are you calling from?" and we told her. Then she said, "I'm sorry you've had trouble with that phone -- I'll report it to our repair center. If you'll please give me your name and address, the Phone Company will reimburse your ten cents." So we did this about twenty times each, and now we're going to get a bunch of free dimes in the mail!

We probably could have done it all day, but then this one Operator said, "Oh, I'm very sorry -- your mother must be very worried about you! What number were you dialing? I'll connect you right now." We got scared and hung up -- but as soon as we hung up, the phone started ringing! We were afraid the police might come, so we ran away.

July 31, 1961

Can you fit your toes into your mouth? No? I can't either, but Bobby Del Valle can. Today we were all at the beach and Bobby said he could put ketchup on his toes and eat it. Nobody believed him, so he made a bunch of bets for a nickel or a dime each, and then when he had a whole dollar bet, he got one of those packets of ketchup from Neeny's Weenies and he put the ketchup all over his toes. Then he stuck his toes in his mouth and ate the ketchup and won a dollar.

That's a cool thing to be able to do -- you could make a lot of money if you could do that, I bet.

August 1, 1961

Colin's a hero! Colin's a hero!

It all started this morning when Colin and Pinky were playing Hide and Go Seek, and Colin was hiding in Old Lady Kroot's back yard. We're not really supposed to go over there, but it was a good thing Colin did today!

Anyhow, Colin was hiding in the bushes underneath Old Lady Kroot's window, and he heard a noise from inside the house. It was Old Lady Kroot and she was groaning and saying, "Help me," so Colin went inside. Old Lady Kroot was laying on the floor and she looked kind of gray, so Colin picked up the phone and called 116 and reported an emergency. Then he got a pillow and a blanket for Old Lady Kroot, and he sat with her until an ambulance came.

Later a doctor called our house and said Old Lady Kroot had a heart attack, not a real bad one but bad enough. He said if she'd laid there all day without help, she might have died. So Colin saved her! Maybe now she won't turn her sprinklers on us when we play on her lawn?

Then at about three o'clock this dorky-looking guy with a pencil and a pad knocked on our door. He was from the newspaper and he asked Colin a bunch of questions about what happened. They didn't take Colin's picture or anything cool like that, but maybe there will be a story in the paper?

Mom was really proud of Colin, which is good because when she finds out he's been banned from the Tocaloma Pool, she's going to be mad. Maybe this will balance it out? Mom says it's good thing she didn't go into labor today with all the excitement on the street.

August 2, 1961

From today's paper:

> ***FIRST AID DEMO PAYS OFF FOR 8-YEAR-OLD.*** *The visit last June by County Firemen to Pacific Street Elementary School paid big dividends yesterday, when an alert 8-year-old boy came to the rescue of an elderly woman who had suffered an apparent heart attack.*
>
> *Eight-year-old Colin McAfee was playing Hide And Seek when he heard cries of help from Mrs. Gladys Kroot, a neighbor across the street. The boy alertly called 116, then comforted the 81-year old woman until the arrival of paramedics.*
>
> *According to County Firefighters, the youngster responded exactly as instructed by firemen during a June demonstration at Pacific Street School. "There's no question he did the right thing," said Paramedic Damian Williams.*
>
> *Asked by a reporter if he had any advice for other children, young McAfee appeared not to understand the question. Finally, after much prompting, his advice to kids was, "Never try to hide a piece of broccoli in a glass of milk."*
>
> *We salute young McAfee both for his clear thinking and 'valuable' advice.*

August 3, 1961

Aunt Gwen came over today and she and Mom were talking about the baby. Mom is really getting huge now. She told Aunt Gwen, "It's awful! I have to pee every five minutes, and I have Hammeroids and now I'm getting Very Gross Veins."

Aunt Gwen said, "I don't know how you do it, Sis. It must be like carrying a bowling ball around in your stomach." Then she smiled and said, "I bet your big boobs are a hit, though..."

Mom said, "Jesus, if they get any bigger I could get a job at Edgemar. I'm scared to turn around fast, for fear of knocking somebody over with them."

"Well, they'll deflate soon enough, so you might as well enjoy them while you can," Aunt Gwen said.

Mom said, "I hope this child arrives soon -- I'm getting too old for this shit."

Mom must be hurting because that was the first time in my whole life I've ever heard her swear! I went into the back yard and made like I didn't hear.

August 4, 1961

It rained this afternoon and there was nothing on TV. Colin was busy looking through the Encyclopedia Brittanica and drawing beards on the women, so I went into the kitchen and told Mom, "I'm bored."

She said, "You know that nice little girl you went bowling with a few weeks ago? Mary-Ann Lindstrom? Why don't you call her up and see if she wants to come over and play. I'll even run over to her house and pick her up..." That sounded OK, so I called Mary-Ann, and then Mom and I drove over and picked her up. I had to meet Mrs. Lindstrom -- I didn't remember her but she said she remembered me from the Kid's Easter Egg Hunt at the Mayfair. I thought, 'Uh oh.'

Mom and Mrs. Lindstrom talked for awhile about the baby, and Mom said, "...Any minute now." After awhile Mary-Ann said bye to her mom, and we came back to our house.

The rain stopped and Mary-Ann and I were playing in the garage, cutting up pictures and making paper mache stuff. She asked about our trip to the High Sierras and I was telling her about fishing, and then we started singing 'I'm Gonna Eat Some Worms.' Do you know that song? It goes like this:

Nobody likes me, everybody hates me,
I'm gonna eat some worms.
Great big juicy ones, little bitty greasy ones,
I'm gonna eat some worms.

First you bite the heads off, then you suck the guts out,
Look at them wiggle and squirm.
Great big juicy ones, little bitty greasy ones,
I'm gonna eat some worms.

Just then Mom yelled, "Liam? Can you please come in the house for a moment?"

So I ran in the house and Mom said, "I don't think it's a good idea for you to teach those awful songs to that nice little girl, do you? What will her mother say when she hears that song?"

I said, "Mom, I'm not teaching it to her -- *she's* teaching it to *me.*"

Jeez, parents can sure be a pain, can't they?

August 5, 1961

Scotty asked me if I wanted to go down to the Santa Monica Pier today so I asked Dad for a dollar, but he said now that he got a pay cut we're too broke for kid stuff. But me and Scotty went anyway, and at the end of the pier there was a big crowd standing around this little stage.

We walked down there to see what was happening, and it was a show with three monkeys -- it was great! First somebody came out and said, "Ladies and gentlemen, please welcome the stars of stage, screen and television, Sabo's International Chimps!"

Everybody clapped and then this guy Sabo came out with three monkeys called chimpanzees. Their names were 'Zippy,' 'Sam' and I forget the third one's name, but they were funny! They played little guitars and they skateboarded, and Zippy did the Hula Hoop.

The funniest one was Sam -- he wore a Davy Crockett hat and kept stealing food from Sabo.

After the show was over, Sabo came over and gave me and Scotty some free pictures of the monkeys. I'm going to put them on my wall.

August 6, 1961

My brother Colin is a weird little kid. Ever since he was about five he's liked to stick M and M's up his nose and then snort them out, but lately he's been trying to put dimes up his nose and I'm afraid one is going to get stuck in there and he'll never get it out.

Tonight one of Mom's pearl necklaces broke into kind of a long string, so Colin wanted to see how far up his nose it would go. Well it went up there pretty far and he couldn't get it out and he started crying, and Dad had to come and pull on it, but it still wouldn't come out. Mom called Dr. Dicksau on the phone and Colin screamed a lot. Dad tried to yank the pearls out of his nose and told Colin to snort, and finally after about twenty minutes they came out.

August 7, 1961

What goes har har har bonk? A guy laughing his head off. Ha ha!

August 8, 1961

Remember I told you about the trailer park they're building at the bottom of the canyon? Well, they're still building it. We don't want them to build it because it'll block us from our shortcut to the beach. So today me and Scotty got a bunch of balloons, then we rode our bikes to the house at the top of the canyon. There's this super rich stupid idiot who lives up there in a humongous house, so we used his garden hose and filled up a bunch of water balloons, then we threw them all down on the workmen. Then we got on our bikes and rode for our lives!

August 9, 1961

About noon there was a big flurry around here because Mom said she "broke water." I'm not sure exactly what that means, but I know it means the baby's coming. Dad called Aunt Gwen right away and she came right over. Then he packed up some of Mom's clothes and books and things into a suitcase, and then he called Dr. Dicksau and the hospital. Aunt Gwen said she'd look after me and Colin, so then Mom and Dad kissed us goodbye and said they'd call us as soon as they knew something. Then they drove off to the St. John's Hospital.

About an hour later they called and said they were all checked into Room 806, but that the baby probably wouldn't be coming til after midnight. I guess babies take their time? Mom sounded OK on the phone, but she said she was pretty uncomfortable. Mom once told me having a baby hurts like the devil.

Aunt Gwen tried to make us a late lunch, but we told her we weren't very hungry. Actually I'm a little worried about Mom, and Colin almost never eats lunch anyway. I remember when Colin was in first grade he never ate the lunch Mom packed him, but he wasn't smart enough to throw it away at school, so he'd get home and realize that most of his lunch was still in his Roy Rogers lunch box. I guess he figured that if Mom found out she'd get mad at him for wasting food, so he'd hide it in the back of our closet. What a genius. After a while Mom began to wonder why the closet stunk so bad, and then she found all these old green hairy boloney sandwiches and junk, piled up in there.

Anyhow, we're all just sort of waiting by the phone to hear about the baby. I hope it comes soon because Mom will feel a lot better when she's not so fat, I bet.

August 10, 1961

Mom had a baby girl! We have a sister!

Last night at about one o'clock in the morning the phone rang and it was Dad calling from the hospital. He talked to Aunt Gwen for awhile, and then he talked to me and Colin. Mom had the baby at 12:25, and it's a girl and they named her Brigid, but they're calling her Bridey just like Gramma. I asked if I could speak to Mom, but Dad said she was sleeping but that we could all come to the hospital in the morning to see Mom and Bridey. It took me a long time to get to sleep, but finally I did. Aunt Gwen woked us up at nine o'clock and we got dressed real fast and we all went down to the hospital.

When we got up to room 806, Mom was in a big white bed and Dad was sitting next to her. She looked tired but really happy. Dad looked like he'd been up all night. The baby was away in the nursery, so a nice nurselady took us for a walk and we got to see our sister through some glass. She was in there with a bunch of other babies, and she was so small I couldn't believe it. She looked kind of yellow and wrinkly, but Mom and Dad think she's pretty. I still can't believe we have a sister! Isn't it great?

Mom has to stay at the hospital for two more nights just so they can make sure the baby didn't pop Mom's guts when it came out, but Dad said he'd be home tonight and that he'd bring some pizzas with him.

August 11, 1961

We visited Mom and the baby again today, and Mom feels much better now. She said, "As long as that *lovely* nurse keeps bringing me those *lovely* pills, I'll be just *lovely!*"

Bridey looks more human today, too -- her head doesn't look as lopsided as it did yesterday, and Mom got to feed her this afternoon. It seems weird to me that milk comes right out of lady's titties like that, but I guess that's what titties are designed for, huh?

So we stayed most of the afternoon at the hospital. Colin got bored and ran all over the place, and I had to go catch him a couple of times. One time he ran into the Emergency Room, and there was a guy in there with a big salad-fork sticking out of his leg. Colin yelled, "HEY! Lookit that guy!" but a nurse chased us out of there.

In the afternoon we went home and Aunt Gwen got us some food to go at the Hot Dog Show. Boy, the phone has been ringing ever since -- everybody wants to know about the baby, but I guess it'll be awhile before the baby can talk to anybody.

August 12, 1961

Today Dad set up a bassinet for Bridey -- a bassinet is a place where babies sleep. It's smaller than a crib but bigger than a mom's stomach. At about two o'clock Dad went and got Mom out of the hospital, and they came home and Mom and Bridey went right to sleep.

Dad says we have to be real quiet around the house for the next few days, because moms and babies need their sleep. That means I can't play my harmonica unless I go out in the garage, but if I do that, all the dogs in the neighborhood start howling. I wonder why dogs do that? Is it because they like it, or because they don't like it?

August 13, 1961

Just now I was writing in this ol' Marty Graw Book, and Uncle Mick saw me and he said, "You writing again? What the hell do you write in that thing anyway, Liam?"

I said, "Nothing really. Just stuff..."

Uncle Mick said, "You're gettin' to be a regular Rude Yard Kipling."

So tonight on the news everybody was yelling about this big wall that got built over in Berlin, Germany. It's supposed to keep some Germans away from some other Germans. I asked Dad why they built it, and he shrugged and said, "For all I care, they should built a wall around the whole goddamn country."

August 14, 1961

A bunch of the neighbors came over today and they were going all goo-goo over the new baby. Mr. Vanderhoeven thinks the baby looks just like Dad, but Aunt Gwen and Mrs. Vanderhoeven think she looks like Mom. I think the baby looks like Winston Churchill.

August 15, 1961

I rode my bike down to the beach today. I was hoping maybe I'd see Deedee Weever or at least run into Scotty or Bobby or Mary-Ann, but none of them were there so I locked my bike and walked down to the pier.

About halfway there I saw a guy sitting on a rock. From behind it looked like he was wearing an Army uniform, so I said, "Is that you, Major Hank?" and he turned around. It was Major Hank all right, and he was crying again.

He said, "Ah, hello young Liam. I'm afraid you've caught me in another weak moment..."

Major Hank didn't look well -- his uniform was dirty, he hadn't shaved in a few days and his eyes had little yellow eyeboogers at the corners and were all red. I said, "Are you OK, Major Hank?"

"Tolerable. Just tolerable, I'm afraid." He wiped his eyes with the back of his hand and said, "Now then. Tell us what brings you down to the beach?"

We sat and talked for awhile, mostly about baseball, and then we were silent while he looked out at the sea. I knew why he was sad. I'm not quite sure why I said it, but I said, "I'm sorry you and Gramma never got to have your time together, Major Hank."

He gave me a funny look and said, "That's a very generous thing for you to say, Liam." He lit a cigarette, then he smiled. "Of course you realize that if Bridey and I had gotten together, she mightn't have married your grandfather. Which means your Aunt Gwen and Uncle Jake and your mother would have never been born, which means you wouldn't even be here speaking to me..."

I hadn't thought of that. It kind of gave me a headache.

Then he said, "I saw Gwen at Bridey's funeral, but I didn't see Jacob. Why wasn't he there?"

At first I wasn't sure who he meant. "You mean Uncle Jake? He's in jail in Texas."

"Oh," said Major Hank. "Why am I not surprised? What did he do, shoot the Governor?"

"He had a lot of loco weed."

Major Hank made a noise kind of like "hrrumpf," and then he was quiet for awhile. Finally he sighed and said, "I'm not doing anybody any good dwelling on the past, am I now?"

I shrugged.

He said, "Your grandmother was a lucky woman, with her three children and her two grandchildren. It's a lonesome life when you have no one, Liam." Then he got up and rubbed his face and said, "I'd better get along home before I scare away the seagulls. I hope you have a carefree summer, you and your brother."

He started walking up to the parking lot and suddenly I yelled, "Major Hank!"

He turned around.

"Major Hank? Mom just had a baby, a week ago! It was a girl and they named her Brigid. Bridey!"

He broke into a big smile and yelled back, "Ahh, sweet symmetry! Thanks for telling me, Liam. I'll sleep better now. See you later sometime?" Then he turned around and went walking across the parking lot and over the bridge. I watched him until I couldn't see him anymore.

August 21, 1961

I couldn't talk to you for a few days – here's why: last Wednesday I had a little crash on my bike. I was coming around a corner really fast and the bike skidded in some gravel and slid right into the curb. I didn't get hurt too bad but I squarshed my harmonica, and the bike got a bent wheel and a broken chain so it had to be taken into the Cycle Shop. Uncle Mick called me a "eejit."

Anyhow, the next day I wanted to go down to the Santa Monica Pier to see if maybe the monkeys would be back, but since my bike was broken I had to take the Blue Bus. I took this Marty Graw Book and the monkey pictures with me, just in case maybe I could get the monkey guy's autograph. But there was no monkey show, and on the way home I accidentally left this book and the monkey pictures on the bus!

Uh oh. As soon as I got home I called the bus company, and they said they'd try to find my book and my pictures. Today they called and said they found them, so I just went into Santa Monica and got them back.

It wasn't like you missed much though. Bridey cries a little, but mostly she just sleeps and slurps up the tittie-milk and makes poop. Life is pretty simple when you're a baby, huh?

August 22, 1961

Roger Maris got his 50th home run tonight! Too bad he's on the goddamn Yankees.

August 23, 1961

In the mail today there were four letters addressed to me from the Phone Company. For a second I thought they'd made a mistake, but then I remembered about the game me and Scotty played, so I opened them up and there was a dime in each letter! It worked!

August 24, 1961

Aunt Gwen is over here visiting. Just now Mom was feeding the baby and she said to Aunt Gwen, "Jeez, will you look at these stretch marks? I look like I've been run over by a tractor! My kids are gonna want to drive their slot cars on these tracks I've got." Aunt Gwen didn't say anything back, she just smiled.

I can't figure out this whole thing with the way babies eat. I mean like, moms make milk, which is food for baby humans, right? OK. But then when we get to be older kids, we're supposed to drink milk that comes from cows. They say it's natural and good for us, but isn't that milk supposed to be for baby cows? So why do we drink it if we're not cows?

Also, if moms make milk and it comes from their nipples, how come men have nipples? What are they for?

August 26, 1961

It's been raining for the last two days so we haven't been able to do much. Yesterday I just hung around the house and watched TV and tried to help Mom.

Today Mrs. Vanderhoeven was out in their garage all afternoon. I don't know what she was doing but since she was gone, me and Pinky and Stinky decided to have some fun with their telephone. We called up a bunch of people and said, "We're calling from Frigidaire and we're conducting a survey. Can you tell us if your refrigerator is running?" and when they said, "Yes," we'd say, "THEN YOU BETTER GO CATCH IT!"

After that we called every store in town that sells tobacco and we said, "Can you tell me if you have Prince Albert in a can?" and they'd say, "Yes," and we'd say, "WELL YOU BETTER LET HIM OUT BEFORE HE SUFFOCATES!" Ha ha!

August 27, 1961

This morning Dad got mad at me because I took my Silly Putty out of it's eggshell and pressed it all over the Sunday Comics before he could read them.

It finally stopped raining, so me and Scotty went down to the beach. It's always fun to go to the beach right after a big rainstorm, because all kinds of weird junk washes up on the sand.

Down at State Beach there's a big lake that gets formed, right where the creek lets out. It's usually stagnant and stinky and full of mosquitoes, so we named it the Polio Pond. If you fall in it you get Polio and die. But after it rains a lot, water gushes down the river and the Polio Pond gets cleaned out, which is nice.

The water in the creek was going so fast it was like in the movies! It was just roaring by, and all kinds of people were standing around looking at it. Some of the kids were thinking they could get air mattresses and ride down the river, but last year two kids from Malibu got drownded doing that, so nobody's doing it this year. Still there were so many people looking at the river, it gave me and Scotty an idea.

We put our money together, then we rode our bikes to the Thrift Store and bought some holey old jeans and a shirt and a hat, and a used Halloween mask. Then we filled up the clothes with wadded up newspapers and with some blown-up balloons (to make it float,) and then we hiked about a half a mile up river and threw our homemade dummy into the water. It took off like a shot -- the river just swept it along!

We ran along the river hoping we could keep up with it, but the water was too fast so by the time we got to the beach, the dummy had already floated by everybody. We asked a bunch of kids if anything weird had come down the river, and one real little kid said, "Yeah! A body came down the river!" but then the older kids said, "That wasn't a body -- it was just a dummy, ya dummy!"

So I guess we didn't fool too many people, but it was a good try.

August 28, 1961

I went into town this morning on my bike and I bumped into Bobby Del Valle at the Mayfair. He said, "Hey Liam, you wanna go to P.O.P.?"

I never told you about P.O.P. did I? Well, P.O.P. stands for Pacific Ocean Park, and it's this big amusement park in Santa Monica, kind of like Disneyland only dirtier. It's real fun -- they have a huge rollie coaster and a haunted house and scary rides, and rides that make girls barf. They also have weird tattoo places where sailors go, and some other places Mom calls "sleazy," but I think the whole place is really cool.

Anyhow, I wanted to go with Bobby but I didn't have any money. But Bobby said, "Don't worry about the money, Liam, I know how to sneak in. You got two quarters for a roundtrip on the bus? That's all you'll need."

I had two quarters, so we locked up our bikes and jumped on the Blue Bus. We had to transfer to get all the way to P.O.P., but that was no problem and pretty soon we were there.

Now P.O.P. is out on a pier over the ocean. Not the Santa Monica pier, but another one. That's what makes it so great -- all the rides look like you're going to fall into the water, but of course you don't because if you did, everybody'd hire Perry Mason and sue the shit out of P.O.P. But anyway, it's on a pier so I didn't see how we could sneak in, but Bobby said, "Trust me."

When we got to the pier Bobby said, "OK, take off your shoes and roll up your jeans," so I did and we walked out into the water for a few feet. Then Bobby said, "Let's climb here," and he pointed up one of those big wooden posts that hold up the pier.

So we climbed up this big wooden pole until we got all the way up the pier, then we put our shoes back on. Bobby said, "Over here, Liam," so we climbed up another pole and then we were on the roof of some building right near P.O.P.

"We're on the roof of the Aragon Ballroom," Bobby said. "It's the place where Lawrence Welk's TV show happens. Look, see that window?"

I looked and there was a big window on a hinge, like in school. I think it's called a 'transom.' I said, "Yeah?"

Bobby said, "That's the window we're gonna sneak in."

So we crawled across the roof and opened the transom, and it was way up high in this building. We slid into it and we pulled ourselves along some beams, then we slid down a pole and we were on a big wooden floor. It was dark and I didn't know where we were, but Bobby said, "Don't worry -- we're in Lawrence Welk's cloakroom!" So I let him lead me around in the dark and pretty soon there was a door.

Bobby went to the door and peeked out and said, "Nobody's looking -- let's *go!*" so we slipped outside and guess what? We were right inside P.O.P.! Bobby knew right where we'd be.

So anyhow we spent the whole day at P.O.P. and we had a good time. We sat underneath the Upside-down Chicken Ride and waited for money to fall out of kid's pockets and we got a few coins that way, so we had a corndog and some French fries.

P.O.P. was really fun, but not nearly as much fun as it was sneaking into it.

August 29, 1961

Do you have Fizzies where you live? You know, those colored, flavored tablets that you stick in a glass of water, then they go all fizzy and make a fruit flavored drink? They're pretty bad, but

Colin likes to stick them right on his tongue and let them fizz away. I tried it once but it burned and it made me sneeze!

So today Colin was trying to eat Fizzies and sing commercials at the same time. He knows lots of commercials, but his best one is the Buster Brown Shoes one with 'My Dog Tige.' Do you know that one? It goes, "Hi! My name is Buster Brown! This is my dog Tige. We live in a shoe!"

So he was running all over the house with this red foamy stuff spilling all out his mouth, yelling, "We live in a shoe! We live in a shoe!" Colin's a pretty funny kid, I guess.

August 30, 1961

Aunt Gwen and Uncle Mick ate over tonight, and Uncle Mick said they're going to go to Ireland together in the spring. And do you want to hear something really crazy? Aunt Gwen and Uncle Mick are thinking about moving in together! Mom says that would be risky for Aunt Gwen's career and might ruin her reputation, but Aunt Gwen says she doesn't care and besides, "Rexall ain't exactly my choice for a career."

And Uncle Mick said, "Who knows? Maybe one day I'll make an honest woman out of her." But I don't think Aunt Gwen is dishonest, do you?

August 31, 1961

Mom was singing to Bridey tonight and rocking her back and forth. She sang for a real long time, so Colin asked Dad, "How come Mom is singing so much to the baby?"

Dad said, "So Bridey will go to sleep."

Then Colin said, "Will Mom stop singing when the baby goes to sleep?"

Dad nodded.

So Colin thought about that for a second and said, "Then why doesn't the baby just pretend to be asleep?"

September 1, 1961

From today's paper:

MAN'S BODY WASHES ASHORE. *The body of a partially clothed man police believe drowned in the waters off Santa Monica Beach was discovered near the pier on Thursday afternoon.*

The man, identified as retired Major Henry "Hank" L. Johnstone (aka Johns) of 142 A Shoreline Ave., Ocean Park, was spotted at 3:20 p.m. last Thursday afternoon by construction workers rebuilding the Santa Monica Pier from last winter's storm damage.

Johnstone, 58, was clothed with only Army pants and had a medium build, gray hair, and blue eyes. The body could have been in the water anywhere between a half-hour or a day, said Santa Monica Fire Lt. William Brennan. Cold water temperatures could have preserved the body and slowed the rate of decomposition, he said.

"It wasn't that beat up for being in the surf," he said. Janet McAllistair from the District Attorney's office said the autopsy did not narrow down the time of death.

Police would not say if they thought Johnstone had committed suicide, but District Attorney Mark Sullivan does not plan to investigate the death further. There was no indication of foul play, McAllistair said. The body was identified as Johnstone late Thursday night.

Once construction workers noticed something floating in the water, they walked to a pierside restaurant and phoned the fire station, who responded in two minutes with a dive team, said Fire Chief Roy French.

Santa Monica firefighters Clifton Woods and Tobias Dumas Jr. suited up for the water rescue. Three other firefighters assisted with the recovery. It took around 15 minutes to retrieve the body from the chilly ocean water.

Santa Monica Police said Johnstone had not been reported missing before being found. Johnstone was retired from the U.S. Army and was a former professional baseball player with the New York Yankees.

September 2, 1961

Mom said it was real sad about Major Hank, and she seemed surprised that I knew him. She thinks it's sort of creepy that an old man would make friends with a 10-year-old boy, but I don't think so. I just think he didn't have very many friends.

When I read the story in the paper I kind of got a weird memory so I went and looked at that old baseball card I got from Gramma's house after she died -- the one she'd kept for 35 years -- and when I looked at it I got goose bumps all over because it was Major Hank! Hank Johnstone and Henry Johns were the same person! Imagine that -- I got to sit and talk to a real Major League baseball player, and he never even told me. Maybe I shouldn't have told him how much I hated the goddamn Yankees?

September 3, 1961

If you want to experience something so totally gross it'll make you pass out, come on over to my house when Mom has to change Bridey's diapers. It's amazing the colors of the goo that comes out of a baby's butt.

September 4, 1961

Do you remember how last year they had Dr. Evil at the Royale Theater for Halloween? Well I just saw a little flyer outside the Royale, advertising this year's Halloween Show. Here's what it said:

COMING UP NEXT MONTH!!
HALLOWEEN SCARETACULAR!
One night only, Oct. 31 at the ROYALE THEATER, 8PM
IN PERSON! DR. NEFF PRESENTS HIS ORIGINAL HORROR
SHOW!
It's scary! It's screamy! It's screwy!
SEE SUTTEE BURNED ALIVE ON AN ALTAR OF FLAME!
SEE THE GODDESS OF VOODOO,
a zombie nightmare with hex appeal!
Magic! Movies! Scares galore!
WE DARE YOU TO BE HERE AT MIDNIGHT WHEN
THE MONSTER WILL BE RELEASED FROM HIS SEALED
COFFIN!! SORRY...WE CAN'T TELL YOU THE TITLES OR THE
CAST OF
OUR SUPER-SCARY FEATURES...BUT THEY'RE SO SCARY
THAT IF YOU CAN SIT THROUGH BOTH OF THEM...WE WILL
REWARD
YOU WITH A FREE PASS FOR A NEAR-FUTURE SHOW!
80 cents admission

Today was Labor Day, which means nobody went to work. So why do they call it Labor Day if nobody labors?

September 5, 1961

In a few weeks it'll be my birthday again. I'm still hoping I'll get a dog, but when I asked Dad about it he said, "You couldn't take care of a dog. Remember the guppies?" That's because a couple years ago we had guppies until Colin put some water softener in their bowl and they softened to death.

So I think I'll ask for a Chemical Set instead -- Chemical Sets are pretty neat because you can make all kinds of experiments. I've tried some experiments already, like did you know that brake fluid mixed with Clorox makes smoke? Lots of it! And I mixed vinegar with baking soda once, and it got all foamy. Then another time I mixed Comet and Dr. Pepper and peanut butter and saf-flower oil, but it just made some goop I had to put down the toilet.

September 6, 1961

Last night I had a dream about Major Hank. He was sitting on the beach in a Yankees uniform, and he took off his cap and a little white bird flew out of his head. It circled all around us and then it flew out over the water and then it turned into the moon, except the moon was yellow.

It was Major Hank, but it wasn't -- does that make sense to you? I mean like it was Major Hank, but he was much younger and different looking. He gave me some advice: he told me that if I ever truly fell in love, not to let it slip away because I might never find real happiness again.

I laid in bed and thought about the dream for a long time, and do you know what? When you really stop to think about it, maybe I just met Major Hank's Monitor?

Anyhow, Aunt Gwen and Uncle Mick ate over tonight and boy were they ever sickening! They kept giving each other goo-goo eyes and winking at each other and saying, "sweetie" and "honey-pie" and junk like that. Disgustomatic, if you ask me. Colin kept faking like he was going to barf.

After dinner I called up Mary-Ann to tell her about my dream and to see if she was going to Marty Graw in a couple days. She said she was. She also said her dad will be coming back from Arabia in a week -- she's real excited about that, because she hasn't seen him in almost a year. I wonder if he'll wear a red and white Italian restaurant tablecloth on his head?

Everywhere now there's the smell of burning leaves in people's back yards -- I really like that smell. I guess it means the seasons are starting to change. It's getting a little colder at night now, and we can't play outside quite as late as we used to because it's starting to get dark earlier. That's all because of the way the Earth rotates on its axle.

September 7, 1961

This morning the telephone rang and Mom answered it and I could tell it was a weird call because Mom kept saying, "Yes, sir? Is that right? Are you absolutely sure there's no mistake?"

Then she hung up and told me it was a lawyer on the phone, and the lawyer said Major Hank left us some money in his will. Isn't that strange? I guess it's because he didn't have any kids of his own and the only person he ever really loved was Gramma, and she can't spend money because she's up in heaven. Mom doesn't know how much money yet -- she says she has to go to a meeting next week and we'll find out then.

Major Hank sure didn't look like he had any money, but I guess you never can tell? And Mom says the family could use some, now that Dad's pay got cut. If it's a whole bunch of money like $250 or something, I'm going to ask if I can get a portable TV so I can watch Rin Tin Tin in peace.

Anyhow summer is almost over, the Dodgers are only one game back of the Reds, and tomorrow is the annual Marty Graw at school. Mom says I have to wear something nice just in case I get to be the Marty Graw King, but I don't think I'll get King.

September 8, 1961

I spent the whole day at the big Marty Graw, and guess what? I just found out I've been spelling it wrong all this time -- it's actually spelled 'Mardi Gras.' I think that's French or something. Most places do their Mardi Gras way earlier in the year, but here at Pacific Street they do it right near the beginning of the fall term.

Mardi Gras was just as much fun this year as it was last year! I played all the games again, and did the penny toss and the darts, and watched the strongman and ate hot dogs and cotton candy. Colin had a great time too -- he especially liked the Cakewalk because he won a cake! It wasn't chocolate, but at least it was a cake.

I also hung out at the General Store and got a few cool records and some books. Even though I've just about filled up this Mardi Gras Book, I didn't buy another one -- they take a long time to fill up and I think I'm done writing down stuff for awhile. There's lots of other things to do, plus I'm getting kind of tired of the other kids saying, "Hey, McAfee! Put down your dumb-ass book and let's play!" And since last years' Mardi Gras is kind of where I started talking to you, I guess I'll just be saying goodbye to you now, and that's that.

School starts up again the day after tomorrow -- I'm really sad to see the summer go by so fast. Next semester we'll be in the A6 so we're the big kids, top seniors, Kings of the Hill! Maybe it will be fun?

Speaking of kings, I didn't get to be the Mardi Gras King. Frankie Dupoy did, and Mary-Ann Lindstrom got Queen. That's the way the cookie crumbles. I don't mind losing to Frankie because I like him and I think it's pretty neat that he woked up this year, and also at least it wasn't ol' Hermie Fleet or Norman Giambalvo. And I'm really happy that Mary-Ann beat Toren Shumaker for Queen.

The only good part of being King would've been that you get to wear a crown and they ask you questions on live TV. Like I saw this woman with a TV camera ask Frankie how it felt to be King and he said, "Do I get to keep the crown?" The lady said, "Yes," and Frankie said, "Neato!"

Then the TV lady turned to Mary-Ann and said, "Your Majesty? There's a huge Livestock Exhibit at this year's Mardi Gras -- so many wonderful animals here on display! Cows, chickens, goats, pigs.... Could you please tell all our viewers at home just what the Queen of the Mardi Gras thinks about all the animals?"

And Mary-Ann said, "I think they stink."